Catherine Tinley has loved reading and writing since childhood, and has a particular fondness for love, romance and happy endings. She lives in Ireland with her husband, children, dog and kitten, and can be reached at catherinetinley.com, as well as through Facebook and on X @CatherineTinley.

T0318054

Also by Catherine Tinley

A Waltz with the Outspoken Governess

The Triplet Orphans miniseries

Miss Rose and the Vexing Viscount
Miss Isobel and the Prince

The Ladies of Ledbury House miniseries

The Earl's Runaway Governess
Rags-to-Riches Wife
'A Midnight Mistletoe Kiss'
in *Christmas Cinderellas*
Captivating the Cynical Earl

Lairds of the Isles miniseries

A Laird for the Governess
A Laird in London
A Laird for the Highland Lady

Discover more at millsandboon.co.uk.

MISS ANNA AND THE EARL

Catherine Tinley

MILLS & BOON

First published in Great Britain 2025
by Mills & Boon, an imprint of HarperCollins*Publishers* Ltd,
1 London Bridge Street, London, SE1 9GF

www.harpercollins.co.uk

HarperCollins*Publishers*, Macken House, 39/40 Mayor Street Upper,
Dublin 1, D01 C9W8, Ireland

ISBN: 978-0-263-34502-5

01/25

This book contains FSC™ certified paper
and other controlled sources to ensure responsible forest management.

For more information visit www.harpercollins.co.uk/green.

Printed and Bound in the UK using 100% Renewable Electricity
at CPI Group (UK) Ltd, Croydon, CR0 4YY

For Clodagh

Welcome to the world

Prologue

Elgin, Scotland,
1797

'Mama, tell us the story about ZanZan and Milady!'
Anna gazed at her mother adoringly.

Mama laughed. 'Again? I declare it is your favourite
story. Very well, but you must promise to go to sleep
immediately afterwards. Now, move over a little, and
I shall sit on your bed.'

The triplets—Anna, Izzy and Rose—shuffled over
in their large, comfortable bed and Mama stretched out
beside them, smoothing her simple dun gown. There
was an ink stain on her hand from her long hours clerk-
ing that day.

'Once upon a time,' she began, 'There were three
little princesses. They lived in a beautiful castle—'

'Not like our cottage!' declared Izzy, briefly taking
her thumb from her mouth.

'No, indeed. Our little cottage is beautiful in its own
way, though, and we are very grateful for it. Now, the

princesses lived in a beautiful castle with their dear friends—'

'Milady!' Rose jumped in with the name.

'And ZanZan!' added Anna. ZanZan was her favourite.

'Yes, the princesses and their mother lived with Zan-Zan and his mama in the beautiful castle. It had nearly a hundred rooms, and the children played and laughed all day long.'

'There was a big, big staircase,' said Rose, lifting her little arms and spreading her hands to show how large the staircase had been.

'And a piano!' said Izzy.

'And secret places. Tell us the part about the secret places, Mama!' Anna could see some of them in her mind's eye: the bookcase in the library that was really a door; the hidden drawer in Mama's desk that would pop open when she pressed the third carved flower from the left; the loft in the stables that no one would know was there. She remembered *everything*.

'And another time,' Mama said, and there was a different tone to her voice, 'The mother of the princesses stayed in an inn for three whole weeks!'

'Why, Mama? Why did she stay there?'

'It was when the princesses' mother was getting ready to be married to their father. Her husband-to-be stayed in a different place, as was proper, and each Sunday the minister read out their names in the church to see if anyone might try to stop the wedding.'

Anna was fascinated. 'Why would someone do that?'

'His family did not wish him to marry. But they did not find them.' Mama shook her head. 'It was a happy time for them both.'

'Like now, Mama?' asked Rose.

Mama smiled. 'Yes, like now.' There were more stories then, until finally Mama said, 'Now, let us sing *The Lady Blue* together, and then we shall say our prayers. But remember, you are never to speak of your father. Now, promise me!'

'I promise, Mama.'

Chapter One

The Lady Blue she points her shoe
You find the line to find the kine
The key is three and three times three
The treasure fine is yours and mine

Cross Keys Inn, Kelso,
Saturday 8th August 1812

I promise, Mama.

Anna awoke, her cheeks damp, her heart aching, and her head full of vague images of churches and danger. What had she promised? She could not recall. Her dream had included a wedding, she remembered, but there had been some danger attached to it.

Her sisters' weddings? Both Izzy and Rose had married recently. But there had been a strange feeling to the dream—a sense of menace.

I promise, Mama.

Her own words still hovered in the morning air. Had she dreamed of her parents' wedding, perhaps? Sighing, she recognised that her disturbed sleep had its origin in the eternal restlessness that haunted her.

There was no proof their parents had ever married, although Mama had been known as Mrs Lennox. As an adult, Anna suspected that had been pivotal. Something had made Mama run away from home and bring up her daughters in a sleepy town in the far north of Scotland, perhaps? But surely such scandal would have been quelled by marriage, even if it had taken place after Mama was with child?

Mama's death from a wasting disease when her triplet daughters had been just ten years old was a loss from which Anna had never recovered. It also meant Maria Lennox's daughters now had no way of having their questions answered, no way of knowing who they truly were. As the years went by, the moments of grief were less frequent, but no less painful.

Never having known their father, losing their mother had been a terrible blow for Anna and her sisters. Thankfully Mama's employer, Mr Marnoch, had become their guardian, and years later his sister, Lady Ashbourne, had sponsored the triplets for a London season.

And now the season had ended, and Anna was on her way to a country house in Scotland for a *ton* summer gathering—still occasionally wondering how she and her sisters had managed to attract such good fortune. They had enjoyed balls and soirées, had been to the theatre and to places of interest in London.

They had even attracted the favour of the Queen

herself—as well as disfavour from some of the more critical ladies of the *ton*. Anna's heart sank a little, recalling the antipathy of people such as Lady Renton and Mrs Thaxby, both of whom had disapproved of three nobodies without family connections being feted by the *ton*. Both ladies, and their husbands, had been invited to the upcoming party in Lammermuir House, and Anna anticipated some tense moments during the next three weeks.

Maybe, Anna mused hopefully, the animosity towards them from certain people would now be reduced, given recent events. Anna's sisters had both made excellent marriages towards the end of the season. The youngest triplet, Rose, had wed James, Viscount Ashbourne—their sponsor's nephew, and Izzy had recently married Prince Claudio of Andernach, a distant cousin of the Queen.

Despite being the eldest of the triplets—by a full twenty minutes!—and being identical in looks and figure to her sisters, at least, to an unfamiliar eye, Anna had not attracted so much as a single proposal of marriage.

Which was why she was sleeping alone in this comfortable bed in a well-appointed room in the Cross Keys Inn, with a serving maid on a truckle bed beneath the window to protect her reputation, while her sisters slept in nearby chambers in their husbands' arms.

As Anna rose and began to prepare for the final part of their journey, she reflected on this. It was hardly surprising, she supposed, that she was the one still unwed.

As the eldest, she had always carried the weight of unseen responsibilities, and as such felt herself to be a little less impulsive than Izzy and a little more practical than Rose, whose dreamy head was often stuck in a book.

Anna was self-contained by will, and design, and intention. Not for her the flirtatious arts; she could no more be arch, silly or full of smiles than she could fly—which was to say, not at all. And, while she had developed a foolish *tendre* for the Earl of Garvald, who was hosting the upcoming summer gathering, she was much too practical to take such a notion seriously.

Recently, the triplets had managed to establish that Mama's maiden name had been Maria Berkeley, and that the formidable Lady Kelgrove was in fact their great-grandmother. She had chosen to recognise the connection, yet Anna knew some high sticklers in the *ton* continued to sneer at the Lennox triplets behind their painted fans.

As she descended to the parlour for breakfast, Anna distracted herself by going over again in her mind some of the faint, precious memories she had retained of her childhood. She remembered the years in their little cottage in Elgin before Mama's death—a house now sadly changed beyond recognition. A local farmer had taken it on, building outwards and upwards until it bore no resemblance to the humble cottage that had been their happy haven while Mama had yet lived.

There was also the wonderful place they had lived *before* the cottage, in some place other than Elgin—the place she remembered as a fairy-tale castle with a huge staircase. She and her sisters had been born there, she knew, for Mama had told them so, many times.

At least I know that much, little as it is.

They had been five when Mama had moved them to Elgin, and ten when she had left them all, to live in heaven. Anna still had happy memories of their life in the castle, though she was now one-and-twenty, which meant that sixteen years had passed.

The Lady Blue, the little song Mama had made up, was haunting her this morning.

Was it in my dream too?

Anna and her sisters had each been given a ribbon by the midwife at birth, tied around their wrists to help Mama distinguish between them—blue for Anna, green for Izzy and pink for Rose. Later, Mama had always sung *Greensleeves* for Izzy, while Rose's song had been *Ring a Ring O'Roses*. Anna's song had been *The Lady Blue*. Eventually the girls had realised that, while both Izzy's and Rose's songs were well-known, no one had ever heard of *The Lady Blue*, and so it had felt even more special to Anna.

There were actions to each of the songs, too—clapping patterns and movement. When they were little, they had loved pretending to sneeze, then throwing themselves to the floor for the 'all fall down' part of Rose's song. For *The Lady Blue* they had followed different actions for each part, first pointing the toes of their right foot as they made a sweeping curtsey, arms outstretched in a grandiose way. They had then woven in and out around each other three times before they'd all finally clapped hands together and against each other's palms as they had chanted about the treasure.

It had been silly and meaningless, and Mama had told them afterwards she had made it up—cleverly crafted in iambic tetrameter, Anna realised later. But in Anna's mind it encapsulated Mama's vivacity and creativeness, and the fact that her girls had been the centre of her world. Even after their tenth birthday, when she had gradually become so weak that she had spent all her days and nights in bed, and Mr Marnoch had sent one of his own maids to help care for them all, she had asked them to sing *The Lady Blue* for her.

'The true treasure,' Mama had told them once near the end, when she had been sleeping most of the time, 'Is the love that we share. Never forget that, Annabelle, Isobel, Rosabella: my belles.'

Anna never had. After the funeral, and Mr Marnoch's awkward kindness in telling them he had arranged for them to live at Belvedere School for Young Ladies on the edge of Elgin town, Anna had known that the three of them needed to look after one another through whatever might befall them.

And now her sisters were married, and she would have to get used to being without them. Rose and James, her viscount, had married in Elgin, in the same chapel where Mama's funeral had taken place. Izzy and Prince Claudio had travelled to Shropshire for a couple of weeks after their London wedding. This had reduced the triplets to pairs, different pairs at different times, and Anna had not yet had to suffer being without them both at the same time. Thankfully they were now all back together, travelling to Scotland for the Earl of Garvald's country-house party.

Anna and her sisters were now one-and-twenty, and so much time had passed that her precious memories were now reduced to impressions and feelings, rather than images. But each time she entered a new building Anna's mind would search out similarities—a door, window, or the sweep of a staircase that vaguely reminded her of the castle. Whitewashed walls, flagstone floors, and large open fireplaces always reminded her of the cottage where they had lived so contentedly.

Last night, the wooden beams in the ceiling of her chamber in the inn had brought to mind their bedroom in the castle. Sadly, the memories were fading by the day, the month, the year. Soon, she knew she would have only the merest glimpses in her mind of Mama, and of the places in which they had lived with her. Too much time had passed.

She had been very little when they had moved to Elgin from the castle, but Anna recalled being happy. In her memory it had been idyllic: games with her sisters and their friend ZanZan; her first piano lessons with Mama and Milady; and even some memories of riding a pony. While she had enthusiastically continued with piano, gaining good proficiency during her years at school after Mama's death, she had not continued to ride, and now suffered from quite a fear of horses.

If we had stayed there, perhaps I...

But no. Anna knew herself to be sensible, practical, logical. There was no point in imagining what might have been. Rose might dream of an idyll, and Izzy might demand and seize every opportunity, but Anna would simply accept her lot. As she always had.

Lammermuir House, Scotland

William Alexander Edward Henderson, Earl of Garvald, entered the breakfast room where a slim, good-looking lady in her middle years was delicately nibbling on some toast, a dish of chocolate by her elbow.

'Good morning, my love,' he announced, bending to kiss his mother's cheek. 'My, you are looking fetching this morning!'

'Do you like it?' Lady Garvald glanced dubiously at her day gown of figured muslin. 'The dressmaker has assured me that my new gowns are based on the latest fashion plates. Not having travelled to London since before you were born, I have no idea of current fashions. Our guests will arrive today, and I know I have made all ready with the staff, but I do not wish to disgrace you with dowdy gowns, Will!'

'You could never do that. And, I assure you, your gown is, er, all the crack!'

She sniffed. 'Well, I am glad to hear it, though I feel I should not approve of such an expression.'

'Ah, but that is why you are a darling, Mama. For you do not chastise me—you simply feel that you *ought* to do so!'

'To be fair, even as a child you rarely needed to be chastised—apart from that horrible year when you turned nine.' Her brow furrowed. 'You were so unhappy, as was I, and I did not know what to do with you!'

Will grimaced. 'To this day I can recall my anger. Children cannot, I suppose, understand such matters.' Mama had sunk into quite a depression at that time, and had not the energy to deal with a deeply unhappy eight-year-old boy. But that had been a long time ago. It would do no good to think of it now. With an effort, he smiled, asking, 'But surely I gave you some grey hairs while at university?'

She rolled her eyes. 'Even in rural Scotland, the tales of your antics reached my ears. Many young men must kick off the traces for a while, I know, but deep down I was certain that such larks would be short-lived. And I was right!' She sent him a sideways glance. 'I imagine you will marry soon. It will be wonderful to have children again in this big house.'

'Now, Mama...' He raised a quizzical eyebrow. 'Do not hold such expectations, for they are sure to be dashed. I am but five-and-twenty, and have plenty of time for such matters.' They had had this conversation many times, he evading what he knew to be his responsibility to marry and produce an heir. It was perfectly reasonable to be unmarried at his age. And since the notion of marriage filled him with unease, he was clearly not ready to tie himself to a bride. At least, not the *wrong* bride.

'Your bosom bows, Lord Ashbourne and Mr Phillips, have both married this year, have they not? Even the prince will bring his new bride to our party—and he is younger than you are!'

He clapped a hand to his chest. 'A hit, Mama! I cannot deny it. But just because they have wed it does not follow...' His eyes widened. 'Did you just *snort*, Lady Garvald? How unladylike! Ah, that is more like it!' She had dissolved into helpless laughter. 'Now, breakfast!'

'I am worried about Lady Kelgrove.'

Izzy, Anna's younger sister, had joined her at the breakfast table in their well-appointed private parlour in the inn.

Anna's heart lurched. Their mama's elderly grandmother had welcomed the triplets into her family, her home and her heart with alacrity and generosity.

'Oh, no! She is unwell?'

Izzy nodded, then clarified, 'Tired, perhaps—too tired. When I called to her room just now, she was in a crotchety mood, talking of her rattling bones and an aching head.'

'Lord, we knew the journey would be too much for her. I do wish she had stayed safely in London.'

'Safe? She is not a person who wishes to be safe.' Izzy thought for a moment. 'It is, I believe, one of the most admirable things about her.'

Having been included in Lord Garvald's invitation to the party at Lammermuir House, and on hearing who else was to be invited, Lady Kelgrove had instantly announced her firm intention to travel. Anna recalled their futile attempts to dissuade her.

'Watch me!' she had challenged, at their protestations. 'I may be eighty-four, but I am not yet underground! Lady Garvald, the Earl's mother, is, as I recall, a pretty-behaved girl with sense between her ears. Such people are rare and must be celebrated. Besides,' she had mused, 'I have a notion to observe certain of the other guests.'

'Who, Great-Grandma? Who?'

'Whom!' Lady Kelgrove had corrected, a wicked glint in her dark eyes. 'It is to do with your father, but we will have plenty of time during the house party to tell you what I know, what I suspect and what I mean to discover!'

This had been decidedly intriguing, given that Anna and her sisters had only recently discovered their mother's family, and Lady Kelgrove had once hinted she had suspicions about who their father had been. Lady Kelgrove seemed to thrive on intrigue, and had once told Anna she liked to keep information for herself as long as possible

'So,' Izzy continued, 'I suggested staying on here for another day or two. The Cross Keys is among the best of the inns we have stayed in so far.'

'Has she agreed?'

'She has, which is both reassuring and concerning.'

Anna knew exactly what she meant. 'Is she breakfasting in her room?'

'Absolutely not! She is indomitable!'

Sure enough, half an hour later Lady Kelgrove appeared, accompanied by her personal maid, Hill. A quick glance towards this loyal servant gave no clues as to her mistress's health, and Anna suppressed an inner sigh. Why must servants always be so unreadable?

They were joined by Prince Claudio, Izzy's doting husband, who sent his wife a warm glance as he seated himself opposite her. Izzy's title was now Princess Isobel of Andernach—decidedly strange, when said princess was one's own sister who had used to pull Anna's hair when she'd lost her temper as a child. As Lady Kelgrove was taking her seat, the parlour door opened, admitting Rose, the youngest of the triplets, along with her husband, the Viscount Ashbourne. His aunt, the dowager viscountess, had declined the invitation, and was instead planning a visit to her brother in the coming weeks.

'I have decided,' announced Lady Kelgrove, after the customary greetings had been exchanged, 'To stay in Kelso for a couple of days. It looks a pretty sort of town, and I am pleased with this inn. Although I have, naturally, brought my own linen, Hill assures me that the beds are spotless!'

At this, they all concurred about the quality of the inn, the pleasantness of the town and the prettiness of the surrounding countryside. No one mentioned, nor did they need to, the gruelling journey they had made thus far from London, nor the fact that only one more day of travel would take them to Lammermuir House. This being Saturday, their intention had been to complete the last forty miles of their journey, for one did not travel on a Sunday. If they did not continue on today that would mean two further clear nights of rest for the elderly lady—a plan of which Anna heartily approved.

But, when they all expressed their support for the entire party delaying their onward travels, Lady Kelgrove would have none of it.

'Absolutely not! Lady Garvald expects us today, and so you must all travel on without me. For one guest to be tardy may be thought an inconvenience, but for such a large party to be delayed would be insupportable! It would be deeply insulting to our hostess, as I should hope my dear Maria's daughters would understand.' She sighed, adding, 'The Kelgrove estate is not entailed, you know.'

They exchanged puzzled glances, but she elaborated. 'My long-suffering lawyer had no need to search through the lesser branches of my husband's family for a male heir when he died, for I inherited all of it—as will you girls. You are all now substantial heiresses, you know, and as such must come under the critical eyes of the *ton*!'

Anna's jaw dropped. Not having thought about the matter much until now, she understood immediately that she did not need to be an heiress, for her sisters had both married well. Of more concern was Lady Kelgrove's hinting at her own demise. Was she more unwell than she was pretending?

Izzy—as ever the quickest to form a response—instantly declared herself to have a headache and, since she had recently recovered from influenza, this could not be gainsaid.

'I do not feel well enough to travel,' she complained, perjuring herself without a blink. 'I am actually relieved that you are staying on, for it gives me exactly the excuse I was searching for!'

Lady Kelgrove sent Izzy a sceptical look but thankfully did not dispute this, and so an hour after breakfast Anna found herself in Lord Ashbourne's coach with Rose, her husband alongside them on horseback. Izzy, Prince Claudio and Lady Kelgrove would follow them in two days.

'Thank goodness our great-grandmother will have some rest before the rigours of the Earl's house party!' Rose commented. 'And wasn't it clever of Izzy to think of a way to remain with her?'

'Indeed!' Anna shook her head slowly. 'Izzy's quickness of mind has proved useful yet again. I could not think of anything to say once she had called into question our understanding of how to go on!'

'It is still so strange to know who Mama was.'

Anna thought for a moment. 'Even stranger to think that in the coming weeks we are likely to discover more about our father—if Lady Kelgrove is correct in her suspicion that she knows his identity.'

'We already know Mama's family has turned out to be wonderful.' Rose frowned. 'Well, Lady Kelgrove is wonderful, at least. Her husband, our great-grandfather, seems rather harsh, based on what little we know of him.'

Anna shrugged. 'All we know is that, rather than telling his wife that their only living grandchild had run away, he pretended she had died in the smallpox outbreak. Perhaps he was trying to spare her feelings, or cover up the scandal.'

'Perhaps. But why did Maria run away to begin with? She cannot have been in the family way, for we were born nearly a full year later. And, even though we came early, she still would not have been with child until at least a couple of months *after* she ran away.'

'We may at least hear more of our father soon. From that we might be able to reason why she ran away.'

Rose's expression brightened. 'True! And Mama always spoke warmly of our father, so if Lady Kelgrove truly suspects who he may be then I am eager to learn more of him—what sort of man he was.'

'A servant, perhaps, or tradesman.' Anna had long since concluded that Mama's sweetheart might have been deemed unsuitable by her family. 'Though our surname—Lennox—seemed unfamiliar to Lady Kelgrove.'

'It is likely to be someone like that, yes. Perhaps a temporary servant by the name of Lennox. Otherwise why not simply marry him, with her family's approval?'

'Exactly. And why did Lady Kelgrove say that she wished to observe some of the guests at this party, do you think? Might it be connected?'

'I have no notion, but I did think it an odd thing for her to say.'

Anna chuckled. 'Our great-grandmother delights in

being odd, and cryptic, and even eccentric, I think! She will certainly add colour to this party!'

'And we are to meet Lord Garvald's mother. Did you note Lady Kelgrove's praise for her?'

Anna nodded. 'Since Lady Kelgrove does not often give praise, we must suppose Lady Garvald to be all that is good.'

'That is indeed encouraging, for I confess her son quite intimidates me!' Rose grimaced. 'Oh, I know I should not say so, for he is one of my husband's closest friends, but...' Her voice tailed away.

Anna nodded sympathetically, but found herself unable to reply, for in truth she had no idea what to make of Lord Garvald. Gazing out of the carriage window, she pictured him as she had last seen him, in the Ashbourne drawing room two weeks ago. His strong form and handsome face were clear in her mind's eye—dark hair, strong jawline and his eyes a shade of blue that sometimes spoke of the sky, sometimes the sea.

Blue was Anna's favourite colour, and she usually chose it to trim her white muslin gowns with embroidery and ribbons—partly because using their preferred colours helped others distinguish between her sisters and her, but partly because blue was genuinely the best colour in nature, in her opinion. The hint of blue in a cloudy sky was hope. The blue-green murmur of the sea at Stotfield or Garmouth, during an occasional excursion from Elgin during her childhood, had always fascinated, calmed, and impressed her with its vastness. And she never forgot that the colour had become hers when she'd been born and the midwife had placed a blue ribbon on her wrist so that Mama could distinguish her from the other babies. Yes, from birth she had been destined to prefer all things blue.

Lord Garvald's coat had been of blue superfine, that last day, she recalled. It had suited him. It had been two whole weeks since she had seen him, and she was no nearer to understanding why he affected her so. During her season in London she had frequently been in his company—at balls, soirées, musicales and the like. The *ton*, after all, was not so large. He was urbane, well-respected and sober, without being staid. He had seriousness, dignity and, occasionally, a hint of dry humour. Yet from the first, Anna had sensed he was playing a role. And from the first, he had had a strange effect on her senses. Each time he looked directly at her, his eyes—those blue, blue eyes—had seemed to search out her soul.

No one else had commented on it, responding to him with joviality, warm politeness or simple courtesy. A few, like Rose, found him forbidding. But only Anna seemed to feel this strange affinity to him. Each time she was with him, her heart seemed to melt and he took up all her attention.

Once again, she told herself she was being nonsensical. Of the triplets, Izzy had always been the one to let her imaginings run away with her, Rose the one most likely to be lost in dreaminess. Anna's approach was simple, straightforward and unaffected by flights of fancy.

Maybe that is exactly why I am drawn to Lord Garvald, she mused now. The Earl seemed equally immune to the fancies, exaggerations and scandals of the season as she.

Perhaps, she thought now, *we share a love for practicality, and nothing more.*

She was certain being in his company for most of the next month would serve to resolve this riddle in her mind. And perhaps she had imagined that he disordered her senses, for she had not seen him in a full fortnight, and could think of him as she did now, without any effect on her senses beyond a barely discernible fluttering in her innards and a slight increase in the intensity of her pulse. Yes, there was nothing out of the ordinary about it. Nothing at all.

Chapter Two

'Welcome, friends.' Lord Garvald bowed formally, then half-turned to the lady by his side—a lady so like him in looks that she could only be his mother. 'Mama, you remember my dear friend, Lord Ashbourne? May I present his bride, Lady Ashbourne…?'

As Lord Garvald began the formal greetings, Anna's mind was in quite a degree of turmoil. The carriage had turned into the entrance somewhere after Haddington, and as the house had come into view her innards had gone into some sort of frenzy—a development as unexpected as it was unwelcome.

His eyes had met hers briefly just now, and a jolt had gone through her, just as though she had been struck by lightning. What on earth was happening? While this was the first time she had ever had the opportunity to attend a *ton* country house party, she had been acquitting herself well in the ballrooms and drawing rooms of Mayfair all season. That being the case, this sudden attack of nerves had caught her by surprise.

Or was it to do with the man himself, and her earlier reflections that he affected her in some particular way? The notion was unwelcome. Yet she could not deny that her attention was almost entirely given to the tall, dark-haired gentleman currently leading the introductions.

Why should she be so affected by seeing him again? The impact was certainly potent. After just two weeks without being in his presence, the urge to allow her gaze to rove hungrily over him was so strong, she had to deliberately quell it, distracting herself by swiftly taking in the facade of Lammermuir House.

Something about its form instantly reminded her of her castle childhood home—although that castle had been much bigger than this one. Despite this, the Earl's home was substantial, pleasing to the eye and well-built. It was square, solid and…reassuring somehow, Anna thought fancifully. Judging by the architecture, she guessed some parts dated back to Elizabeth's reign, while others were clearly more recent additions.

'And this is Miss Lennox.'

Anna made her curtsey, reassured to see a kindness in Lady Garvald's eyes that was not always there among *tonnish* people. The Earl's mother was petite, warm and engaging, and she had clearly passed her eye colour to her son. They were much alike, which would account for the stab of familiarity that had struck Anna on first seeing her.

Viscount Ashbourne was now explaining that Lady Kelgrove, Prince Claudio and Princess Isobel would arrive on Monday, two days later than planned, and that he hoped it would not put Lady Garvald out too much.

'Not at all, my lord—our guests may arrive according to their own preferences. And it is far easier, after all, to have *fewer* for dinner than to add extra people, do you not agree?' Her eyes danced, and Anna felt herself relax a little. Given the Earl's habitual stiffness, it was a relief to find his mother to be so engaging.

Viscount Ashbourne agreed most readily, and their hostess led the way indoors.

'Lord and Lady Renton have already arrived,' she offered. 'As have Mr and Mrs Thaxby. The Thaxbys came directly from their house in Edinburgh—a delightful mansion, by all accounts. They plan to return there following our little party. Now, then, I shall introduce you to Gibson and Mrs Lowe.'

She indicated the elderly butler and the housekeeper standing inside the hallway. 'I am sure you are all desirous of a rest before dinner, so Mrs Lowe will show you to your rooms.'

After expressions of thanks and gratitude had been properly made by the party, Anna followed the rest up the wide staircase. It had two turns, windows along the middle section and an archway along the landing—a common arrangement, and one that definitely stirred something in Anna's memory. Her castle must have had something similar, perhaps. Lord, would her life always be like this—always searching in vain for a time that was past? *Now* was what mattered, surely?

Yet, as Mrs Lowe led them along the upper hallway

containing the guest bedrooms, a small door on the right caught Anna's eye. It was just a door, narrower than the others and with a traditional latch, yet something inside Anna made her keep her eye on it as they approached then passed. She shivered, realising she had had a sudden attack of goose flesh. Scottish castle architecture from mediaeval times until the present day had clear commonality; Lammermuir House must date from the same era as the place where she had been born.

'Here you are, miss.' The housekeeper opened the door to what would be Anna's bedchamber. 'Your maid will ensure all your things are unpacked.'

'Thank you, Mrs Lowe. What a pretty room!' The bed was large, ornately carved in dark wood and with a canopy. A matching screen, side tables, desk and chair completed the set, and there was a soft armchair positioned by the small fireplace—an arrangement almost begging for Anna to sit and read in comfort. The hangings were of blue and gold, the wall coverings a gentle golden hue.

Once the housekeeper left, Anna made her way to the window. Outside was the front of the house, and she leaned forward to see the hum of activity below, the servants removing the trunks from the various coaches.

Sally, Anna's own personal maid, had accompanied her from Ashbourne House in London. Anna had never had the services of a maid until this year and was most heartily glad. Sally knew how she liked her hair to be dressed, and which gowns were most suitable for which occasions. Anna was determined not to let herself and her family down during her stay at Lammermuir House.

It was also important that she look her best at all times. Something about this thought bothered her, for she was unused to particularly caring about her appearance. Pushing the thought away, she kicked off her slippers and dropped her reticule onto the chair. Yes, she would be comfortable here. She just knew it.

'Tell me, Miss Lennox, have you been to Scotland before?'

With some effort, Anna focused on the young gentleman beside her. Mr Ashman was the son of Sir Walter Ashman, the local magistrate, and both he and his father had been invited to dinner, presumably to counterbalance the fact that both she and Lady Kelgrove were 'extra' ladies in the party. Given that Lady Kelgrove's arrival had been delayed, the dinner group had ended up imbalanced anyway—a fact to which Lady Garvald had airily referred, then dismissed as they were all being seated. She was at the foot of the table facing her son, as was correct, and Lord Garvald had Rose and James on either side of him, they being the highest-ranking guests present. The honour would be passed to Izzy and Claudio after Monday. Regardless, Anna was unlikely ever to be placed beside him at dinner. Not that she cared about such things.

'My sisters and I actually grew up in Scotland. We attended Belvedere School in Elgin until this year.'

His eyebrows shot up. 'Indeed? I have heard Elgin

described as a fine town, though sadly I have never visited it.'

'We are very fond of Elgin.' There was a silence. Knowing her obligations, Anna added. 'And what of you, Mr Ashman? Have you always lived in the district?'

'I have, and like you with Elgin, I am fond of it. There is something most agreeable about maintaining a connection with the place of your birth, is there not?'

'Indeed—but I must tell you that I was not born in Elgin. We lived somewhere else for the first five years of our lives.'

A gleam of humour lit his eye. 'Am I permitted to know where? Somewhere else in Scotland?'

'Yes, definitely Scotland, but in truth I do not know where exactly. Such information was lost when my mother died.'

'I am sorry to hear that. My own mother is also deceased.'

They shared a momentary glance, acknowledging the connection, then he moved on to begin telling her about the beauties of the district. Anna's gaze flicked briefly to the head of the table, as it had frequently during dinner, and her jaw sagged briefly as she met the Earl's gaze. How long had he been looking at her? Had he been listening to her conversation with Mr Ashman? And why did he look so displeased?

Rose said something and he turned his attention to her, just as the footmen began serving the next course. This was the signal for Lady Garvald to turn the table, so Anna turned to her right to converse with Lord Renton—an affable gentleman, quite undeserving of such an acerbic wife—and the conversation moved on.

Afterwards Lady Garvald led Rose and Anna out of the grand dining room, along with Lady Renton and Mrs Thaxby, into the yellow drawing room which she explained was where she and her son usually conversed after dinner. The gentlemen left to their port would join them in due course, but this was Lady Garvald's moment. Anna chose a satin-covered sofa near the piano, glancing at the instrument covetously. She loved to play, and wondered if Lady Garvald might permit her to practise on what looked to be a fine instrument.

Glancing around, Anna subtly eyed the others as they took their seats. Rose was nearby, glowing with contentment in a pink silk evening gown—her recent marriage undoubtedly the source of the contentment. Lady Renton had marched straight up to claim a wing-backed armchair near the fireplace, quite the most comfortable seat to be had, and probably normally occupied by their hostess. Anna would not have dreamed of doing such a thing, but Lady Renton clearly had no such qualms.

Anna's gaze roved on. Mrs Thaxby was eyeing the furnishings and art with an assessing air, her habitual frown in place. No doubt she would shortly have something to say about the decor, the paintings or some such thing. Finally, Anna met the gaze of their hostess, who smiled warmly.

'I cannot tell you how delighted I am to have guests in the house again! I often receive my neighbours, but it has been an age since I welcomed old friends and acquaintances from London. And of course new friends too!' She gestured towards Anna and Rose, and would have said more, but was forestalled by Lady Renton.

'I remember being here around fifteen years ago,' she announced, rearranging her silk skirts. 'As I recall, my daughter did not travel, being unwell at the time. I had left her in the safe hands of her nurse, for who wants a small child hanging on one's skirts while trying to enjoy an extended house party?' Her gaze became unfocused. 'I always thought I would have more children.' She brightened. 'Still, at least I was not barren.'

No one quite knew how to respond to this—particularly since everyone present knew Mrs Thaxby had no children.

After a brief silence, Lady Garvald offered, 'Like you, Lady Renton, I have only the one child, but a son such as Will is all a mother could wish for. I am so proud of the man he has become, though I sometimes miss the boy he used to be!'

So the Earl's given name was Will. It did not suit him, somehow. It was at once too…too *informal* and too *English*. One of the things Anna genuinely admired about Garvald was his pride in being Scottish at a time when all things English were thought by the *ton* to be innately superior. And the Earl's general demeanour was rather more characteristic of a *William* than a *Will*.

Naturally this brought her thoughts back to the way he had seemed to glower at her earlier. She shrugged inwardly, shaking off the discomfort at the notion he might be displeased with her. Somehow it had mattered briefly that he approved of her, but such notions contradicted her knowledge that her worth lay not in the approval of any individual—even a glowering Earl who was far, far too handsome. Instead, her value was in knowing herself to be Anna—a good sister, friend and, in this situation, house guest.

Besides, she must have imagined anything *specific* in the Earl's expression, given that it was Garvald's...er, *William's*...habit to glower. And William was a Scottish name too, she reminded herself: William the Lion; William Wallace.

'But would you not have wished for a daughter, Lady Garvald?' Lady Renton once again spoke with a particular bluntness.

Lady Garvald's gaze flicked briefly to Anna, then Rose. She nodded. 'I would, but sadly my husband died soon after my son's birth.' She smiled. 'I pray Will chooses a suitable wife, for she will be the nearest thing to a daughter I shall ever have.' She touched the diamond bracelet on her wrist. 'I shall be delighted to pass this heirloom to her.'

'A pretty piece, to be sure.' Mrs Thaxby's eyes gleamed with hardness. 'Have you had it valued?'

'No, I have not,' Lady Garvald replied firmly. 'Its true value lies in the meaning it has for this family.'

Mrs Thaxby gave a short laugh. 'Its true value rests in those stones, Lady Garvald, and in the gold they hang upon. We had a similar treasure in my family— the Fletcher necklace. A cluster of diamonds around a large, pear-shaped sapphire. Unfortunately, it was stolen many years ago and was never seen again.'

Clearly shocked, Lady Garvald asked, 'And did they ever catch the thief?'

Mrs Thaxby shook her head. 'All that wealth, gone forever!' Muttering, she added to herself, 'That necklace was worth a dashed fortune!'

Anna's jaw hardened. Mrs Thaxby cared only for wealth, and the *ton* knew it. But was there nothing of sentiment in her for a family heirloom lost after who knew how many generations?

'Does your son seek to marry, Lady Garvald?' For once, Anna was glad of Lady Renton's plain-spoken manner as well as her tenacity, for she too wished to know the answer to this particular question.

'Oh, no. But he will marry eventually, of course.' Their hostess gestured vaguely. 'This place, and the family name, require it.'

I had not thought he might marry!

Anna was conscious of a strange tension within her. The word 'eventually' was reassuring, though. The sudden anxiety began to drain out of her, even as her mind caught up with her nonsensical reaction. Why should she care when the Earl married, or whom?

'And if you were to choose his bride, what would you require in the next Lady Garvald?' Mrs Thaxby's tone was piercing.

Lord, what a pair!

Anna exchanged a brief glance with her sister. Lady Garvald was facing quite the inquisition.

'Oh, I should not dare to meddle in such matters.'

'Ah, but it is hardly *meddling* to ensure our children make good marriages—that they choose someone of consequence, with clear lineage and an air of distinction, yes?' Lady Renton was persistent, that was certain.

Mrs Thaxby gave a sweet smile. 'Your daughter, of course, is lately married, Lady Renton—to Mr Phillips.' She added, in a confidential air, 'Dear Lady Garvald, you may not know Mr Phillips, not being part of the London set.' She tilted her head to one side, as if considering the matter. 'I am not sure Mr Phillips could be said to have an air of distinction, but he clearly met your standards, Lady Renton.'

Ouch! Lady Renton had not been pleased with her daughter's choice and the *ton* knew it. Anna was conscious that her shoulders were now decidedly tense.

Lady Garvald's chin lifted. 'I have met Mr Phillips here on a number of occasions, and I think him an excellent young man. As to whom our children marry, that is a matter for them, I think. For my part, I should much prefer if my son chose a lady of character. Family background is of course important, yet we generally judge people by how we find them, do we not?'

Lady Renton sniffed, her eyes flashing fire. 'I must disagree with you there, Lady Garvald. I most certainly judge people based on their connections. Those with… shall we say *questions* about their paternity…in particular can never be fully accepted by right-thinking people, no matter how well they marry.'

Shocked—for this barb could only be aimed at her and her sisters—Anna froze, noting that Mrs Thaxby was attempting to hide a smirk at Lady Renton's words.

Lord, they care not who is hit by their arrows!

The two ladies constantly baited one another, as well as casually striking anyone else within earshot.

Lady Garvald intervened with an air of calmness. 'I must clarify something, Lady Renton. You were here *sixteen* years ago, not fifteen. I remember it well, for my son was eight years old that summer—almost nine. That was also the last time I saw a dear friend.'

My, she is bold!

She'd corrected Lady Renton so smoothly, and diverted attention from anyone in the room with questionable parentage, all in one sentence. Anna felt a surge of admiration for their hostess. Though unused to the viciousness of the London drawing rooms, Lady Garvald was clearly both formidable and quick-thinking.

'You are correct, Lady Garvald.' Mrs Thaxby took the opportunity to lob another rock in the general direction of Lady Renton. 'I was also present at that house party, and I remember it was 1796. But, tell me, who was the dear friend whom you never saw again? I recall the Kelgroves were also present, and of course Lord Kelgrove is since deceased, but he cannot have been your *special* friend, surely?'

Something about her emphasis on the word 'special' set Anna's teeth on edge. The woman's insinuation was obvious, and highly insulting.

Why on earth has Lady Garvald invited these two odious women to disturb her peace?

It made no sense—unless perhaps the ladies had been kinder sixteen years ago. Reflecting, Anna doubted it. Lady Renton's character was well-known, and the lines on Mrs Thaxby's face signalled a lifetime of grievance and complaint.

'Of course not!' Lady Kelgrove's tone was sharp, but she continued with a milder manner. 'She was a friend who moved away. She was not part of our party.'

'I find female friendship to be unnecessary,' declared Lady Renton. 'While I have many acquaintances among the ladies of the *ton*, I should not describe any of them as *friends*, I not think.' Anna's jaw sagged again at Lady Renton's statement. The woman seemed entirely oblivious to the fact that the principal reason for her lack of friendships was her own demeanour, nothing more and nothing less.

'I, on the other hand, have more friends than I can count,' declared Mrs Thaxby, making Anna blink. While the Thaxbys were received everywhere, given their lineage and wealth, Anna would struggle to identify anyone who might call Mrs Thaxby a friend.

'Including the Dowager Viscountess Ashbourne,' Mrs Thaxby continued, 'Who is a dear, *dear* friend.' Anna caught her breath at the sheer scale of the falsehoods being presented. 'I am *so* disappointed she is not here. As chaperone for Miss Lennox, she really ought to be.'

Now they were all looking at Anna. 'My sister, the

new Lady Ashbourne, is more than capable of chaperoning me, I think,' she offered quietly.

Lady Renton sniffed. 'In my day such a young woman could never be held to be an adequate duenna. My, you are *exactly* the same age!' She laughed at this, just as though she had said something witty.

Anna resisted closing her eyes in despair. The weeks ahead stretched out endlessly. Perhaps they should never have come. But Ashbourne and Garvald were bosom bows, and Anna had secretly been pleased at the notion of spending the summer here in Garvald's home—partly because she wondered if she might see another side of him here. Now though, with the Thaxbys and the Rentons disturbing everyone's peace, it did not seem worth it.

Thankfully, at that moment the door opened, admitting the gentlemen. Instinctively, Anna's gaze went to Garvald. As their eyes met he frowned, as if sensing something of her distress. Instantly she veiled her emotions, smoothing her expression into what she hoped was inscrutability. His gaze immediately went to his mother and his frown deepened.

'Will, here so soon!' Was there something of relief in Lady Garvald's tone? Anna certainly thought so. Glancing about, she realised that both Mrs Thaxby and Lady Renton seemed oblivious to, or uncaring about, the air of tension in the room.

'We could not stay away!' declared Lord Ashbourne gallantly, making straight for his wife and kissing her hand as he took his seat beside her. Mr Thaxby and

Lord Renton chose seats as far away from their spouses as was possible in the drawing room, while Garvald sat with his mother, and Mr Ashman and his father joined her on the satin settee.

What on earth has happened?

Will sensed the tension in the room immediately. Miss Lennox was on edge, as was his mother—although both ladies had hidden it behind a veneer of politeness.

Taking the empty seat next to Mama, he hoped the return of the gentlemen might alleviate any tension among the ladies. He knew the Rentons and the Thaxbys of old and, of the four of them, the beleaguered Lord Renton was the only one he had any time for.

'We have been discussing Garvald's lands,' Lord Renton informed him. 'We can hope to ride every day, so long as the weather holds up.'

At this, Miss Lennox exchanged a rueful glance with her sister.

What does it mean?

Mrs Thaxby, it seemed, had also spotted their exchange.

'What? You do not like our plans, Miss Lennox?' Mrs Thaxby sent her a piercing look, quite matching the tone of her question. Will began to suspect the character of the conversation prior to his entering the drawing room.

'I am afraid I and my sisters do not ride, Mrs Thaxby.'

Miss Anna's tone was calm. 'Still, no doubt we shall find other diversions while you are all out.'

'Not ride?' Lady Renton was all astonishment. 'Young ladies who do not ride? My, what is the world coming to?' She shook her head sadly. 'Once again I must be proud of my own daughter's accomplishments.'

'Including her stellar marriage?' This was clearly a reference to Lady Renton's daughter having married Mr Phillips.

Mrs Thaxby never failed to miss her mark, Will thought, watching as her husband handed her a glass of wine procured from one of the impassive footmen flanking the fireplace. Will had hinted to his butler a few days ago that Mrs Thaxby's relationship with wine was perhaps more focused on quantity, not quality.

'I am very happy with Mr Phillips as a son-in-law.' Lord Renton spoke firmly. 'As sensible and responsible a young man as I ever encountered. Our daughter chose well.'

Mrs Thaxby's mouth tightened but she subsided. *Well said, Renton!*

As host, Will found himself biting back one of his usual acerbic remarks. Mama had warned him to have a still tongue, and he would do all he could to promote whatever harmony could be achieved among the guests.

Briefly, he glanced at Miss Anna, and together they shared an instant's wry acknowledgement at the recent exchange. As he met her gaze, her blue eyes brimming with humour, he was disturbed to find his heart suddenly pounding and his mouth dry.

How does she do that?

'I shall teach you to ride, my love.' The affection in Lord Ashbourne's tone was plain as he looked adoringly at his new wife. 'And your sisters, too.'

With a small cough, Garvald drew his friend's attention. 'I have a couple of quiet mares that would suit Lady Ashbourne and her sisters. They are at your disposal, Ashbourne.'

'Oh, no!' Rose protested. 'I would not keep you from your sport, James!'

'We shall speak of it later, then,' Lord Ashbourne assured her, clearly undeterred.

The group was now large enough to enable multiple smaller conversations and, as people began speaking informally to those seated nearest, Will was able to share a few words of reassurance with his mother.

Miss Anna was sitting with Mr Ashman and Sir Walter, he noted, and they seemed to be conversing easily and naturally together—so much so that he noticed her shoulders loosening and her smiles become natural rather than forced. While he could only be pleased that she was feeling comfortable, something within him could not help wishing that it had been he and not the Ashmans who had taken the trouble from her brow.

Eventually, tea was served, and then they all dispersed—Will to the billiards room with some of the gentlemen, Mama accompanying Miss Anna to her chamber. He watched them go, his heart a mix of worry, hope and delight. What would the coming days and weeks bring?

* * *

Anna climbed the stairs to her room alongside her hostess, relieved the evening was at an end. While Lady Garvald and her son had been pleasant hosts, and the Ashmans delightful company, the bickering warfare between the Thaxby and Renton ladies had unsettled her.

In addition, the news that riding was to be the main day-time occupation was concerning. She and her sisters would be sorely disadvantaged, and she was daunted by her brother-in-law's offer of lessons. While Anna would dearly love to be able to ride, the thought of learning—of being near those large, prancing, unpredictable creatures—made her decidedly nervous. Rose would be fine if her doting husband was there, for James would ensure she came to no harm. Given the way the Ashbournes were so fixated on each other, though, Anna doubted that James would even remember her own presence, never mind her safety.

'Is your chamber to your satisfaction, Miss Lennox?'

'Oh, indeed, my lady. It is pleasant, and comfortable, and with as beautiful a view as I have ever seen!'

'I am glad.' She paused. 'My son tells me you have always lived in Scotland until this year—Elgin, I believe, and another place before that?'

'That is true.' She could not recall ever speaking to Garvald directly about it, but it was no secret. 'We moved to Elgin when we were just five years old and have no clear memories of the place we lived before that.'

'I see. There is something I wished to say to you. Many years ago, I had the—'

'My lady!'

They both started, turning on the stair.

'Sincere apologies, my lady.' It was Mrs Lowe, the housekeeper. 'One of your guests has just requested a bath—at this time of night! I dunno how I'm supposed to get gallons of hot water up three flights of stairs at eleven o'clock at night. Most of the servants are already in bed, for I shall have them up at five to see to all the extra duties!' She did not look pleased.

'I see.' Lady Garvald's brow was creased, as well it might be. 'Please excuse me, Miss Lennox.'

'Of course!'

As Lady Garvald descended with her housekeeper, Anna shook her head ruefully. Although she could not know for certain, she was willing to guess that the identity of the demanding guest could be narrowed down to two people: both female. And, what was more, it was likely that Lady Renton or Mrs Thaxby—whichever one of them it was—had demanded a bath deliberately, in order to test Lady Garvald's servants, hospitality or patience.

Outrageous!

If only she could help in some way! But, no, there was no role for her in this. She could help best by going to her room and staying there—and not requesting a midnight bath!

Chapter Three

The breakfast room at Lammermuir House was as pretty as the rest. Morning sunlight slanted through the tall windows, setting patterns dancing on the gleaming silverware. Indeed, the whole house had a warm, welcoming feel to it. Adhering strictly to the time set out by their hostess the night before, Anna arrived around five minutes after nine, smoothing her day gown of fine embroidered muslin as she entered. Surprisingly—or perhaps not, now she came to think of it—Lady Garvald was as yet the only person there.

'Good morning, Miss Lennox!'

After exchanging greetings and confirming that she had slept very well, Anna took her seat, requesting eggs, toast and porridge with honey.

'Ah, a woman after my own heart!' observed Lady Garvald, indicating her own bowl of oatmeal. 'The London chefs have not persuaded you to have fish or meat for breakfast, then?

Anna shuddered. 'No, indeed! I find I must breakfast lightly—especially since my sisters and I were raised on plain food.' She frowned. 'Please do not think me ungrateful, for I assure you our dear Lady Ashbourne—the dowager, that is—has been so welcoming and so generous.'

Lady Garvald smiled. 'Naturally! I understand she is your guardian's sister and that he is a solicitor in Elgin. Is that correct?'

She is remarkably well-informed.

'Yes. My mother clerked for him for five years and rented a cottage near his office for us to live in. She often spoke of her gratitude for his kindness.'

'Some people,' mused Lady Garvald, 'Being kind themselves, seem to attract kindness wherever they go. While others…'

They shared a look, knowing there was no need to finish the thought, for they understood one another perfectly. Just then, the door opened and the Earl entered, causing the usual response in Anna's foolish innards. As she responded to his greeting, she was conscious of her cheeks burning with heat—quite why, she could not imagine, but it was dashed inconvenient.

Lady Garvald, watching, seemed briefly to still, an arrested expression in her eye, before responding to her son.

'How was the billiards last night, Will?'

He grinned. 'With Ashbourne abed, there was no one who could beat me. Still, I let them play one another.'

'How generous of you!'

He laughed. 'As host, one must suffer these indignities!'

Anna joined in, enjoying the wry, self-deprecating tone. She and Lady Garvald shared a similar sense of wit, it seemed. What surprised her was that Will—that the *Earl*—had the same sense of humour. In London he had only ever been stiffly remote—which was why she could never fully understand why he, of all gentlemen, had sparked such an inconvenient *tendre* within her.

Her gaze swept over him briefly. Yes, he was handsome. Thick dark hair, strong jawline, deep blue eyes—all were present and correct, as was his fine form, currently displayed to advantage in buckskins, a crisp white shirt, cravat and a morning coat of deep-green superfine.

She suppressed a sigh. It was unfair that one man should be so…so *beautiful*! Particularly when he was so habitually closed—closed, unreadable, inscrutable… Briefly considering her new brothers-in-law, she reflected that both James and Claudio were much more transparent to her in their thoughts and feelings. Unlike the Earl, who…

Actually, to be fair, thought Anna, his current repartee with his mother was showing her an entirely different side to him.

Perhaps it was a good idea, coming here.

Anna had long recognised the Earl's intelligence, worldly knowledge and insight, but now she was also developing an understanding that, like her, he seemed to share a love for absurdity. This was a side to him that was decidedly lighter. Briefly, she remembered the look they had shared last night when Lord Renton had put Mrs Thaxby firmly in her box, and once again her heart skipped a beat. Clearly, he and his mother shared true affection, a notion that gave motherless Anna a brief pang—which she ruthlessly ignored. But his affectionate tone, open expression and relaxed good humour were entirely new—and entirely welcome. Perhaps, after all, he could be a Will rather than a William.

The conversation continued, Lady Garvald apologising for stifling a yawn at one point, which made Anna wonder just what had happened with the requested bath last night. Waiting until the room was briefly empty of servants, both footmen having been dispatched on errands, she asked with an innocent air, 'Was your housekeeper able to solve her dilemma last night, my lady?'

'Eh, what's this?' The Earl glanced sharply at his mother. 'Did something occur after we left the drawing room?'

'Oh, it was nothing, Will. One of the guests requested a bath, that is all.'

'A bath? A *bath*? At near midnight?'

'Oh, no, more like eleven o'clock.'

His jaw hardened. 'Never tell me that Mrs Lowe had to drag servants from their beds at that hour of the night!'

'Actually, no. I was able to persuade the guest in question to wait for morning. Even now, the extra footmen are processing to that bedchamber with hot water.'

He rolled his eyes. 'Lord save us! Good for you—your powers of persuasion are legendary!'

She gave him a rueful look. 'Not always, Will. Not

always.' There was a pause, Anna frowning in confusion as some meaning passed between them. 'But, in this instance, yes.

'Miss Lennox,' she continued, 'I shall speak plainly, for I think we understand one another. I care not whether I fail some arbitrary test of hospitality set by a demanding person. The request for a bath was an opportunity to show my teeth, and the boundaries beyond which I and my servants will not go. And I took it.'

'I am glad to hear it,' Anna replied. 'And I must tell you how much I admired your ability to hold the conversation after dinner, despite the missiles being flung about!'

'Missiles? What missiles?' The Earl's curious look was soon replaced with rueful laughter as they informed him of some of the verbal barbs being hurled around his drawing room while the men had been at their port.

'Lord!' he declared. 'I did wonder what had been said when we first joined you. There was an air of disquiet, I think.' He shook his head. 'The viciousness of the *ton*, exported to rural Lothian! Still, so long as we choose to be entertained, their arrows cannot pierce too deeply.'

'A good tactic, and one which we employed last evening, I think!'

'I do hope you will enjoy your time here, Miss Lennox.' His tone was curt, reverting to the familiar cadence she knew from London. 'It is important to me,' he continued, 'That you—that *all* our guests—may spend a pleasant few weeks at Lammermuir.'

'You love this place very much, do you not?' Anna's tone was low, her throat strangely tight.

He nodded, eyeing her directly. 'Aye. As a house, and my home, it is special to me.' Their gazes held and something between them swelled and resonated, taking the breath from Anna's lungs.

'You should take Miss Lennox on a tour of the house after breakfast, Will.'

Startled, Anna broke his gaze and looked at Lady Garvald. For an instant, she had forgotten Will's mother was present. 'Indeed,' the lady continued, humour dancing in her eyes, 'I insist on it.'

And so half an hour later Anna found herself walking by his side through room after room, covering every nook and cranny of the ground and first floors, until she was quite dizzy with it all. The building was a random collection of older parts and more recent additions, from thick, stone-built castellations to an elegant modern wing. As usual, some of the sights reawakened hints of old memories: the winding staircase to the castle tower; the library with its numbered sections outlined in gold paint; one of the drawing rooms done out with green hangings; even some paintings—a still life, a rural scene with a herd of cattle and a portrait hung above the fireplace in the Earl's study.

'My grandmother,' he explained, seeing her focus on it. 'A strong character, they say. I had it moved here. I quite like having her with me as I work on my documents and accounts.'

'Her strength of character is obvious,' Anna murmured. 'Just look at the vivacity in her eyes!'

The lady had a tall coiffure, an elaborate gown *à la française*, and a familiar diamond necklace on her wrist. No doubt Mrs Thaxby would have commented on the latter. Instead, Anna stood there, studying the portrait more attentively.

As was customary the artist had contained multiple details hinting at the life of the sitter: a book on the table beside her; a harpsichord in the background; a window revealing an idyllic scene of fields and sky. There was even a little dog peeping out from behind the lady's cerulean silk skirts. It all looked decidedly familiar, and a search for the painter's name provided an explanation.

'Gainsborough!'

'Yes. My grandfather hounded Mr Gainsborough until he agreed to paint her portrait. He was, I understand, already busy with multiple commissions, but my grandfather had his way in the end. He was excessively fond of my grandmother, by all accounts.'

'Gainsborough's style is so distinctive, I almost feel as though I have seen this painting before.'

He seemed to freeze in place. 'Many *ton* houses contain Gainsboroughs.' He paused. 'Do you remember anything of your first childhood home?'

'Almost nothing.' She shook her head sadly. 'Even my memories of the cottage we lived in afterwards are fading.' She pressed her lips together. 'It is all we have of our mama, those memories.'

'But—Lady Kelgrove…?'

'Of course, we are delighted to discover our connection to her. She has begun to tell us of Mama's childhood—though has said almost nothing as yet of the time when she ran away. Previously she had told my sister Rose how Mama's brother died—killed by brigands on the Heath, and his friend left for dead alongside him. She lost her daughter, then both grandchildren.'

He shook his head. 'Lady Kelgrove has had much tragedy to deal with.'

'Which is perhaps why she is so delighted to have found us.' Anna frowned. 'I just hope that her insistence on travelling does not make her too ill. She was determined to come here, you know!'

'Perhaps having another rest day today may aid her?' He opened the door, indicating she should precede him back out into the hallway.

'I do hope so. Oh, are we to go below stairs?' He had pressed something in the panelling, opening a hidden, narrow doorway off the main hallway which she realised led downstairs via a simple stone staircase. Again, she was reminded of the similar door upstairs. Why it had stayed in her mind, she could not say.

His eyes danced. 'I always abhor those who show only the public rooms. As master, I am responsible for ensuring the kitchens and storehouses are adequate for their purpose—just as much as I am responsible for ensuring the acquisition of art and furniture with which to grace the drawing rooms and library! A tour should of course show the inner workings of a house, I always think. And, as master, I am prodigiously well-informed about such matters as ovens and chimneys!'

Fascinated, Anna followed as he showed her through kitchens, sculleries, wine stores, dry rooms and even the laundry. Everywhere they went they encountered startled servants who curtseyed and bowed, and who seemed to find it highly unusual that the Earl was showing a young lady around the servants' quarters. Perhaps, despite his protestations, he did not get the opportunity to show visitors around very often.

'Apologies, sir!' The housekeeper bustled towards them, a hint of outraged dignity about her. 'If I had known you wished to inspect our work below stairs, I would have made all ready!'

'Not to worry, Mrs Lowe.' He smiled. 'Just an informal walk about, that is all.'

His calm tone seemed to mollify her a little, and she glanced towards Anna, as if taking in the Earl's companion for the first time. Her eyes widened briefly, a gleam of speculation in them. 'I hope you find everything to your liking, Miss Lennox.'

What an odd thing to say.

'The house is delightful, Mrs Lowe. And everything is very clean and well cared for.'

She preened a little. 'Well, we do have a good group of hard workers here, that I will say, miss. Of course, we have added extra staff for the house party, and they are still under my eye, I assure you.'

'I have no doubt that you and Gibson have everything in hand, Mrs Lowe.' The Earl's tone was firm.

Seemingly satisfied, she nodded, asking if she might assist them with anything else.

'Oh, no, no,' he assured her, opening yet another door. 'Now, Miss Lennox, this staircase will take us directly to the upper floors of this wing.'

Smiling a farewell to the housekeeper, Anna followed him up a long, dimly lit staircase, pausing to let footmen pass with empty jugs. Presumably they were still engaged in filling the bath for Mrs Thaxby or Lady Renton—whichever of them had so outrageously demanded such a privilege at nearly midnight.

Gasping in surprise as they emerged on the landing where the bedchambers were located, Anna observed, 'We are so far up! You know, I think my childhood home was rather like this—lots of hidden staircases and passageways.' Out of the corner of her eye she saw the narrow door, wondering if he would take her through it, but instead he led her down the landing.

He shrugged. 'Most larger houses have a warren of runs for the servants to move about unobtrusively. Now, let me show you the chambers we have set aside for Lady Kelgrove, and for the prince and princess.'

The bedchambers were like her own, comfortable and richly furnished. She made appropriately admiring noises, then, as they began returning to the main staircase, commented, 'Thank you for showing me around. I believe I have seen everything!'

He laughed. 'Not quite, for we have not visited the attics or the outbuildings. Another day, perhaps.'

Attics. So her instincts were probably correct, and the

narrow door must lead up to the top level of the house. 'Do you know,' she offered, 'I believe this is the longest conversation we have ever shared? How strange!'

He shrugged. 'London events do not facilitate conversation, I find. At least, not meaningful conversation. And I myself have not the happy knack of being an easy conversationalist in company—which I have no doubt is commented upon frequently.'

'Oh, no,' she lied politely. 'But surely everyone is more able to be open and at ease in their own home?'

'That is certainly true. Now, we are back at the breakfast room.' He indicated the door, surely the hundredth they had just passed through. 'Let us see,' he added softly, leaning down to speak softly in her ear, 'How many of our lay-abed companions have managed to rise, for it must be nearly ten!'

She gave a short laugh, quickly stifled. His breath was on the side of her cheek, his lips so close to her ear…

Dash it all! Now her heart was racing, her senses tingling, and no doubt she would be flushed again, just as they were about to engage with company. The weather was fairly warm, to be fair, so hopefully no one would think anything of it.

Fixing a polite expression on her face, she stepped inside where the whole party was present, save Lady Renton. It seemed Lady Garvald had already informed them that she was being given a walk around, and some of the others immediately clamoured for the same privilege. Laughing, the Earl agreed, and it seemed to Anna that he had never looked more handsome.

Taking her seat, she joined in the general clatter and hum of breakfast and conversation, remaining when the Earl left with Rose and James, the Thaxbys and Lord Renton, leaving only Anna and Lady Garvald along with Sir Walter and his son. Lady Renton, she deduced, was currently enjoying her bath.

The day passed in a mixture of conversation, food and wine. The party attended church in the little chapel on the grounds, and once again Anna was struck by a sense of familiarity—something about the layout, perhaps, or the way the light came in through the glorious stained-glass windows. Walking out with Rose in the late afternoon to explore the pretty gardens to the side of the house, Anna took the opportunity to speak to her sister about the strange feelings she had been experiencing since their arrival.

'I think wherever we lived for those first five years must have been very like this house, Rose. I have half-memories all around me here. Have you felt it too?'

Rose shrugged. 'Not really. But you were always the best at remembering things from long ago, Anna.'

Anna frowned. 'There must be many such houses, but this one has a decidedly Scottish feel to it. The architecture is distinctive, I think.'

'Which means we probably lived in Scotland for those first five years.' They shared a look. 'I am glad.'

'Me too. Although Mama was English, and in all

likelihood our father was too, I have always felt Scottish in here.' She jabbed at her chest.

'As have I.' Rose frowned. 'Now you come to mention it, I did think there was something familiar about the main staircase. The one here is much smaller than the one in our castle, but something about the turns and the windows…'

'I thought exactly the same! And yet, there are only a limited number of ways in which one can design a grand staircase, so we must not read too much into it.' She sighed. 'I am glad of anything that connects us to memories of Mama, no matter how vague.'

Rose slipped a hand into the crook of Anna's arm. 'We three will always have each other. We are all Mama's daughters, and while we remember her she will live on.'

'And now we also have Lady Kelgrove.'

'Who believes she knows something of our father!'

'That is true. While we might never discover our first childhood home—for Lady Kelgrove cannot know of it—would it not be wonderful to know who he was?' She giggled. 'I suggest he was a handsome groom, turning Mama's head with his strong body and his oh-so-handsome face!'

Laughing, Anna joined in the speculation, suggesting an earnest vicar with a lively mind and a loving heart.

'Yet,' Rose objected, 'Mama was never *pious*, so I hardly think he could have been a vicar!'

On they went, Anna enjoying the simple pleasure of spending time alone with Rose who, naturally, had been distracted by her recent marriage. Emerging from the pretty rose garden with its statues of Poseidon and Athene, they turned a corner, entering what was clearly the kitchen garden. Two gardeners were currently engaged in harvesting vegetables—vegetables which would no doubt grace their table today. One of the best things about being back in the country was the freshness of the food—from garden to fork in just a few hours. Anna was convinced it tasted better.

Seeing them, the gardeners paused their work to bow and await their passage. Anna and Rose nodded smiles in their direction and carried on. Ahead, in the small yard between the kitchen garden and the house, a laundry maid was vigorously scrubbing something made of linen—a petticoat perhaps—while a valet or footman was beating a reddish-coloured coat.

Curious, Anna looked closer, wondering if it was Lord Garvald's, but a pang of disappointment went through her as she realised the coat was too small to belong to the Earl, who was a head taller than both Lord Renford and Mr Thaxby.

Lord, I am even interested in his coat! Really, this fixation was proving mightily inconvenient! She had no thought of marriage, no indication that he liked her, nothing—only her own random notions.

Like the gardeners, both servants paused politely as the girls passed. Strangely, Anna wondered for a brief instant if the valet wished to say something to them. The way he looked at them seemed rather intent. There was nothing sordid about it; it was just a look. She eyed him curiously. He was a trim, well-presented man with grey hair and a face filled with lines, suggesting his age to be more than sixty. He held himself well, with a quiet dignity. A servant, naturally, could not address a guest of the family without a clear reason to do so, but...

They walked on towards a small orchard. Just as they reached the first trees—the apples beginning to ripen nicely on their low, twisted branches—Anna's thoughts about the owner of the coat were confirmed. Mr Thaxby stormed round the corner, making for the valet, and seemingly unaware of Anna's and Rose's presence.

'John! Why did you not come when I called?'

The valet bowed, his brow furrowed. 'I apologise, sir.' He indicated the coat. 'I am readying the mulberry jacket in preparation for this evening, as you requested.'

'As my valet—my *current* valet—you are expected to understand and anticipate my needs.' Lifting a hand, he slapped the man hard on the side of the head. Anna winced and stepped a little closer to Rose.

'Do you understand me?'

'Yes, sir. How may I serve you?'

'We have decided to ride out. Bring my boots to the room near the servants' quarters where the others are already making ready. Well, why are you still standing there, gaping at me like the feeble-minded ninny you are? Go!'

'Yes, sir.' The man went, briefly rubbing his left ear, which surely must still have been ringing with the force of his master's blow.

Anna and Rose remained stock-still until Mr Thaxby had disappeared around the corner, then shared an angry look.

'Only the worst of men abuse their servants so!'

'He hit him as hard as he could, knowing the valet could not fight back.'

'And John—the valet—had done nothing wrong! How was he to know they would go out riding?'

'One thing puzzles me...' Rose's brow was furrowed. 'Why did he not send another servant to fetch him?'

They eyed each other in dawning horror. 'Because he wanted to do it himself.'

'Because he wanted to hit him.'

Anna shuddered. 'I have always heartily disliked the Thaxbys. Now I have even more reason to do so.'

On they walked, and it took some time for the sick feeling in Anna's stomach to subside. Eventually, though, they spoke of other things, their conversation eventually circling back to Anna's half-memories revived by aspects of Lammermuir House.

'Now,' declared Rose, 'This seems familiar to me!'

She indicated the stables with a hand, and Anna chuckled. 'Well, naturally, for most stable blocks look the same to me. I do recall you were particularly enthusiastic about learning to ride when we were little.'

'Whereas you were nervous around the ponies at first—though, as I recall, ZanZan was very patient with you.'

'He was.' Anna sighed. 'So, you do still remember some things, then.'

Rose shrugged. 'Very little. Not like you. I do wish I could recall more of Mama.'

Anna squeezed her hand. 'Me too, Rose. Me too.'

Chapter Four

Descending via the main staircase later, clad in an elegant evening gown of white silk adorned with tiny blue rosebuds along the hem and sleeves, Anna took particular notice of the elements of Lammermuir House that seemed familiar: the layout of the turns in the stair; the position of the windows... Yes, this staircase was smaller, but surely she remembered peeping through banisters like these at a hallway below?

Lost in thought, she made her way to the drawing room, there to await the dinner gong. Entering, she was surprised to find the Earl and his mother deep in conversation.

'But you *must* tell them, Will, and soon. After all, that was the whole purpose in bringing them all here.'

The Earl had a definite air of agitation about him, Anna noticed. *How curious!*

'I shall, Mama, once they are all here. Indeed, I wondered if Miss Lennox—'

'Miss Lennox!' intoned the footman, and mother and son whirled to face her.

'Miss Lennox!' echoed the Earl, covering any confusion he might have experienced by striding towards her and taking her hand. 'You look delightful this evening. Does she not, Mama?'

'I suspect,' offered his mama with only a hint of dryness, 'You would find Miss Lennox to look delightful even should she come adorned in sackcloth!' She indicated a nearby settee. 'Come, my dear, and sit with me. Did you enjoy our gardens earlier?'

'I did, my lady,' Anna confirmed, even as their earlier words were sinking in. *What must he tell me? And what was Lady Garvald's purpose in bringing us here?* 'The roses are exquisite!'

Naturally, she could say nothing of the incident involving Mr Thaxby. Dropping the Earl's hand—which left her own feeling bereft—she moved to sit with her hostess, who beamed.

'You have hit upon exactly the right thing to say to my mother, Miss Lennox.'

His eyes met hers, and as usual there was a sense of breathlessness within her. 'How so, my lord?'

'The rose garden is my mother's particular pastime, and I believe it fair to say it owes as much to her as to the efforts of the gardeners.'

'Oh, stuff!' retorted his mama inelegantly, but a telltale flush stained her cheeks. 'I only do a little.'

'Every day!'

'Well, yes, but one absolutely must keep deadheading to keep the flowers coming.'

'But your dedication means you can take at least some of the credit for the garden!'

'I suppose. Have you any interest in gardening, Miss Lennox?'

'Truthfully, I have never had the opportunity to try.' She thought for a moment. 'But I see how it could be fascinating, working with one's hands, doing something which leads to the development of such a beautiful garden... Yes, I believe I could have an interest, given the opportunity.'

'Your true interest is music, is it not?'

Now it was Anna's turn to blush.

My, she is well-informed on everything! He must have...

'I do enjoy playing—although having to play at *ton* recitals and musicales is quite the most terrifying thing I have ever experienced.'

Lady Garvald indicated her own piano. 'Feel free to practise or perform any time while you are here—or not to perform, if you truly do not wish to.'

'Oh, no, I am happy to play if you wish it.'

She nodded, satisfied. 'Perhaps after dinner, then.'

'You are in for a treat, Mama. I have heard Miss Lennox play, and her talent is remarkable.' Anna's eyes flew to his face, seeking any evidence of polite exaggeration. But, no, he seemed entirely sincere. Swallowing, she realised abruptly his opinion mattered to her. It mattered very much.

'Lord and Lady Renton!' They turned at the footman's announcement, Anna inwardly bracing herself for whatever level of acerbity Lady Renton would unleash tonight. By the time greetings had been made, Rose and her viscount had arrived, and before long the whole party was assembled and the gong sounded for dinner.

Afterwards, they retired to the drawing room—first the ladies, the gentlemen joining them relatively quickly. Mr Thaxby was wearing a mulberry-coloured jacket, Anna noted. Anna played and was complimented by everyone—even Lady Renton, who for once had no caveat or indirect insult with which to shadow any words of praise.

Relieved that her performance had gone well, it was only when she was climbing the stairs for bed at nearly midnight that Anna recalled the Earl's strange conversation with his mother earlier.

That was the whole purpose in bringing them all here...

Lady Garvald's words made no sense. Unless...

Anna stopped halfway up the stairs, uncaring of the footmen below, who must surely think her behaviour odd. Bending, she peeped through the banisters as she might have done as a small child. Of course, the proportions would seem different. To a four-or five-year-old, this staircase would have seemed positively enormous.

Sally was waiting in Anna's bedchamber, and Anna submitted to her ministrations while inwardly her mind was awhirl. Was it possible? The library, the chapel, the paintings... Images whirled through her mind like leaves in autumn. The mysterious door on the landing… The staircase…

The maid left and Anna went to bed. If this *was* the idyllic first home of their childhood—which of course she could not say for certain—that would mean that Lady Garvald was 'Milady'. *My lady.* Yes, that would fit.

And was ZanZan… Milady's son? Will was probably about the right age and ZanZan, her dearest friend, had had dark hair. Had his eyes been blue? She could not recall. She only knew that she had missed him terribly after they'd gone to Elgin. A loss that had become part of her, compounded by Mama's death five years later. Loss rippled through her, a familiar pain sharpened by what were no doubt fanciful notions.

Had she not spent a lifetime unconsciously searching for her first home and the happiness she had enjoyed there with ZanZan? The yearning within her might well be making her mind wish for things that simply were not true.

Another notion struck her. If the Earl had recognised them on their arrival and presentation in London, why had he not said something? No, the mysterious matter his mother was urging him to speak of must be something else.

Anna took a deep breath. She was no dreamer, like Rose. Nor was she passionately romantic, like Izzy. She was Anna—plain-spoken, logical and always practical. She should not be dreaming of impossible things, for the very reason they were impossible. That way led to heartache and yearning, and the reopening of deep wounds that were slowly scarring over.

No. She must put all speculation from her mind. Just because she was in a house that was architecturally similar to one she had lived in a long time ago meant nothing, really, nothing at all. Blowing out the candle, she turned on her side and allowed sleep to claim her.

Will lifted his glass, idly noticing how the glow of the brandy was enhanced by candlelight. When the others had retired he had sat on, needing some solitude and quiet before seeking his own bed. A reckoning was coming—probably tomorrow, when their final guests arrived. Was he ready for it? He did not know.

Since Anna and her sisters had made their presentation earlier in the year—astonishing the court by being identical triplets—he had been on edge. There were so many questions, so much riding on the answers. What if he was wrong to have done things this way?

Ah, but what if I am right?

So far, the house party was going exactly as one might have predicted. Anna and Rose were perfectly well-behaved, Mrs Thaxby and Lady Renton rather less so. The gentlemen were a mix of bemusement, indulgence and studied ignorance. Why his mama had invited these others was not entirely clear to him. Obviously they had needed to invite enough guests to make the thing a party, but there were some surprising specimens among them. While Lord Renton was generally well-liked—and rather pitied at times—he knew no one who genuinely liked the Thaxbys.

Sighing, he took another sip. It was late. Riddles could wait.

She is peeping through the banisters.

The staircase is enormous, the central feature in this house-like castle. Or is it a castle-ish house?

Below, Lord Garvald glowers at her. Shrieking, she runs upstairs, making for the narrow door. On she goes, up and up to the top floor, where there is safety.

The corridor is narrow, daylight pouring in from the two skylights. She opens the door on the left and dashes inside, to the safety of the nursery. Her sisters are there, and ZanZan.

'Oh!' She feels surprise. 'Were you not just down-stairs?'

Anna awoke, her mind and heart racing. Without thought, she sat up, leaving her bed. Feeling for the unlit candle on her side table, she made her way across the room and opened the door. The house—*or was it a castle?*—was quiet. Clearly, everyone had retired. Lighting her candle from the large candelabrum illuminating the landing, Anna hurried towards the narrow door. It was not locked, and she lifted her candle to survey the narrow stairs leading upwards. *Yes!* Her heart pounding, she ascended, her bare feet making no sound on the wooden steps. At the top she lifted her candle again, surveying the ceiling above. There were two skylights, now wreathed in darkness. The door on the left loomed into view. With a shaking hand, she opened it and stepped inside.

Yawning, Will made his way along the landing. That last brandy had hit the right spot, and he now had every hope of sleeping tonight, despite the worries that plagued him. The Lennox sisters. His mother. Anna.

He stopped. The door to the attic floor was open. Frowning, he took the branch of candles from the side table and made his way up the narrow staircase. The door on the left was open, the one that led to the nursery, and a glimmer of candlelight shone from within. With a sense of inevitability, he pushed the door wide open.

She whirled around, candle in hand. Her eyes were wild, hair unbound, face as pale as her thin nightgown.

'What is your name?' Her tone was demanding, though her voice cracked.

'William. Will.' His throat felt tight, and it seemed as though his heart would leap from his chest at any moment.

This is the moment. It had finally come.

'No. Your *full* name.'

'W-William Alexander Edward Henderson.'

'Alexander. Xander. Was that your mother's childhood name for you?'

'Yes.' He took a breath. 'You called me ZanZan.'

Chapter Five

He stood immobile, silence stretching between them as his words sank in. His heart was thundering; his breath caught. She reached out a trembling hand, and all the while her eyes searched his face.

'ZanZan.'

Their eyes locked. 'You—you remember me?' His throat felt tight, his voice cracking. Everything, his past and present, revolved around this.

'I do now. And I have never forgotten—' She broke off, putting her free hand to her forehead. 'Oh, lord, I feel strange. I…'

As her knees buckled he managed to catch her with one hand, wrapping his arm around her and setting his candelabrum down on the dresser to his left. Her own candle had fallen to the ground, and he stamped on it to snuff it out while simultaneously wrapping his other arm around her. Her head lolled awkwardly against his arm, and his stomach felt a little sick at the wrongness of it.

She was clearly unconscious—well, why should she not be, given the shock she had just experienced?

Dash it all, I should have told her before!

Glancing about him, he realised he had few options. The three wooden bed frames that had served the triplets so long ago were still there, bare of mattresses and looking sadly neglected. But then, no one ever came in here. He himself had avoided the place, associating it with the dreadful sense of loss he had felt for years after they had gone away.

His only option was to sit on one of the small beds and hold her on his lap. He was not prepared to lay her on a hard, dusty floor, and carrying her downstairs might lead to dramas neither of them would wish for. A shudder rippled through him as he briefly imagined what the Thaxby or Renton ladies would have to say about such a shocking turn of events! No, somehow he had to keep this private, and hope she would be well again soon.

He sat gingerly, but the bed held their combined weight without protesting. Although it was furthest away, he had chosen the bed to the right of the small fireplace, and as he readjusted her on his lap he understood why. This had been her bed. How many hours had they all played here together, here and throughout Lammermuir House? Anna, Izzy and Rose had been more than companions to him. They had been friends and family in one. And he and Anna…

Afterwards he had tried to explain it to his mother. Through the tears and distress of an eight-year-old boy, he had expressed outrage that Anna had been taken away by her mother.

'She—she is my twin!' he had protested.

Mama had tried to understand. 'Do you mean that, of the three of them, Anna is the one you liked best?'

'Yes! But no! I like all of them. B-but they are t-triplets. And me and Anna are the *same*. We are triplets together—I mean t-twins. And I am going to m-marry her when I g-grow up.'

'Speak slowly, Xander. You're tripping over your tongue.'

At this, he recalled stamping off in frustration. And it seemed every time Mama had told him to 'slow down', 'take a deep breath' or think about what he was saying, his stammer became worse. He'd known she was trying to help, but it had only made him more aware of it.

By eleven, there'd been times he could barely get a word out, and his time at boarding school had been dominated by boys, and occasionally teachers, mocking his speech. At fifteen, realising that his own name was one of the hardest things to say, he had retired the name Alexander and adopted his birth name of William. He had also dedicated himself to practising his speech, realising that he could be completely fluent while reading aloud or singing, and building confidence from there.

Despite working on his speech, Will's wounds from the loss of the Lennox girls had only faded, not healed. When they had left, his mother had sunk into low spirits for a long, long time, compounding his hurt. Somewhere deep within him, he had known one thing: *people leave.*

By the time he had left university, most of his friends had not even realised he had a stammer, so adept had he been at managing it—including covering it up by changing a word if he knew it would trip him up. He rarely relaxed his guard—except with his mother and a few close intimates—and had developed something of a reputation for being closed and distant. Aloofness was now part of his nature—partly to hide his speech defect, partly because he could never seem to risk being hurt. He had male friends, good friends, but until recently he had never allowed a woman to touch his heart.

It did not bother him—most of the time. But, when it came to *wanting* to be open, wanting to speak to a certain person about the fact they had known each other as children, it had proved impossible. The very thought of speaking the truth to Anna had caused his body to tense in fear. Naturally, he had had no way of knowing how she or her sisters would react—they might well have been delighted to meet someone from their past again. But none of them had recognised him. To be fair, their names and the fact that triplets were so unusual had made him certain: Anna, Isobel and Rose Lennox, the triplets.

To them, though, he was an unremarkable gentleman whose given name—if they even thought to ask someone for it—was apparently William, not Xander. And their mother had clearly never told them their first home had been Lammermuir House, the seat of the

Earl of Garvald. Given all of that, why should she— *they*—have realised?

Yet *something* had brought Anna to her old bedroom tonight. He had deliberately shown her around the house, hoping she might recognise something. He had not, though, had the courage to bring her up here, for the nursery had barely changed in the sixteen years since they had left, travelling by Mama's coach to meet the stage at Haddington. That was a strong, clear memory for him—the sight of their coach disappearing down the drive. It was the last time he had seen them—until they had appeared in the Queen's drawing room as beautiful young ladies, leaving him briefly stupefied.

Their beauty—Anna's beauty—had quite knocked him back, his mind and heart swirling in confusion as they'd made their curtseys before the Queen. Afterwards he had danced with her, incapable of much speech, bowled over by the knowledge that the beautiful woman holding his hands was none other than his very own Anna.

Refocusing on the present, he felt the warmth of her body against him. There had been no sign of recognition in her earlier. Once again, the thought could not be denied. Something must have sent her here, to her old chamber after midnight. *She remembers!*

Gently, he smoothed back her hair from her face. She was breathing evenly, and had it not been for her extreme pallor he might have been able to pretend she was asleep.

My, how beautiful she is!

Eight-year-old Xander had had no point of reference, but twenty-five-year-old Will knew that objectively Anna and her sisters were beautiful—the Queen's diamonds, no less.

She stirred, lifting a hand to her head, then her eyes opened. There was a brief moment of what looked like—was that *wonder*?—then she struggled to raise herself up.

'My goodness!' Her voice trembled. 'Did I faint? I never faint!'

He helped her to sit, but now her face was close to his, her bottom pressed into his lap. *Too close.* 'You did! Let me help you.' He smoothly lifted her off him and placed her carefully alongside him on the small bed, exhaling in a curious mix of relief and disappointment.

'Now, are you feeling faint again? Perhaps sitting up so quickly was too much.' His hand was still on her back, in case she should once more be overcome, and he could still feel the warmth of her skin through the thin nightgown. Now that she was recovering, his treacherous body had decided to notice every detail: the swell of her bosom hinted at in the warm candlelight; the delicious scent of her beside him; the sight of her kissable lips.

Sending a stern rebuke to his nether regions, Will focused on her health. Such concern, he hoped, would prevent his body from fixating on other matters.

'Yes, I… But I shall be well presently. Let me just sit a moment.'

'Of course.'

She looked at him, and he at her. Time seemed to stand still. The urge to kiss her was becoming unbearable, but before he could lean in she shook her head, as if to clear it from confusion.

'You are ZanZan.'

'I am. I am relieved you remember me.'

She clasped his free hand, declaring fiercely, 'I would never have forgotten you! Never!'

He swallowed, unsurprised to find his eyes stinging. 'I knew you all from the first, at your presentation.'

She nodded thoughtfully. 'The Lennox sisters. Triplets.'

'You are fairly distinctive, to be fair. I danced with you that day, but you clearly had no idea who I was.'

Her hand was still on his, and now she squeezed it. 'I am sorry, Zan—I mean Will. I mean, my lord.'

He waved this away. 'I am delighted to be ZanZan again.' He smiled. 'Or Will, if you prefer. Anything but "my lord". We have too much history between us for formalities.'

Her brow was furrowed. 'Looking back, there was always something about you. When I saw you at soirées or balls, I always… But I did not… I think,' she finished slowly, 'That something within me half-recognised you.'

'Perhaps.'

She smiled at him through eyes wet with tears. 'You were our best friend, and Milady like a second mother to us.'

He flinched inwardly. Something about her emphasis on the word 'friend' was bothering him.

'And your mama, Mrs Lennox, was so good to me. Why...?' He swallowed. 'Why d-did she leave, take you away?'

She frowned. 'We do not know. Some danger, never specified.'

His jaw loosened. 'Danger? Here?' *What on earth...?*

'I know. It seems unlikely.' Shrugging, she squeezed his hand. 'ZanZan! It is—it feels like a miracle to find you! I missed you so much, and for so long!' Her eyes searched his face, as if seeking to find whatever faint memories she had of the boy and map them to the man. 'My recollection is that you and I...' she faltered.

'That we were *particularly* close? Yes, we were. I told my mama after you left that you were my twin.' He thought for a moment. 'She never understood it.' His face twisted. 'And your departure affected me for a long time. I felt abandoned.' He rolled his eyes to lessen the sting, but she caught her breath.

'Of course you did! I had Izzy and Rose, and we each had our mothers, but you lost your three best friends. "Abandoned" is exactly the word.' She bit her lip. 'No doubt you were angry with us.'

'Angry is an understatement,' he admitted ruefully. 'I was lost in rage for a time. But all is well now.'

'It is.'

There was a silence as they simply stilled for a moment, his heart swelling with a fierce mix of unknown emotions. They rose then by unspoken agreement and he walked her back to her room. Somehow her hand stayed in his all the way. At her door he bowed and kissed her hand.

'Sleep well, Anna,' he murmured.

'You too, ZanZan.'

Walking down the landing, he felt compelled to look back. She had not moved, and at his turning she smiled. Heart soaring, he matched her, and continued on to his chamber feeling as though he were walking on air.

Anna awoke, realising from the light at the edge of her curtains it was morning. *Finally.* All night she had slept in brief snatches, being too full of astonishment, emotion and *questions* to rest deeply.

She was suddenly, unexpectedly, angry with Will. Or ZanZan, as she now knew him. He had known, all along, for months. Yet he had never so much as hinted at the truth, leaving Anna and her sisters in the wilderness of ignorance all this time.

I thought him a stranger. Was he playing games with me?

Thank goodness Izzy would come today, for one thing was certain: her sisters must know as soon as possible! Should she tell Rose this morning or wait and tell them both together? Might Izzy feel left out?

Recently, at the request of both Lady Kelgrove and Lady Ashbourne, they had held secrets for a time, to be revealed at a key moment. The *ton* liked its drama. And so they had delayed revealing the fact they were identical triplets until their presentation, not leaving

Lady Ashbourne's house until their day at court. Later they had also allowed Rose and James to share the news of their marriage. And just a few weeks ago Lady Kelgrove had held a ball for the express purpose of revealing that the Lennox sisters were her great-grand-daughters. Was that so different from what ZanZan had done—keeping the secret of their connection all this time?

Yes. A few days, a couple of weeks…not months. They had been presented in March, more than five months ago. And, she now realised, his mother had clearly been urging him to tell them yesterday. Yet he had not. And, if she had not realised and gone to the nursery, she would still not know the truth.

Still, for now it would be good to keep this news to herself, so as to tell Rose and Izzy at the same time later today.

Keep it to herself and ZanZan.

I must speak with him.

Rising, she twirled about the room to the sounds of an invisible orchestra. Joy was everywhere—inside her, in the air about her, in the beautiful day now beginning. She opened the curtains, gazing at the gardens below with a fresh eye. Should she have recognised the view? It mattered not, for her search was over. She had found Lammermuir House. Found Milady. Found ZanZan. Even though she was cross with him, it did nothing to diminish her joy at having rediscovered her first home. It was as if she'd found a missing part of herself.

I was born here.

Yes, she would tell Izzy and Rose together, later today. Oh, how wonderful it was going to be! But first she should write it down. Something this momentous must not be forgotten. Sharpening a pen, she sat at the small desk in the corner of her bedchamber, committing to paper the astounding sequence of events which had unfurled last night. As she wrote, she realised she was addressing it to her mother in the form of a letter. She told Mama all about it—Lady Garvald's warm welcome, Lammermuir House itself and the Earl who was really ZanZan. Mama had always encouraged her girls to keep a journal, and Anna was well used to writing about the events, thoughts and feelings she was experiencing.

Eventually, she was done. Crossing the room, she rang the bell for the maid, then returned to the window and the beautiful day outside.

Half an hour later she was in the gardens—alone, for of course it was terribly early and only the servants were about. Softly humming to herself, she wandered amid tall gladioli, proud hollyhocks and Milady's roses until he came, as she had known he would.

'Good morning, Miss Lennox.' Her heart stilled, then raced. How handsome he looked! His coat was blue and brought out the colour of his eyes.

ZanZan has blue eyes.

The knowledge satisfied something deep within her. Joy at seeing him warred with the crossness within her, and joy won—at least for now.

She made a curtsey. 'Good morning, my lord.'

They laughed then, and he stepped towards her. 'Anna!'

'ZanZan!'

Taking her hand, he placed it in the crook of his arm. 'Let us walk together.' He leaned towards her. 'I saw you, from my window.'

She sent him a sideways glance. 'I hoped you might.'

'But you have a dimple!' Raising a finger, he touched her cheek. 'How did I not know this? And why have not seen it before?'

'Ah, my elusive dimple! It is one of the few things that distinguishes me from my sisters. It apparently only appears when I adopt certain expressions.'

'Very well. I shall endeavour to make a study of it, for I wish to know everything about you. And I mean everything.'

'As do I. About you, I mean.' She exhaled, her earlier anger briefly forgotten in the face of his warmth. 'How fortunate we are to have found one another again! Dear friends reunited.'

Was he frowning? Perhaps not, for his tone was even as he offered, 'I know I really should have made myself known to you from the first. I...'

'Yes, why did you not say something? All this time you knew, yet you said nothing.' Inwardly, Anna recognised that what she sensed felt almost like betrayal. No wonder she had been angry earlier. This was Zan-Zan, and he had said nothing. Why?

'Well, at first I was in shock, and you clearly did not

recognise me. I was, to be honest, at a loss—and I am unused to being out of control in that way.'

Interesting. Control was clearly important to him.

'I suppose,' she offered, 'It would have been very difficult for you to casually mention in conversation: *by the way, did you know we grew up together*?'

'True. But there is more to it than that.' He took a deep breath, and Anna abruptly realised he was about to say something of significance. 'When I told you before I am not blessed with the happy knack of being an easy conversationalist in company…'

'Yes?' Her attention was entirely on him, so much so she was almost holding her breath.

He grimaced. 'The truth is that I have a s-stammer, which I manage to hide fairly well most of the time.'

A stammer? She had had no idea. She nodded thoughtfully. 'I see. So is that why…?'A number of things now came to her: his aloofness; his reluctance to speak to a larger group; the air of tension she had sensed in him at times.

'It is.' He smiled. 'I do not even know for certain what you are trying to say. I just sense that you understand.'

For answer, she nodded and squeezed his arm. She did. So much made sense now.

'So,' he began in an entirely different tone, 'Are we to tell the others? My mother already knows who you are, but I think she will be delighted to hear that you have remembered.'

'I would prefer to tell my sisters first—before the Thaxbys and Rentons, I mean.'

'This afternoon, then, when the prince and princess arrive?'

She nodded. 'And perhaps we can tell Lady Kelgrove and your mama at the same time?'

'A capital notion. Let us attempt to contrive it, then.'

The next few hours were a heady mix of joy, wonder and frustration. Thoughts flew through Anna's mind like a river in torrent, bustling and roaring over one another so that she hardly knew what was what. Somehow, she made it through breakfast, a walk in the woods and a long and dreary lecture from Lady Renton on the freedoms allowed young ladies now that would never have been permitted in her day. It was little wonder Mama had run away, if that had been the case, thought Anna dryly.

Rose naturally sensed something different about Anna. To be fair, Anna thought, the air of suppressed excitement within her must be apparent to anyone who knew her well. But, when Rose sent her a questioning look when no one else was watching, she only shook her head and gave a look which she hoped was mysterious and mischievous in equal measure.

Late in the afternoon Prince Claudio and his bride arrived, followed a few moments later by Lady Kelgrove in her large and comfortable travelling coach. Their servants had already arrived and were currently engaged with Lord Garvald's footmen in bringing trunks and bandboxes to the respective bedchambers.

Standing on the drive with the others, Anna took part in the exchange of greetings with a strange feeling. What she had to tell her sisters would change all their lives forever, for it had changed hers.

Once inside, Lady Kelgrove requested tea in her bed-chamber, making Anna exchange a look with Will. Anna then sent him a nod to indicate they should go ahead with sharing the news regardless, and Will sent her an answering nod. In that moment it did not occur to Anna to notice how attuned they were.

While the others were engaged in conversation, he took the opportunity to ask Anna in a low voice, 'Well? Shall we await Lady Kelgrove's return?'

Anna shook her head. 'I can barely wait a moment more. We can tell Lady Kelgrove later.'

He nodded. 'I suggest the morning room in…ten minutes? I shall bring my mother.'

'Agreed.'

The conversation had been swift, but they had understood one another perfectly.

That is because Will—the Earl—is my ZanZan. She hugged the notion to her, enjoying the excited warmth within her chest and stomach. *Happy butterflies.*

Ten minutes later, Anna led Rose and Izzy to the morning room by the simple expedient of bidding them to accompany her. Rose looked a little confused, to be sure, but since Izzy was currently dominating their conversation with an account of how their coachman had almost missed the entrance to the estate, even though it was perfectly obvious, the moment passed without any precipitate questioning.

Lord Garvald and his mother had clearly just arrived, for as they entered she was saying, 'I really should not be away from my guests, Will. I must ensure Lady Kelgrove has all she needs— Oh!'

She blinked as the three Lennox sisters entered, bringing a hand to her chest. 'Your Highness! Lady Ashbourne! Miss Lennox! My, you are so alike! I know I commented upon it outside, but it really is quite striking!' Pausing, she turned to her son. 'What is amiss, Will? For this looks suspiciously contrived.'

He laughed. 'As sharp as ever, Mama.' He took a breath. 'Nothing is amiss. Indeed, what I have to say will, I hope, be received was good news. Yesterday Miss Lennox and I...'

'Oh, my goodness!' Izzy clapped her hands, even as it dawned on Anna what she must be thinking. She stood helplessly in horror as Izzy clattered ahead with her customary lack of foresight. 'Are you to be *married*?'

Chapter Six

Izzy looked from Anna to the Earl and back again, delight apparent on her face. 'How wonderful! I—'

'No!' Will cut her off, then grimaced ruefully. 'I apologise, Your Highness. It might have seemed as though that was the announcement I was about to make.'

Anna was frozen to the spot, overcome by mortification. The way his mama was looking at her...and as for Izzy!

How could she?

The Earl was still speaking, and belatedly she returned her attention to what he was saying... 'She felt as though she half-recognised some of the parts of Lammermuir House.' He paused, looking at her expectantly.

She took a breath. 'Lord Garvald has now confirmed that a lady called Mrs Lennox lived here for five years. And she had triplet daughters.' Her words dropped into the silence like stones in a well. The impact was deep, resonant, and shocking.

'What—here?'

'This is where we lived?'

Izzy was quick to make the connection. 'Then you are Milady, Mama's dear friend!'

'I am,' said Lady Garvald tremulously. 'I missed her dreadfully when she went away.'

'Wait,' Rose said thoughtfully. 'So are you the boy who was our friend?'

He grinned. 'You called me ZanZan.'

He used exactly those words last night.

A shiver of something tremendously powerful washed over Anna at his statement. His words had immediately proved to her who he was, for no one else could have known their childish name for their friend.

'ZanZan! Oh, my goodness!' Izzy enveloped him in a brief hug, then turned to his mother. 'Milady!'

Lady Garvald opened her arms, and Izzy embraced her. Rose and Anna did the same, Anna feeling in that moment a strong connection not just to Milady and her son, but also Mama. Rose also hugged Will, but Anna did not even move towards him. Well, how could she, when it was clear her moment of revelation with him had already passed? And, besides, much as she wished to embrace him, something within her did not want an audience—particularly after Izzy's recent, mortifying assumption.

'This is astonishing!' Izzy eyed Will. 'When did you realise, my lord?'

'When the Queen's major-domo announced the three Misses Lennox at your presentation and you walked towards her, as alike as peas in a pod! *And*—' he emphasised '—I danced with each of you that day, and not one of you recognised me!'

Rose's hand flew to her mouth. 'How dreadful! I apologise, my lord!'

He waved this away. 'Call me Will. Or ZanZan, if you prefer.' He gave a rueful laugh. 'Realising there must be some reason for it, I said nothing, but immediately wrote to my mother, who was, naturally, delighted.'

'All season he has been keeping me apprised of your progress, my dears,' said Lady Garvald. 'As well as details you revealed of your life in Elgin, as the *ton* came to know of them. I heard of your tremendous success in society—the Queen called you her "diamonds" at your presentation, and I can understand why. My dear friend Maria would be so, so proud of you!'

'You are too kind!' Izzy took her hand. 'But I am so happy to see you again after all these years. I remember little of this place, but I remember it as a happy time.'

'Yes.' Anna's voice was little more than a croak, so she coughed briefly before continuing. 'I recall this was a place of love and of safety. We were happy here.'

Lady Garvald gave a look that was half-glad, half-sorrowful. 'Your mother was happy here too—until that day when she was suddenly *unhappy*, and agitated, and declaring she must go. Nothing I said could persuade her to stay.'

'But why? Did she say why?'

'Not enough for me to fully understand, no. I was

hoping you might be able to enlighten me. Did she ever explain it to you?'

'No. But she told us bedtime stories of this place, and both of you.' Anna swallowed. 'She wanted us to remember you both with fondness.'

'And did you?' Will was looking at her directly, and the yearning in his eyes sent a feeling of weakness through her. 'Did you remember us with fondness?'

'Oh, yes!' Izzy replied fiercely. 'In her stories, Mama described us all as princesses, and you the young prince.'

'And now you have married a prince and become a princess in real life!'

Izzy giggled. 'I know. Astonishing, is it not? As astonishing as finding Milady and ZanZan after all these years.'

Anna was still holding on to a previous thread. 'What reason did Mama give you for wanting to leave, Milady?'

Lady Garvald took a breath. 'That she and her girls—you three—would be in danger if she stayed.'

Exactly as Mama had hinted to them. On the occasion of Rose's marriage, Mr Marnoch, their dear guardian, had shared a letter from their mother with them—a letter containing words of love and sorrow. A letter which Anna nearly knew by heart, for she had painstakingly copied it from Rose's original, and had read it dozens of times. In the letter, Mama had said:

There were people who wished us harm...

And:

*The old danger had returned, and so I had no
choice but to flee again.*

There had been no further details as to who the people were, or what form the harm might take, but clearly
Mama had judged it to be clear and imminent enough
that she had been forced to leave the sanctuary of Lammermuir House and begin a new life with her children,
cutting all ties to her dear friend Lady Garvald.

Anna's sisters were clamouring to know more. What
had she meant? What danger? What had made her
leave?

Lady Garvald looked thoughtful. 'I had been planning a house party, much like the one I am hosting now.
It was to be the first party I had hosted since my husband's death, as I worry dreadfully about such matters.
Maria had gently encouraged me to host small soirées
with the neighbours, so I had decided to be brave, in-
viting some of the leading members of the *ton*.

'I had thought to surprise Maria with the details,
assuming she would be excited to be receiving *ton*
visitors. I showed her my list of guest names and she
immediately went pale. She then looked at me—I shall
never forget her stricken expression—and said she had
to leave.

'And she did, the day before the guests were due to
arrive. During the two weeks in between, she would
tell me nothing of her motives, nor where she was

going. Indeed, I believe she did not know where she was going, for she had lived here as my companion for five years by then. My coachman brought her—brought you all—to the staging inn at Haddington, but I knew not whether she would travel north to Edinburgh or south to England.'

'How curious!'

Danger! Anna's stomach felt a little sick. There it was again. What troubles had poor Mama faced? To what lengths had she gone to keep herself and her daughters safe? And why?

Lady Garvald's eyes were distant, as she recalled her friend's words from long ago. 'I remember she said to me, "I hope to return one day. Or perhaps my daughters shall. I have left something of myself here and I hope that it will endure"...'

'Poor Mama! To have to run away not once but twice!' Rose had tears in her eyes.

'But running from what? Or whom?' Izzy's expression was fierce, as if she would avenge Mama's pain right then and there.

'We cannot know that now,' Anna offered with her usual practicality. 'What we do know is that this was our home for a time.' She turned to Will. 'Now that we have realised this, I should like another tour please. May we?'

'Absolutely.' He turned to bow to Izzy. 'Perhaps after you have rested after your journey, Your Highness?'

'Stuff!' declared Izzy inelegantly. 'As if I could rest now! Lead on, ZanZan!'

So once again Anna made her way through the house, which was distinctly castle-like in parts, this time accompanied by her sisters as well as Will, while Lady Garvald went to check on Lady Kelgrove's comfort.

ZanZan is Will. Will is ZanZan. There was something perfect about it—about finding her dearest friend again after so many years.

A notion struck her and she caught her breath. *That must be why I was so drawn to him in London!* Although her mind had not recognised him, something deep inside had known him.

Not a *tendre*, then. Good, for that made more sense. Why would she have developed a *tendre* for a gentleman so reserved? In reality her feelings for him had been present from the moment she'd met him again in London, for he was her dearest childhood friend. And she was far too practical to daydream and indulge nonsensical notions.

The Earl's reserve, too, had been explained. ZanZan's speech impediment as a child had affected Will's demeanour in social situations in adulthood. It made perfect sense. And there was something about the fact he had told her about it—something moving, and precious.

She stole a glance at him. His face was relaxed, his expression open as he laughed with Izzy about her ongoing expressions of shock, surprise and delight. Something inside her warmed at the sight. *He can be open and easy with us, for we are his childhood friends.*

On they went, Rose and Izzy exclaiming at half-memories in key places. 'These cattle look decidedly familiar,' Rose mused, standing in front of the bucolic painting in the library. 'Although I may well be putting notions in my own mind.'

Anna's heart skipped. 'I thought that painting seemed familiar, too! That one, and another—the one in your study, my lord.'

'Will.'

She tutted at herself. 'Will.' Although she knew it, somehow her mind was still slowly accepting that Lord Garvald was ZanZan and that their previous connection gave her the right to use his given name. Warmth ran through her at the thought, and she shook her head. 'It still seems so strange.'

He grinned. 'Strange, but delightful.'

She smiled back. 'Agreed.' A moment later, she realised that there had been a silence, and that her sisters were exchanging a glance.

What?

'Shall we go there next?' she babbled, suddenly unsure. 'I should like to know if my sisters are drawn to the other painting.'

On they went, and by the time they had reached the Earl's private study she had managed to regain control of her mortification. Her sisters—themselves both recently married and strongly enamoured of their husbands—were seeing things that were simply not there. Yet to speak to them of it might make it seem more real, for they could pretend that it was she who was raising the issue and possibility.

She frowned, remembering confessing to Izzy a few

weeks ago that she had something of a *tendre* for Garvald. Perhaps she should say something, for Izzy might not otherwise understand that it was not a *tendre* after all but something entirely different.

'Here she is!' Will indicated the Gainsborough above the fireplace. 'My grandmother.'

'She is beautiful!' Izzy's eyes searched the painting.

'And formidable,' added Rose. 'I am not certain… There is something about it…'

'The dog! I'm sure I remember that little dog!' Izzy remarked, eyes shining. 'How wonderful!'

'Really?' Anna's heart skipped in hope. 'Then, like the rural scene, perhaps we do remember these somehow.' She took a breath. 'There is somewhere else—a place that I have recognised with certainty.' She looked at Will. 'May we go to the nursery next?'

He assented, and as they made their way to the narrow doorway leading to the staircase Anna could feel excitement build within her. Even if Izzy and Rose failed to recognise the room, she had, and besides there was no real need to search for proof, as they now knew for certain they had been born here in Lammermuir House. Still, when they entered the room, she took in the familiar scene with a quick glance, her gaze flicking to the wooden beams overhead. Just days ago the beams at the inn had reminded her of this very room.

She need not have worried about her sisters' memory. 'Oh, my goodness! This was my bed!' Izzy marched straight to one.

'Yes! And this one was mine!' Rose pointed to the

bed to the left of the fireplace. 'Mama used to sit in an armchair just there at bedtime. We said our prayers and sometimes she would tell us stories.'

'Yes!'

'And our clothes were kept in that cupboard.'

'And we had books! They were kept in there.' Marching across to a corner, Izzy opened the door of a small cupboard, then shrieked with excitement. 'Look!'

She held up a dusty tome which Anna recognised straight away. '*Tales of Mother Goose!* Oh, Lord, I remember!'

'Little Red Riding Hood!' Rose added, her voice trembling. 'And the one about the glass slipper!'

The gates containing the emotions within Anna abruptly gave way, and she found that she was crying and smiling all at once. With perfect timing her sisters too were overcome, and they gathered together in an embrace, heads touching and arms around one another, while Will stood to the side, grinning with joy.

After hugging and making use of their handkerchiefs, the sisters returned to the book, exclaiming at the illustrations and the stories within.

Will, who had been silent throughout, now commented to say that he remembered clearly Mrs Lennox reading the stories to them. 'I used to sit on the small carpet before the fireplace.'

'Yes!' As he said the words, the memory came clearly to Anna—Will listening intently, his dark hair and serious expression as he sat by Mama's chair. 'I can picture you in my mind.'

'This is…this is wonderful.' Rose's voice trembled. 'I cannot tell you how happy I am to find this house again—the place that was our first home.'

'You are welcome here any time. Lammermuir House will always, in some way, be your home.' Will's voice was gruff, and Anna's throat tightened at the emotion in it.

'Thank you.'

They lingered then, sharing memories and hearing Will's stories of their time with him. Every word was vital, and Anna focused intently, feeling as though she were an incomplete painting slowly being coloured with wholeness.

Chapter Seven

Eventually they left the nursery, Izzy clutching the dusty book tightly to her chest. The servants informed them that Lady Kelgrove was taking tea with Lady Garvald in her chamber, so they all made their way there, including Will.

When their great-grandmother heard what they had to say she was all astonishment and delight. 'So this—' she sent Lady Garvald a piercing look '—is why you have convened this house party. To meet the triplets again.'

'It is—and it is not only that.' Lady Garvald again told the story of Mama's abrupt decision to leave and Lady Garvald's assumption that it had had something to do with an earlier house party, sixteen years before.

'I wondered if bringing the same people back together might help us all unravel the mystery.'

'Hmm...' Lady Kelgrove's brow was furrowed. 'Her grandfather and I were among your guests, but it would make me sad to think Maria saw herself as being in *danger* from our discovering her.' She sighed. 'My husband could be…difficult. Family pride was every-thing to him. But I like to think if he had found Maria again—alive and well, with three beautiful daughters—he would have forgiven her for running away. Although, he had put it about she had died, so perhaps…'

Her gaze swung to the triplets. 'I am glad for you, my dears. I have no doubt you were safe and happy here, and how wonderful that Lady Garvald realised who you are!'

'It was not especially difficult,' Lady Garvald of-fered dryly. 'Triplets, surname Lennox, exactly the right age… My son realised straight away at their presen-tation.'

'Of course he did.' Lady Kelgrove sent Will a sharp glance. 'Yet you said nothing.'

'They did not recognise me and I wished to proceed with caution.'

Lady Kelgrove gave a nod of agreement. 'That was sensible, given what we now know—scant as the in-formation is. Bringing everyone here—a place full of your own loyal servants, a place that is well-known to you—was entirely fitting.'

Anna felt the hairs on her arms stand to attention. Lady Kelgrove was not suggesting there was present danger to them, was she?

No, I must be imagining it.

'No doubt you girls will be ranging all over the house, seeking memories. But you must not inconve-nience Lady Garvald!'

Anna was now smiling inside. Lady Kelgrove was

acting as though they were eleven, not one-and-twenty. But it was heart-warming to have a family member to chastise one, after so many years when they had only had each other.

'I honestly do not mind, my lady. The girls are welcome to treat Lammermuir House as their home, for once it *was* truly their home.' She sighed. 'I had a great fondness for them, and for Maria.'

'Did she ever speak of the girls' father?'

'Yes, but not in a way that I might work out who he was. He was a gentleman, that I know, and he died just before she arrived here.'

Anna exchanged glances with Izzy and Rose.

A gentleman! Not a servant, then. So why...?

'I had suspected it.' Lady Kelgrove's eyes held a far-away look. 'I even suspect I know his name. But the young gentleman in question was perfectly eligible. So why did she run away from home?'

Lady Kelgrove's words speared through Anna. *She knows who our papa is!*

Lady Garvald shrugged. 'Something to do with his trustees.'

'Was he under-age?'

'Yes.'

'Hmm.' She pursed her lips. 'As I thought.'

'They married in Scotland, Maria said.' Lady Garvald frowned. 'Indeed, I vaguely recall her suggesting they had wed somewhere near here.'

'So they were properly married.' Lady Kelgrove

grew thoughtful. 'That may be significant. No proof, of course.'

Izzy was clearly unable to contain herself any longer. 'Who is our papa?'

Lady Kelgrove sent her a look that was half-sympathy, half-mischief. 'I shall tell you of my suspicions soon, I promise. You must be patient, child. You have waited twenty-one years. You are perfectly capable of waiting a little longer, for there are matters I must confirm.' She frowned. 'One cannot simply make allegations without some modicum of proof.' She rose briskly. 'You must all leave me now, for I have some urgent letters to write.'

Having been summarily dismissed they departed, exchanging wry glances at Lady Kelgrove's autocratic demeanour.

'She is such a forceful character,' Rose mused. 'I wonder if that is where Mama got her strength from?'

'Not just your mother,' Will murmured. 'You all have it. By the time you are in your eighties, I have no doubt the *ton* will be in awe of all three of you!'

Izzy tossed her head. 'People often recognise that I am strong. It takes perception to see the strength in my quieter sisters.'

He eyed her steadily. 'We all knew each other as children. Perhaps there is something in that.' His gaze moved to Rose and Anna. 'When you all left, my mother and I were like vines whose tree had blown down in a storm. We had each other, but missed you all dreadfully.' He pressed his lips together. 'It took time, but I re-grew myself.'

A pang of pain went through Anna as she tried again to imagine how bereft he must have been. 'I am sorry, Will. We still had a sense of family, since there were four of us. You and your mother had only each other.' The words seemed inadequate, and she had said them before to him. Still, it was all she had.

He shrugged. 'I took no permanent harm.'

Anna was not sure she agreed with this but, while she was trying to think of a response, he continued.

'What of Lady Kelgrove's assertion she knows the name of your father?'

'Yes!' Izzy's eyes were ablaze. 'We shall soon know of him!'

'She said she *suspects* it, Izzy.' Anna's tone urged caution. 'She did not say she knows for certain.'

'But Milady's account seemed to match her suspicions entirely.' Izzy ticked each element off on her fingers. 'A gentleman, under-age, eligible…by which we must assume her family would have eventually supported a match.'

'So perhaps it was *his* family who did not approve.'

'Maybe.' They all stood for a moment, realising they lacked the information with which to consider or guess further.

'We shall simply have to wait,' said Anna, knowing it fell to her to contain the speculation.

'Oh, Anna!' Izzy's brow was creased. 'Why must you always be so *practical*? This is one of the most exciting days of our lives, and all you can tell us is that we must wait! Well, you know how dreadfully poor I am at waiting!'

Anna touched her arm. 'I know, love, and, believe me, I am just as excited—and just as frustrated—as you are. I too wish we did not have to wait.'

'Lady Kelgrove has some plan in mind—that much is obvious.' Will's deep voice was reassuring, yet Anna's innards responded to it just as they had all year—with butterflies and a racing heart. Clearly her body had yet to catch up with the news that he was *not*, after all, simply a handsome eligible gentleman for whom one might develop a *tendre*. Instead he was her dear childhood friend, and the connection she shared with him was because of that, nothing more.

It was important that she not let her feelings and notions run away with her, for he too would see her as a friend. Just because she was surrounded by newlyweds should not encourage her to allow herself to be overcome by sentiment.

They discussed Lady Kelgrove's cryptic comments for a moment more, then parted on the landing—Rose and Izzy to find their husbands and share the news, Lady Garvald going in search of her housekeeper.

Anna and Will, left standing together, walked to the front door by unspoken agreement, and from there to the gardens to talk, speculate and wonder together about recent events. Anna even told him about the incident between Mr Thaxby and his valet—a tale that left Will frowning.

He glowers to great effect, she thought, laughter bubbling up inside her.

But his words sobered her. 'A man who abuses his servant is no gentleman. The valet had no choice but to take his chastisement—even though his master was quite clearly in the wrong.' He frowned. 'I would never have invited them—it is only because they and the Rentons were to be part of the original list.'

'The one that made my mother take us and run away...'

'Yes.' They were silent for a moment.

'Might they be something to do with our father?'

'Or the danger?'

She nodded. 'Or both?'

'And what of the Rentons? Lord Renton is a good man, and sensible. His lady is outspoken and rather single-minded, but I cannot imagine any harm in her. I could, however, imagine her threatening to cut off a young man who wished to marry someone not meeting the lady's approval. She would be of a similar age to your mama, I expect.'

'Had Lord Renton a brother, perhaps? A brother considered too young for marriage? But Lady Renton would not have been able to prevent a marriage, surely?' Anna shuddered. 'Family connections are everything to Lady Renton. Why, as you know she objected to her daughter marrying Mr Phillips, who is one of the kindest, smartest gentlemen I know.'

He sent her a quizzical glance. 'So you find kindness and intelligence to be important qualities in a gentleman.'

'Does not everyone?'

He shook his head. 'There are some who would have mentioned Mr Phillips's connections and fortune first.'

'Sadly, I believe you are correct.' She sent him a sideways glance. 'And what of young ladies? What are their important attributes, do you think?'

'As what? As a friend? A bride?'

Something within her almost choked at his choice of words, but she managed to respond. 'Is there a difference then? Or are there some attributes a young lady must aspire to irrespective of the relationship?'

He considered this for a moment. 'The core qualities apply to both gentlemen and ladies—kindness and discernment being chief among them. But I suppose most men would seek something *more* in a bride that would certainly not be present in a friend.'

'Something more? Is friendship not then enough of a basis for marriage?'

'Some marriages undoubtedly are built on a firm friendship—and are all the better for it. But many of the current generation have a notion for…for *love*.'

The word hung in the air between them, and Anna's heart was now pounding.

'My sisters,' Anna offered, speaking firmly for fear of an unbecoming tremble in her voice, 'Have both married for love. And I believe they will be happy.'

'Agreed. Prince Claudio and the viscount are both lucky, I think.'

The hairs on the back of Anna's neck were standing to attention.

What...what is he saying?

Laughing lightly, she offered, 'Rose will always be pleasant and even-tempered, that is for certain. Prince Claudio, though, will soon discover that our Izzy has strong opinions on many matters, and it is difficult to steer her from her course once she has fixed on something. But she adores him, so they will do very well together.'

He gave a bark of laughter. 'Oh, you may be certain that Claudio knew *exactly* who Izzy is when he married her. Indeed, I believe it is the reason why he married her.' He thought for a moment. 'Knowing one's spouse is rather important, do you not think?'

'Undoubtedly.'

'And, of course, you and I...'

'My lord!' A young page was hurrying towards them.

'Yes?' Will's tone was a little brusque, as though he had not welcomed the interruption. 'What is it?'

The page bowed. 'Her ladyship requires your presence, sir. In the drawing room.'

'Very well.' He offered Anna his arm. 'Shall we?'

She assented and they walked together in perfect harmony, making their way to the drawing room to have tea with the Thaxbys and Rentons—whom Anna had almost forgotten were here, in the excitement of the last two hours. No one mentioned the rediscovered connections—it was all too new, and they needed time to understand it. With some difficulty, Anna managed to quell her inner agitation, and by the time her sisters and their husbands joined the party she felt perfectly calm inside.

Having enjoyed a brief hack earlier with the other gentlemen, it seemed her brothers-in-law had been playing billiards together. The raillery between them—which Will now joined with wit and enthusiasm—warmed Anna's heart, for Claudio had only recently befriended the other two gentlemen.

They are alike in so many ways, mused Anna now, glancing from one to the other. Good men, with handsome faces, lively minds and kind hearts.

Her mind went back to her conversation with Will.

My sisters have married well.

She did not finish the thought, for something about it was unsettling, and soon afterwards the party dispersed to dress for dinner.

Chapter Eight

Dinner itself was uneventful. Sir Walter and his son attended once again, and tonight Anna found herself seated between Prince Claudio and Sir Walter, so was able to enjoy perfectly cordial conversation with her food.

When the gentlemen came to join the ladies in the drawing room, young Mr Ashman made directly for her, pulling up a chair next to hers and engaging her in light, pleasant chat. Mr Thaxby brought her a drink—he often served the ladies in this way, even in London, despite the fact that there were always footmen aplenty ready to provide wine or ratafia on request. Privately, Anna had frequently wondered if it was because Mrs Thaxby was excessively fond of wine but did not like to single herself out by requesting a refill very often.

'It is a delight to see you again, Miss Lennox.'

Smiling politely, she thanked Mr Ashman, a little concerned that his attentions were particularly towards her. In the general hubbub of conversation there was no need for concern that others may read anything into his attentions, surely? While he spoke in detail about the new book he had lately received from Hatchard's, she subtly glanced about…

She froze. Will was glaring at her—at them! But why? Nothing untoward was occurring, and Mr Ashman must be perfectly amiable since Lady Garvald had invited his father and him to dinner for the second time. Perhaps she had imagined it, for as their eyes met briefly Will's expression became masked, then he bent his head to listen to whatever Mr Thaxby was currently saying to him. Her eyes went to Thaxby, sporting a familiar maroon jacket, and she swallowed.

'Do you not think?'

'Oh, undoubtedly,' she offered, hoping it would suffice.

'I knew you would agree, Miss Lennox! I shall make the arrangements with Lady Garvald, then, and we will enjoy a delightful excursion!'

An excursion? *To where?* Naturally, she could not now ask. Lord, what had she agreed to? She was not normally so scatter-brained.

From across the room, Lady Kelgrove hailed her. 'Annabelle! Please play for us.'

'Of course!' With a polite smile of farewell to Mr Ashman, she made her way to the piano, thinking about what she would play. As her fingers touched the keys, she knew. Here was a piece she knew by heart—one of Mr Mozart's beautiful, mellow piano sonatas. Mama used to play it on the dilapidated little piano they had had in their cottage, and Anna had practised and practised it after Mama's death until her fingers knew it by instinct. Closing her eyes, she lost herself in the notes, feeling as though she were bringing Mama back into the room with them.

The music soared and softened, and she felt every emotion, every need: Mama's struggles; she and her sisters, orphaned too soon; Lady Kelgrove, who had spent years alone, believing she was the last of her family; Will and his mother, who had grieved when they had gone.

Her heart sore, she now played with hope. Love was here, and people reunited. This place was her first home, and her soul felt it. As the last notes died away, she allowed herself to return to the present and opened her eyes.

There was a silence. Bewildered, Anna looked around her. Will's gaze was fixed on her, his throat working with emotion. She swallowed, breaking his gaze. Both her sisters, as well as Lady Garvald, were making use of their handkerchiefs, while Lady Kelgrove was gripping the arms of her chair so tightly that the knuckles were showing white.

'Brava!' Lord Renton applauded, supported with enthusiasm by Sir Walter and his son, and with politeness by Lady Renton and the Thaxbys. 'A virtuoso performance, Miss Lennox!'

Anna, still shaken by the feeling that Mama had been right beside her as she played, could only manage a tremulous 'Thank you,' before making for the nearest empty seat, next to Lady Kelgrove.

'Your mother loved that piece.' Lady Kelgrove spoke softly.

Lady Garvald managed a sad smile. 'She often played it here as well—and on that very piano.'

'What is this?' Lady Renton's tone was sharp. 'Maria Berkeley visited here?'

'More than that,' replied Lady Garvald calmly. 'She and her girls lived here for a number of years.'

'Indeed?' Lady Renton's gaze jumped from one to another, presumably in an attempt to assess who had been privy to the information. 'How interesting! I knew her a little. Did you know her, Mrs Thaxby?' Her eyes gleamed as she threw what sounded like a challenge to her rival.

'I did not. At least… I believe I met her on only a few occasions.'

'You must have known her, Mrs Thaxby, for she had a season. But perhaps you did not then move in those circles?'

'I always moved in those circles, being a Fletcher!' Mrs Thaxby, her lips white, continued in a calmer tone, 'I knew Maria's brother, Mr Richard Berkeley, who was then heir to the barony. He and my brother George were great friends.'

Lady Renton, clearly undeterred, continued. 'You must tell me more, Lady Kelgrove. I remember your Maria was a *sweet* girl!' Lady Renton's attention was engaged, for she leaned forward with an interested air. 'But how did your granddaughter come to be living here, in the middle of nowhere?'

Anna flinched at the implied insult to Lady Garvald, her son and the entire Scottish nation, before another notion struck her. A sweet girl? If Maria's love had been a member of the Renton household, and the young Lady Renton had wished to prevent a marriage, there was no sign of it in her honeyed tones. Unless—and this was entirely possible—Lady Renton was extremely accomplished at pretence and dissimulation.

'No.' All eyes swung back to Lady Kelgrove. 'Tonight I wish to speak not of Maria, but her brother—my grandson, Richard, whom Mrs Thaxby referred to just now.' Her voice trembled a little. 'He always loved that piece when Maria played it.' Sitting straighter, her tone now became brisk. 'Your uncle, my dears, was as promising a young man as ever lived. He died very young, you know.' She paused. 'Murdered.'

Something strange was happening, Anna noted. While most people's expressions signalled shock, Mrs Thaxby's bearing had gone rigid, her eyes glassy, almost frozen. *What on earth...?*

'Is that not correct, Mrs Thaxby?' Like a hawk swooping on its prey, Lady Kelgrove's tone and words were directed with arrow-like precision at Mrs Thaxby.

As Anna watched, fascinated, the woman mastered control of herself. With a sad sigh, she nodded. 'Indeed, Lady Kelgrove. A *dreadful* tragedy. Dreadful.'

'And your brother was involved, was he not?'

Now Mrs Thaxby's brow was furrowed. 'Involved? I am unsure of your meaning, my lady.'

'He was there that night, I understand, on the Heath. When the brigands attacked your coach.'

'My coach? I was not there!'

'How clumsy of me! I meant to say, your *family* coach, with its rather distinctive crest. The Fletcher crest.'

'Well, yes. Richard and my brother George were great friends, as you will recall. They were going to a card party at Kenwood…' She made use of her handkerchief and, as if on cue, Mr Thaxby crossed to sit with her, taking her hand with a sorrowful sigh.

'If only they had dined with us that night,' he said, shaking his head slowly, 'Instead of insisting on travelling out to Hampstead.'

'So you knew of their intentions? They had spoken beforehand of this card party?'

'I do not recall exactly…' His face took on a sorrowful mien. 'But Mr Berkeley died that night, and George was seriously injured by those thieves.'

'They even murdered the coachman and groom, did they not?'

At Mrs Thaxby's nod, Lady Kelgrove leaned forward. 'Did you not think that strange?'

'I… What are you saying?'

'Robbers do not normally *murder* their victims—particularly not when those victims are gentlemen of consequence, riding in a crested coach. The risks would not be worth it. Nor do they typically murder the servants. The coachman's weapon was still in its place, indicating they were taken by surprise. Indeed, George said so afterwards.' She shook her head. 'I have ruminated over it many times over the years. It simply makes no sense.' Her gaze swivelled to Mr Thaxby. 'Did you not wonder at it, Mr Thaxby?'

'Well, I…that is to say… I had not thought of the possible significance. I…'

'We were grieving, Lady Kelgrove!' Mrs Thaxby's look held something of triumph, mixed with relief. 'We could not even think clearly at the time. Our poor, dear George had been left for dead and took many months to recover.'

Lady Kelgrove nodded regally. 'This I know. Some of his recovery took place at my country home, where as I recall he felt happy and safe.'

The hairs were standing to attention on the back of Anna's neck as a preposterous notion formed within her mind. Instinctively her eyes sought Will's. His look was steady, and she understood she should not give voice to any suspicions just now. She dared not look at her sisters. Besides, Lady Kelgrove seemed to be managing the situation masterfully. It did not occur to her to notice that, once again, she and Will had communicated without words.

Mrs Thaxby, whose jaw had dropped at Lady Kelgrove's last words, now brought a hand to her forehead. 'I declare I am feeling decidedly unwell! These memories are awakening old wounds.'

'My dear!' Mr Thaxby was all solicitousness. 'I shall take you to your chamber immediately.' Helping his spouse to rise, he bowed to the assembly, then slowly walked his lady to the door.

The door closed behind them and Lady Kelgrove nodded.

'Exeunt stage left!' she murmured, but with an air of satisfaction. 'Mrs Thaxby,' she announced with a casual air, 'Was several years older than her brother George. Indeed, she and her husband were trustees for his fortune until he could come of age, along with a very elderly lawyer. Of course, George Fletcher died just before he reached his majority. And, since he died unmarried and childless, his fortune went to his sister and her husband.'

Anna's mind was working furiously. *Trustees... Fortune... Murder... The Kelgrove country estate...* And something else: *danger.*

'But let us speak no more of this!' Lady Kelgrove's tone was firm. 'Anna, play something lively and light-hearted, if you please!'

With some initial difficulty, Anna complied. By the time she had played two more pieces, and various members of the party had performed a song, the Thaxbys' presence was no more than a ghost among the assembly. Later, after tea had been served, Anna and her sisters managed a brief conversation about Lady Kelgrove's comments.

'Was George Fletcher our father?' Izzy, naturally, went straight to the point.

'That was my thought too.' Rose's expression was full of wonder. 'I recall Lady Kelgrove telling me how

Mama and Richard and George were great friends, and that George spent every summer at Kelgrove Manor. She also said that Mama nursed him through his recuperation after Richard died.'

'After Richard was *murdered*,' Izzy clarified. 'And Lady Kelgrove seemed to be suggesting—'

'Hush!' Anna glanced about. 'People may hear you. Let us speak of this another time.'

Satisfied they were aligned in their thinking, Anna returned to her seat, where Mr Ashman proceeded to regale her with tales of his university days. He was an entertaining companion, and made her laugh more than once. Thankfully, he then made reference to his suggested excursion in a way that gave her clear information. They were to travel out to a place called Gifford, two days hence, and would walk through some woods to see a ruined castle.

At length he and his father departed while there was still light in the sky, and Anna was gratified by his making a point of kissing her hand—a gesture which he did not perform for anyone else. While she would not wish to give Mr Ashman the wrong impression, she did like him, and had been grateful for his entertaining company in helping dissipate the uneasiness following Lady Kelgrove's probing questions. Should she ever marry, perhaps someone like Mr Ashman… But, no; something within her rejected the notion. Besides, despite her sisters' recent nuptials, she was in no hurry to marry. There were more important matters to be resolved first.

The remaining young gentlemen, including Will, made for the billiards room soon after, and no sooner had the doors closed behind them than Izzy rose, beckoning her sisters. 'Excuse me,' she announced to the remaining assembly, 'But my sisters and I must go. There is something I wish to show them.'

Ignoring the speculative look in Lady Renton's eye, and the disapproval—or was it concern?—in Lady Kelgrove's, Izzy took them by the hand and ushered them out of the door.

'Quickly!' This was Izzy at her most excited.

What on earth...?

'Where are we going?'

'To ZanZan's study. I've just had the most tremendous notion!'

Allowing herself to be propelled along, Anna was almost breathless when they reached the room. Sunset lent the view outside a rosy glow, and the room itself was twilight-dim. Izzy had snatched a branch of candles from the hallway as they entered, and now she thrust them aloft, illuminating the painting above the fireplace.

'What is it, Izzy?' Her eyes searched the Gainsborough, ZanZan's grandmother's eyes seeming to be dark and mysterious tonight in the half-light.

'What colour is her dress?' Izzy demanded, her voice tight with excitement.

Rose was frowning. 'Blue. Why?'

The hairs on Anna's arms were suddenly alive, and

standing to attention. *'Blue!* And look, her right foot is peeping out from under her skirts.'

'Oh, my goodness!' Rose's hand flew to her mouth. 'She points her shoe!'

'"The Lady Blue she points her shoe…".' Izzy was all excitement. 'I do not know why it suddenly came to me. Something to do with this place, and Mother Goose, and Lady Kelgrove's probing. Can Mama have been thinking of this painting when she made up the rhyme?'

'Yes! It is obvious now!' Anna's heart was pounding. 'I felt close to her earlier, when I was playing piano. This just adds to it. I feel like we are finding her all over again.'

'But do you not see? There is a message in it!'

'In what? The rhyme?' Even as she spoke, distant memories were coming to her, including those triggered by wooden beams in an inn. '"The treasure fine is yours and mine…".She often spoke of hidden treasure, but always in an oblique manner. Can it really be a message?'

'She always said how clever we were, and how she knew we were skilled at solving riddles. Do you recall at Christmastide she often made up little rhymes and riddles that led us to sweetmeats hidden somewhere in the cottage or the garden?'

'Yes! And *The Lady Blue* is very similar to those, now that I think of it!' Rose's eyes were shining. 'But what treasure?'

'We know she was not wealthy…' began Anna, thinking it through, 'And she often talked about our little family being her most precious treasures… Perhaps a letter, like the one she left with Mr Marnoch for us?'

'That would be wonderful—but we must not dare to hope!'

'First,' Anna asserted, trying to focus on logic, 'We must solve the riddle—if indeed it is a riddle. Then we will know the form of the treasure.' She frowned. '"The Lady Blue she points her shoe…".It seems clear now that Mama refers to this painting. Next is, "You find the line to find the kine".'

'*Kine* is cattle. Are there cattle in the background?' Izzy held the candles higher but, disappointingly, the countryside visible to the left in the painting showed only fields and sky—a few birds the only living creatures outside.

'Points!' Rose indicated the delicate satin slipper emerging from beneath the wide skirts of ZanZan's grandmother. 'She *points* her shoe!' Whirling round, she assessed the invisible line created from the angle of the shoe. It led directly to the window opposite. 'She is pointing outside!'

As one, they rushed to the window. Below was the rose garden. '"Find the line to find the kine",' breathed Rose. 'Finding the line from the pointed shoe leads…' She looked back at the painting, then outside again, carefully assessing the angle. 'It leads *there*!"

Chapter Nine

'What is that exactly?' asked Izzy, as they peered at the object at the end of the path, following the line of Rose's pointing finger.

'It's the statue of Poseidon,' said Anna. 'But what has that to do with cattle?'

There was a silence. 'Let us go down. We shall have to inspect Poseidon. Mama will have left us another hint; I know it!'

Anna sighed. 'Should we not wait until morning? No, do not give me that look! But it is nearly dark, and we… Oh, very well!'

A few moments later they were hurrying through Lady Garvald's precious rose garden, Poseidon and his trident looming above them as they reached the end of the path.

'What's the next line? "The key is three…".'

'No.' Anna interrupted Izzy's enthusiasm. 'We know how Mama's riddles worked. We cannot move on to the next until we have fully solved this one. We must find the *kine*—the cattle—first.'

'She is right, you know,' Rose agreed, bending down to peer more closely at the plinth. 'We dare not think about the numbers until we know we have found the cattle.' Straightening, she made a frustrated sound. 'Nothing. No engravings or letters.'

'None that we can see, leastways,' said Izzy. 'Too dark for such a detailed search.'

Resisting the urge to say *I told you so*, instead Anna offered in a conciliatory tone, 'It was worth a try. Let us meet in the morning before breakfast and search again.'

All in agreement, they turned...to see a trio of handsome young gentlemen standing at one of the large windows, laughing fondly at them.

'The three husbands!' said Izzy, blowing a kiss to the prince.

'Er—no.' Anna spoke flatly. 'Two husbands and a friend.'

'At present that is the case. But who is to say what may happen in future?' She and Rose exchanged a sly glance. 'It would be perfect if you and Will—'

'Stop right there!' Turning to face them, Anna put her hands on her hips. 'Such foolishness is not to be tolerated—and especially when we have just learned that Will—that the Earl—is our dear friend ZanZan!' She took especial care to emphasise the word 'friend'.

Her sisters, however, were having none of it. 'What has that to do with anything?' Rose's expression was one of genuine puzzlement. 'Will is our friend, yes, but he is also a man. A man who is not a relation, and so is perfectly eligible!'

'Exactly!' Eyes blazing, Izzy put a hand to her heart. 'Oh, it would be just *perfect* if you married him, for he and Claudio are becoming fast friends.'

'And of course James and Will are already bosom bows!' Rose cast Izzy a sideways glance before continuing. 'Naturally, we would not wish you to marry where your heart is not engaged, but it seems to us that you and Will are ideally suited.'

'And so you told me yourself!' Izzy asserted triumphantly.

'I did not!' Anna retorted hotly.

'Well not, perhaps, in so many words. But I clearly recall a day a few weeks ago when we were walking in Green Park and you confessed to feeling a *tendre* for him!'

I knew she would mention that!

Anna waved it away. '*Pfft!* That is nothing. A maiden is perfectly entitled to feel a passing fancy for any good-looking young man and then change her mind if she chooses.' She tossed her head. 'And I do so choose!' Deep within, she sensed fear—fear of believing them. Of daring to hope, then finding such hopes crushed.

Izzy laughed. 'Some maidens may, yes, but you are *Anna*—always cool-headed, always sensible! For any man to capture your fancy he must indeed be special.'

Anna rolled her eyes. 'Logic was never your strong

point, Izzy. Have you not thought that there may be another explanation for that *tendre?*''

'Another…? What on earth do you mean, Anna?'

'Yes, speak plainly.' Rose added her urgings to Izzy's.

'Simply this.' She ticked off the points on her fingers. 'First, my memories of our childhood have always been stronger than yours. Agreed?'

They nodded.

'Second, my…*curiosity*…about Will goes right back to the day we first met him at our presentation to the Queen. There was something about him, *something* that made me look at him more, or focus on him more, than anyone else. That *something* was clearly that I remembered him, not that I felt…*feelings* for him. Why, I did not even know him!'

Her sense of triumph was short-lived. Making an exasperated sound, she asked, 'Why the knowing smiles?'

'You were drawn to him.'

'You *looked* at him more.'

'But no, I—'

'You were beginning to love him, even then.' Rose's gaze grew distant. 'It was the same for me, when I was beginning to love James. My heart fluttered and my mind raced every time he was near.'

'And I thought of Claudio constantly, even when he was not present.'

Anna's eyes widened. Some of what her sisters described was disturbingly close to her own experience.

Lord, I hope they are wrong, for I do not wish my heart to be broken. To love is to be vulnerable...

'In fact,' Rose concluded firmly, 'I loved James even when he vexed me.'

'And I loved Claudio even though I despaired at his hedonistic lifestyle. So, you see, it is all a hum. For you to have a *tendre* for Will is entirely perfect, as we said.'

'But he is just a friend to me!'

The words came out with more vehemence and volume than Anna intended, but at least it had an effect. There was a brief moment of shocked silence during which Anna had the satisfaction of seeing both her sisters' jaws drop, even if she wondered briefly if she had just told an untruth—to herself, as well as them. It was an unwelcome thought, so she swiftly banished it.

'Just a friend? But...'

'Well, naturally that is how *we* see him, but *you*... A friend...' Izzy looked decidedly crestfallen. 'Oh, dear.'

'What? What "oh, dear"?'

'Well, he may not see you as simply a friend.' Rose's tone was tentative. 'And so he may be disappointed—hurt, even. I would not like him to be hurt.'

A pang went through Anna at the thought of Will suffering any hurt from any source, alongside wild hope. But there was nothing—*nothing*—to suggest that Will saw her as anything other than a friend. Why, he did not even offer her gallantries, such as Mr Ashman did! Yes, he had kissed her hand after bringing her to her bedchamber on the magical night when she had found the nursery. But that meant nothing, for they both had been overwhelmed by her discovery. Will was reserved and unreadable, but he was also her own dear ZanZan. Surely she, who knew ZanZan so well, would be able to tell if Will liked her in a particular way?

No. It cannot be.

She shook her head. 'I am certain of it. So you need not be concerned that he will take any hurt from me. Now, let us go inside, for it is becoming chilly!'

Head held high, she led the way, almost *hearing* the dubious looks being exchanged by her sisters behind her back and conveniently ignoring the fact that the late summer air was anything but chilly.

Next morning after breakfast the sisters reassembled in the rose garden, this time accompanied by the three gentlemen—the two husbands and a friend. Anna had awoken determined to stop thinking too much about complex matters over which she had no control, and which made her feel decidedly confused. She did not like to feel confused, and had always valued her own mind over what some people might fancifully describe as their 'gut'. No, logic and order ruled the day.

And Anna's mind was busy with the puzzle of *The Lady Blue*. It was her own rhyme, and she therefore felt under an obligation to solve the riddle of it—regardless of whether there was treasure at the end. Feeling connected to Mama again was treasure enough.

Izzy had made the first discovery, and together they had followed the invisible line from the direction indicated by the lady's satin slipper. Today's task was to solve line two—the elusive cattle. The home farm was not near, and Will had said that cattle would never have been near the house. He remained rather mystified about what was causing the three sisters to babble so incoherently on their way outside, so as Izzy and Rose forged ahead with their husbands it was left to Anna to explain.

'Mama always wrote riddles for us, leading to little surprises like sweetmeats—especially at Christmastide. There is a rhyme that we used to sing, and we know she devised it. We now believe it is a riddle based on this place.' She gestured about her. 'That is why Izzy was asking if cattle were ever allowed near the rose garden. We believe the statue of Poseidon is the first sign, and we are seeking the second, which is something to do with cattle.'

'How intriguing! So what is the part of the riddle related to the statue?'

'It says,"You find the line to find the kine".' She laughed lightly. 'Perhaps it sounds foolish to you, but for us it is an unexpected opportunity to solve one last puzzle set by her.'

'Not foolish in the least! And, remember, your mama was important to me too.' Their eyes caught and held for a breathless moment, making Anna's heart pound in her chest. What if her sisters were correct and he too…?

His forehead creased. 'But what makes you certain the statue is the correct starting point?'

They had reached the statue. Just then, Izzy asked,

'Will, has this statue always been here? Might it have been moved since Mama's time?'

Her words struck Anna with the force of a thunder-clap, making her gasp. 'Will! Where was your grand-mother's portrait hung before you had it moved?'

'Excuse me?'

'You said you had it moved. From where? Where was it during our time here?'

His eyes widened. 'The library. On the right-hand side. Nothing else has been moved or changed in that room.'

'The library!' Anna spun to face her sisters. 'The room where we saw the painting of the cattle!'

Then they were off, skirts flying in their wake, ac-companied by the gentlemen. Anna's pulse was now racing for entirely different reasons. The portrait would originally have been hung opposite the rural scene. It had to be the solution to the second line.

Breathless, they raced to the library, making directly for the idyllic painting showing a herd of highland cat-tle grazing contentedly amid trees and ruins. A craggy mountain was visible in the background, and a river to the left. There was nothing unusual about the painting, and the gilt frame looked entirely usual.

'I *knew* there was something about this!' declared Rose. 'I just knew it!'

Anna's eyes, having searched the scene, were now looking at the space held by the painting. It was in a plaster cartouche with bookshelves either side, above and below. Inwardly, she was murmuring the last two lines of Mama's riddle.

The key is three and three times three.
The treasure fine is yours and mine.

Whatever the treasure was, they were so close she could almost *feel* it!

Chapter Ten

Three cows grazed in the foreground of the painting. *Three.* Was that significant? The artist's signature was visible on the bottom right. Noris or Norie—not anyone Anna had heard of. There were three lines of books below it and two above. *Three again.*

Gilt numbers were on the shelves. Desperately, her eyes scanned them. 'Three and three times three...' Three and nine...twelve. She gasped, pointing a shaking finger. The digits one and two were clearly visible on the shelf above the painting.

Rose had also worked it out. 'Twelve!' Her voice was shaking.

'The key is three and three times three. Yes!' Izzy's eyes were shining. Stretching, she tried to reach the shelf, then dropped her arm in frustration. 'Mama was not very tall, I think. How did she reach up there?'

'Perhaps I can assist.' Will made for the corner, returning with a set of three steps on tiny metal wheels which he manoeuvred into position.

Three steps. Did that mean anything? *Lord, I am seeing threes everywhere.*

And yet, it was fitting. As triplets, the number three had been their lodestone throughout life.

With a flourish, Will gave way to Anna. He offered a hand to steady her, and she took it, noticing his warmth and the tingle that went through her at his touch—a connection based on friendship, not a *tendre*, she reminded herself.

With a deep but ragged breath she mounted the steps to explore the section marked with a twelve. Running a hand along the books, she eyed the titles. Gibbon's *The History of the Decline and Fall of the Roman Empire*—in six volumes. Ovid's *Metamorphoses.* Sheridan's *Rivals...* Nothing stood out. She did not even know what she was looking for.

Very well. This would have to be done with method. 'I shall pass you down each book in order. Search it for hidden documents. Be sure to keep the sequence, just in case it is significant.'

Starting at the left, she pulled out the first book—something by Goethe. Eyeing it briefly, she passed it to Will, who in turn gave it to Claudio. Rose, James and Izzy clustered around the large library table, opening the book and searching through it. While tempted to pause and await the results of their search, Anna persisted, knowing logically that would use their time most effectively. Next were volumes by Rousseau, Kant, then Adam Smith, all clustered together by author. Now the section with Gibbon, Ovid and Virgil. *Nothing.* A good deal of the shelf was now empty, with nothing concealed behind. Refusing to be daunted, Anna continued, until it became too far to reach safely.

'Let me move the steps,' Will offered, and Izzy then pounced, announcing it was now her turn to search.

Half an hour later, they had to admit defeat. Having removed all of the books from the section and searched within for hidden notes or letters, they had been sorely disappointed. They had found nothing more than dust, a recipe for arrowroot sauce and a folded note which had initially caused them to exclaim in hope, but which had proved to be nothing more interesting than a list of places taken from the book *Travels through France and Italy* by someone named Tobias Smollett.

'I do not understand it!' complained Izzy, stamping a little foot in frustration as they carefully replaced each book in order, 'It should not be this difficult! It never was in Elgin.'

'Elgin,' offered Rose thoughtfully, 'Was our apprenticeship. We learned the craft of solving riddles at Mama's knee, but perhaps all the while she was teaching us to master the skill as children so we might decipher the most difficult of riddles if the opportunity came our way as adults.'

Izzy sniffed. 'It is not that difficult. I found "the Lady Blue" and, if she had still been where she was supposed to be, the kine are obvious.'

Will grinned. 'I apologise for moving my grandmother's portrait and almost spoiling the riddle. But do not be disheartened. I have no doubt you—we—shall solve this before long.' He frowned. 'There is a hidden door here. Might that be of significance?'

Smiling at their gasps, he crossed to the fireplace, turning a small wooden handle that had been almost invisible against the shelf. Anna gasped as the entire section opened, revealing another room behind it. 'But I knew this! I vaguely remember it.'

Will grinned. 'You and I often hid in here when we did not wish to be bothered by Izzy and Rose.' He bowed. 'Apologies, ladies.'

'But this is astonishing!' declared Izzy, waving away his apology. 'So clever! May we go inside?'

In they trooped, to exclaim and explore. Unfortunately, the room held nothing more than more books, a small table and a hard chair. 'We believe this was our priest hole, back in the day,' Will shared. 'It may also have served to hide some Scots from the Duke of Cumberland's men.'

'Jacobites!' James laughed. 'I would never have taken you for a rebel, Will.'

'Would you not?' Will answered mildly, and Anna stifled a smile.

Returning to the library, they considered the gilt numbers painted on each section of shelves.

'My grandfather apparently had a desire to systemise and organise his library,' Will explained. 'He intended to keep an index of all his books, organised by category and author, hence the numbers on the shelves. It came to nought, though, as he had underestimated the time necessary to complete such a task.'

Anna studied the numbering. The top section was numbered from one to twenty in sequence. The middle and lower sections however were punctuated by the door, fireplace and various works of art, so the numbers beneath did not line up mathematically. The neatness and accessibility sought by Will's grandfather did not even extend to the appearance of the numbering, never mind their purpose. Perhaps Mama's plans would be similarly doomed.

'I wonder how Mama thought we might come to be here?' Anna mused. 'She went to great lengths to keep us hidden, it seems to me.' It was only the fact that they had gone to London and mixed with the *ton* that had led them to discoveries—first, Lady Kelgrove and now, ZanZan and Lammermuir House.

'I suspect,' pondered James, 'She worried about you being discovered through some misadventure and hoped that if your identities did become known you would find your way to this place, where you have friends.'

'I think you might be right,' Rose replied, her voice thick with emotion. Anna, too, had a lump in her throat. All these years they had had no notion of the lengths to which Mama had gone for their sake to protect them.

'Right!' declared Claudio briskly, perhaps intervening before his own wife became caught up in the poignancy of the moment. 'Are we continuing with our plans for this morning?'

'Riding lessons?' Anna shuddered. 'Not for me,

thank you. I intend to stay here and continue to search the library. But you all may go ahead without me.'

This set off a clamour of debate, which only ended when Will said that he would stay to keep Anna company, while Izzy and Rose would venture out to the stables to what was promised to be a gentle introduction to the art of horse-riding, involving only the quietest of mares.

'Are you frightened of horses?' The door had finally closed behind them, leaving behind a quietness which was causing an unexpected reaction within Anna. Why was her heart suddenly pounding so? And why was she abruptly unable to think?

He was still looking at her, awaiting her answer. Not for him, then, a heart-pounding realisation they were now alone together.

See? He clearly sees me as a friend. It is only my own foolish notions that say otherwise.

Conscious of a stab of disappointment, Anna shook herself enough to respond to his question. 'Yes, they terrify me. I do not know why.'

He nodded thoughtfully. 'I believe I know why.'

She caught her breath. 'What? I do not understand.'

His eyes held sympathy and a hint of humour. 'You might say, once I have told you, that it is my fault.' Now the humour brimmed over. 'So perhaps I should not tell you!'

The playfulness in his expression was reflected in his tone. Playful—the taciturn Earl of Garvald? Briefly, she recalled his typical demeanour in the ballrooms and drawing rooms of London, before tilting her head at him. The soul of a rebel hidden beneath an urbane exterior? Perhaps.

'Well, you must tell me now. You cannot tease me so cruelly!'

Sighing dramatically, he took her hand and led her to a settee covered in cherry-coloured satin. 'Very well. Just before you left here, when you were five and I was eight, I let you ride my gelding. You had only ever ridden ponies until then, and you were extremely accomplished.'

'Was I?' The notion was unsettling, contradicting as it did all her beliefs about her relationship with members of the equine family. He had retained her hand, and she allowed it, hoping he would not notice and take it away. He seemed entirely distracted by his tale, and his expression now grew serious.

He nodded. 'You had your very own pony. He was called Tumblethumb.'

She stilled as memories flooded through her. 'Tumblethumb. Lord, how could I have forgotten him? He was so beautiful, and I loved him so much!' Her eyes were now stinging and her throat tight with emotion. *More loss.*

'He is dead, of course.' It was not a question. Tumblethumb had been an elderly pony when she had ridden him sixteen years ago and more. Each new and wonderful discovery she made seemed to be tinged with sadness. Mixed emotions coursed through her—happy memories of her beloved pony, and the knowledge she would never see him again.

Will nodded. 'But he had children and grandchildren. You shall meet them later.'

'Thank you.' Her voice cracked.

With a muffled exclamation, he opened his arms and she went into his embrace gratefully. As her tears flowed he procured a handkerchief from somewhere and passed it to her, and she gave way to the sorrow running through her. This place, Mama's music, the riddle…and now Tumblethumb.

She had adored her pony, and had shed many tears for his sake after they had left. Later, she must somehow have built a wall around those memories to keep them from hurting her. Yet the loss of her beloved pony had stayed with her, unrecognised, all this time.

It is too much. I am only one girl. I cannot endure it!

His arms were soothing, his hands pressed lightly on her back and his heart beating loudly beneath her cheek.

'Thank you,' she mumbled against his coat, suddenly realising she was in the embrace of a man! Will might have comforted her when they were children in this way, but…

'We are not children any more.' Had she really just said that aloud? Their eyes met.

'No.' His voice was tight. 'We are not.' His face was impossibly close. It would take only the slightest of movements for her to press her lips to his. The impulse to do so throbbed within her. It was more than an impulse, it was desire. It was *need*. It was terrifying.

But a lifetime of good sense could not be ignored. Reason asserted itself, and she shuffled away from him, breaking eye contact and dabbing at her cheeks with her handkerchief. 'What you must think of me! I am not normally such a watering pot, I assure you.'

'What I think of you? Only good things, I assure you.' His voice was deep and low, and set her insides trembling.

'You are too kind. But I know that gentlemen do not like it when ladies...' She faltered, for he had raised a quizzical eyebrow. 'When ladies are...'

'Are what? Do pray continue, Anna. I should like to know what you have divined about all gentlemen, based on your worldly experience.'

She shook her head, managing a tremulous smile. 'You are right, of course. What can I possibly know of such matters? But it is a widely held belief among *ton* ladies that *ton* gentlemen find displays of emotion unseemly.'

Her tone was light, following his lead. Inwardly she was telling herself to be calm. Between remembering the loss of her beloved pony and the unexpected and unlooked-for desire running through her, it was difficult to regain her equilibrium.

Now he shrugged. 'Some men, perhaps.' He thought for a moment. 'But authentic emotion, such as true grief, could never be belittled.'

She swallowed. 'He was a dun bay, Tumblethumb.'

'Yes. A Highland pony, sturdy and gentle.'

Now it was her turn to raise an eyebrow. 'And your gelding?'

'Not so much. But you were determined you wished to ride him, and so I agreed.' He grimaced. 'To my later regret.'

Vague hints of memory were beginning to surface in her mind. 'What happened?'

'All was going well. We were in a clearing in the woods beyond the rose garden. I mounted you on him, and you walked him beautifully in a gentle circle.'

'And then?'

'Something spooked him. A bird in the under-growth, I think. He reared and you were deposited on the ground. You had been riding astride, and unfortunately your skirts got caught in the stirrup as you fell.'

She gasped. 'I remember! He panicked and ran, dragging me behind him!'

Will nodded grimly. 'Thankfully I had him attached to a leading rope, which I quickly wrapped around a branch before he took off. I knew it was my only chance to stop him, for I would not have had the strength. He did not get far, thank the Lord!'

'Was I injured?' She frowned. 'I seem to remember a lot of blood.'

He closed his eyes for a moment. 'A head wound. It bled profusely, scaring the life out of me. Turned out to be quite small, but at the time all I could see was your face covered in blood.' He shuddered. 'I can see it yet, in my mind's eye. I thought you were going to die.'

He opened his eyes again and Anna saw there pain—

pain, sorrow and grief. Like her, he was reopening old wounds, long buried. It had all happened a long, long time ago, yet only now were they able to speak of it.

'I did not die, but then I went away.'

'Yes.' A muscle twitched in his cheek, and Anna realised his jaw was tight. 'The day of your injury, I recall begging you not to die. The day you left, I could say nothing, for it had all been decided already.'

Reaching out, she took his hand. 'I am so sorry, Will. And so glad to have found you again.'

'I, too.' The silence this time was fraught with emotion as well as desire.

Here is where I am supposed to be. Here is my home. The notions flooded through Anna with a sense of rightness.

'Your mother loved it here. She must have had good reason for going away.'

Anna frowned, thinking again of Lady Kelgrove's exchange with the Thaxbys. 'That much is certain. But nothing can be proven, nothing is certain. That is why it is so important we solve this riddle. We must hope that Mama left us more information.'

'Indeed.' He turned his head to look at the painting and she drank in the strength and perfection of his profile before following his gaze. 'Might your mother have hidden something behind the painting itself?'

'Of course! What a great suggestion!'

As one, they made for the painting. Will gently tilted the bottom corner towards him, peering behind. 'I cannot see properly. I shall take it down.'

This he did, carefully loosening the wire from its sturdy nail and laying the large painting directly onto the thick carpet. Judging by the effort evident in his demeanour, the painting in its frame weighed a considerable amount. Kneeling, he then raised it from the top, allowing Anna to crouch down and peer behind it.

'Something is written there!' She made a frustrated sound. 'I cannot make it out.'

'One moment. I shall endeavour to turn the whole thing over.'

Once he had done so they both knelt to read the script etched onto the backing board.

Landscape with Highland Cattle
James Norie 1730

Anna's heart sank.

'I am sorry, Anna.' His eyes held such sympathy it was almost her undoing. Determined not to cry again, she sought refuge in nonchalance. 'We cannot force this.' She managed a smile. 'Now, how are we to restore the cattle to their rightful place?'

He rose, offering a hand to assist her. She took it gratefully, as ever wondering why his touch affected her so.

'I have no intention of even attempting it. I think it will require at least two footmen to raise it to the right height and attach it by its wire. You and I may safely leave it here.' Walking across the room, he rang the bell for the servants.

Anna's mind had returned to her pony, and the incident with Will's horse that had clearly affected her for years. 'Perhaps we should go to the stables after all. Oh, not to ride! I am not ready for that. But I think I must be brave and simply walk among the horses today, in honour of my dear Tumblethumb.'

His eyes blazed with what looked suspiciously like admiration. 'That's my Anna,' he said softly, sending a delicious shiver through her. 'I shall be at your side in every instant. You may rely on me.'

'Thank you.' Now warmth flooded her chest—the warmth of an emotion she was not ready to name. Together, they left the library side by side.

Chapter Eleven

Will was as good as his word, gently guiding Anna through the stable block and out to the paddock. Her heart pounded with fear as the enormous horses moved around her, but she endured, keeping a hand on Will's arm at all times. Knowing that she'd once been a promising rider helped, as did the knowledge of the single incident that had brought terror to her heart.

'I believe,' she mused, 'That, if I had had the opportunity to keep riding after that day, I might have overcome my fear.'

'I do not doubt it,' Will replied, giving her *that* look again—the one that made her feel as though she was special in some way. It made her strong inside, as though she could accomplish anything. Mama had used to make her feel like that, she recalled, and now Will.

'The best thing to do after a fall is keep riding.' He gave a rueful grimace. 'Because of your wound, I took you straight to the house to be tended to, otherwise I would probably have put you straight onto your pony— not my gelding, who would have still been agitated. As it was, our mamas banned you from riding until your wound healed, and by that stage it was time for you all to go.' He shook his head. 'We all knew you were to leave. I recall a sense of confusion from you, and help-lessness from me. Neither of us could change it. I was only eight, after all.'

'And I was five. I probably had no real notion what leaving even meant.'

Their eyes met, and once again Anna felt that sense of deep connection to him. Inside this handsome—so handsome!—kind, and thoughtful man, was her dear friend ZanZan. The boy had become a handsome man and she a grown woman, and the feelings swirling inside her were much more complicated than simple friendship.

She was all confusion, and her mind kept circling back to her sisters' insinuation that there could be some-thing between them. For her part, she could admit he was fast becoming something of an obsession with her, but once again her logical mind asserted itself. It had been only a couple of days since her discovery that this had been her childhood home, and that the Earl of Gar-vald was ZanZan. Naturally, her mind had focused on it. Reason dictated that she hold fast, avoid dramatic assumptions and conclusions and simply wait for the maelstrom of emotion within her to settle. Only then would she have a clear head and would be better able to understand what was happening to her.

He brought her to the ponies then, and she delighted in meeting Tumblethumb's offspring. Although they moved unpredictably around the paddock, they were small enough for her to enjoy the encounter without giving way to fear. She walked beside them, stroked their smooth necks and gave them treats which Will had procured from the kitchen while she had been donning her half-boots.

Afterwards she was in alt, a mix of relief and a sense of accomplishment which she tried to articulate to Will.

'I understand entirely!' he told her. 'And I am proud of you.'

The warmth that rushed through her at these words was like nothing she had ever experienced. Not many people in her life were close enough to claim pride in her actions—her sisters, her guardian, Lady Kelgrove and, now, Lord Garvald and his mother.

However, when he repeated the sentiment later to her sisters and their husbands, she felt only mortified. The men took it in good stead, offering her congratulations and a hope that she would catch up with Izzy and Rose, who by their husbands' account had done remarkably well today. Anna's sisters however exchanged a knowing look which made her momentarily want to pull their hair as she had when they were children. Instead she bunched her hands into fists and offered mild bashfulness, delivered, she hoped, in an unassuming manner.

'You are too kind. I walked through a stable and a paddock, that is all. Now,' she added briskly, 'We should find the other guests, for I fear we are neglecting our social duties.'

At this, Rose simply nodded, while Izzy blatantly

rolled her eyes. Determined not to argue, Anna led the way to the drawing room. They were all there—Lady Kelgrove, the Rentons, the Thaxbys and Lady Garvald, who flashed them a look of relief or possibly gratitude when they arrived. Anna felt a pang of guilt. They had truly been neglecting Lady Garvald, who had been left to shepherd and manage the conversation of her more challenging guests for far too long.

The arrival of the three young couples enlivened the conversation, keeping the discourse light and cordial. Anna had no clue what had been discussed before their arrival, but hoped Lady Garvald could now be a little more comfortable.

Mrs Thaxby was in affable mood, with no sign of the distress she had displayed the night before. Was that because the distress had been feigned? Something within Anna felt rather sick at the notion that one could feign distress at the death of a sibling, yet that was the clear impression she had been left with. And was it possible that such an unlikeable character as Mrs Thaxby might be their aunt? Her gaze drifted to Lady Kelgrove, who was currently enjoying a conversation with Prince Claudio. The two seemed to get on particularly well.

Lady Kelgrove knew, or *suspected* she knew, what had happened to Richard, and if George was their father. But their indomitable great-grandmother would tell them what she knew or suspected only when it suited her to do so. Anna clamped down on inner frustration. The game-playing among the *ton* was wearying at times—although in this case it was more likely to be based on Lady Kelgrove's requirement for more proof.

Her mind drifted back to that day in February when Mr Marnoch had told them what he knew of their mother, and had set each of them a task to complete. Rose was to discover their mother's true name and identity, which they had now confirmed. Mama had been Maria Berkeley, granddaughter of Lady Kelgrove.

Izzy's task had been to find the name of their father—a task which was surely about to be completed.

Anna's own quest was in some ways the most challenging. She was to discover the circumstances behind Mama leaving their first home and going to Elgin—although how on earth she was meant to accomplish this she had had no idea. And yet…the story was slowly, gradually, coming to light. Lady Kelgrove knew some of it, and Lady Garvald too.

But they needed more information. That was why it was vital they solve the riddle and find whatever it was Mama had hidden for them. The one letter they had—the letter left with Mr Marnoch for them—had mentioned Lady Garvald with great affection, although not by name.

I hate to leave you now, but I know you are safe with Mr Marnoch—one of the kindest people I have ever known.

Others have been kind to us too, like the Lady we lived with for the first five years of your lives. You may not remember her, but I do, and I can as-

*sure you she is as good-hearted and as generous
a person as I have ever encountered.*

Anna resolved to tell their hostess of Mama's kind
words as soon as the opportunity presented itself. But
it was Mama's next words that she ruminated over constantly. Once again she repeated them in her mind.

*It was hard to leave that place of safety, that
haven, that sanctuary, but the old danger had returned, so I had no choice but to flee once again.*

The inference was clear: the same danger that had
caused Mama to run from her family and hide goodness knew where for the best part of a year before she'd
gone to Lammermuir House had reappeared, forcing
her to run away again. The Thaxbys were unlikeable,
certainly, but were they truly capable of acts so heinous as to make poor Mama afraid for her safety and
the safety of her daughters? They were received everywhere, and were surely no worse than tedious? Anna's
brain could not take it in.

'What is vexing you?' Will came to sit with her, and
she flashed him a smile. 'You are frowning and ruminating. I could sense it from across the room.'

'I was thinking of my mother and wondering about
the danger she was running from.' Briefly, she told
him about Mama's letter. He was interested, and asked
clever questions. Worryingly, his conclusions matched
Anna's.

'I do think it possible that the Thaxbys may be the source of that danger. Lady Kelgrove strongly hinted at it. Of course, your great-grandmother is full of guile, and she may well have been indirectly targeting the Rentons, while seeming to focus on the Thaxbys. Who knows? I would urge you to be wary of *all* of them, Anna. Do not confront them or ask questions, for we do not know what these people are capable of.'

He thought for a moment. 'Lady Kelgrove plays a dangerous game, I think.' He shook his head, as if to clear it of dark thoughts. 'Now, tell me, what else did your mother include in her letter? There may be riches not yet discovered there.'

'Oh!' A sudden notion had come to her, triggered by his question. 'There was something about our names. Let me think…yes. Mama said, "Your father loved me very much, as I loved him. There were people who wished him harm, so he sent me away for my own safety, for fear they would harm me too. I wish I could share with you my true name, and his, but I cannot assume you are safe, even now. My belles, my beautiful belles: Annabelle Georgina; Isobel Judith; Rosabella Hemera. By these names you will be known…".'

Saying Mama's words aloud was interesting, for the words were striking her in new ways.

His eyes widened. 'So much information in just a few lines!' He marked them on his fingers. 'First, she is telling you that Maria Lennox is not her true name. Second, that your father sent her away initially. And then I understand he died soon afterwards?'

Anna nodded. 'We believe he had already died when Mama came here.'

'And she arrived here the day you were born?'

'Yes. Lady Garvald took her in that day—Mama had already started her labour. Your mother is all generosity.'

He glanced towards her and Anna glowed at the warmth in his eyes.

There is love in him for his mother—another sign of a good man.

'She is that. They were well met, I think; two good souls. Now,' his tone became brisk, 'Back to your names. I understand why she called you her "belles", for there is Bel and Bella in there. But she also included your middle names. Have you ever wondered why?'

'I was just wondering about it now. And that phrase: "by these names you *will be* known". She might have said "you are known". The words "will be" sound significant. They must mean something, surely?'

'The eldest child in a family is traditionally named after their father, you know.'

She gaped. 'I did know, but I never thought to apply it to me. Georgina. *George.*'

He nodded. 'Yet more evidence that you may unfortunately be closely related to Mrs Thaxby.'

They exchanged a rueful glance, then returned to the puzzle. 'Judith; Hemera—a common name and an uncommon one.' Anna shrugged. 'I would wager they are linked to the Kelgroves or the Fletchers.'

'Let us check in Mr Debrett's book, then. I have a copy in the morning room.'

He indicated the archway at the side of the room, leading to the next chamber. It would be perfectly un-exceptional to wander through into there for a few moments. They rose, making polite conversation as they passed the others, who remained engrossed in their own conversations. Once in the morning room, Will took a heavy tome from the bookcase and together they searched through it, quickly discovering that Maria's mother had been called Judith, while George Fletcher's Mama...

'Look! Anne Margaret Hemera Fletcher!'

They eyed one another, smiling at their joint discovery. 'And there it is.' Anna sighed. 'I am Mrs Thaxby's niece. It is practically certain.'

'I am sorry for your trouble.' There was a glint of humour in his eye.

She sent him a wry look, then frowned. 'We should say nothing about this for now in company. I shall tell my sisters and Lady Kelgrove, and you may wish to ensure your mother is fully apprised of everything.'

'I shall. And for now, it is probably better not to pursue it, as you say.' He sighed. 'Lady Kelgrove has some plan; I am certain of it. Let us hope it does not take too long to come off, for the waiting is frustrating for me. I cannot even imagine how it must feel for you!'

She sent him a grateful glance. 'Frustrating, yes, and exciting, and a little frightening, if I am honest.

So much has happened since we arrived on Saturday. And it is only Tuesday!'

He laughed. 'Indeed. Who knows what the next three weeks will bring?'

They returned, he to converse with Lord Renton, Anna to find a seat by herself, allowing the conversations to wash over her. Three weeks; three more weeks of being in his company, in this place of her dreams. The two were entirely entwined in her mind and heart.

Three weeks of bliss. And then it would end.

Where would she go? Back to London? To Elgin, to see Mr Marnoch? Both her sisters had invited her to live with them—Rose and James at Ashbourne House, Izzy, Claudio and Lady Kelgrove in Kelgrove Manor. She had so many options. And yet, at moments like this, she felt unsure, confused and quite, quite alone.

Chapter Twelve

Yester Castle was little more than a ruin, aboveground at least, but the excursion was enjoyable nevertheless. Mr Ashman had made it his business to accompany her on the walk through the woods, enlivening the trek with entertaining stories and gallant compliments.

The party had set out after nuncheon, the carriages taking less than an hour to reach the end of the tracks. They had all descended then—Anna and her sisters, their husbands, Will and Mr Ashman. He and his father were staying for dinner again, and Sir Walter and Lady Garvald were currently leading the older members of the house party on a gentle stroll around the Lammermuir grounds, the Renton and Thaxby ladies having proclaimed that the trek to Yester sounded far too energetic. Mrs Thaxby had declared herself to be full of aches, but allowed herself to be persuaded to be part of the gentle excursion.

At Yester, the group paused by a pretty waterfall on Gifford Water, the silvery splash of the water contrasting prettily with the verdant canopy all around them. After that, the paths improved, and they were able to walk three abreast. The combinations changed frequently and, just as they reached the ruins, Anna found herself flanked by Will and Mr Ashman.

There was something a little uncomfortable in the air—she could not quite say what, but perhaps it was that the gentlemen's comments to each other felt a little barbed. She shrugged. Mr Ashman was a local man, and presumably he and the Earl had known one another for a long time. Who was to say what history might lie between them? For her part, she continued to find Mr Ashman to be perfectly amiable.

'The architecture,' he was saying, 'Was so advanced for its day, that a rumour started locally that Sir Hugo de Gifford had entered into a pact with the devil.'

Her eyes widened. Chuckling, Will took up the tale. 'There is a vast underground hall at the bottom of yon staircase—' he indicated an archway to their left '—and they call it Goblin Ha'.'

'Goblins?'

'Yes.' Mr Ashman waggled his eyebrows theatrically. 'Or Hobgoblin Hall. The space is so vast and well-built for its time that they said no human hands could have constructed it. Ah! Here is my man.'

He walked across to a servant lugging a sack who had just arrived. It proved to contain torches and a tinder box, and before long each of the gentlemen bore a lit torch. Instantly, Prince Claudio feinted with it towards James, who grinned and mimed a counter thrust. At this, their wives rolled their eyes, Izzy murmuring something about men remaining boys for eternity. Play-acting done, they approached the arched entrance to the staircase. The darkness yawned below, maw-like and sinister. Anna shivered.

'You do not have to go down there, you know,' Will murmured to her.

'I know. But I should like to see it.'

'Very well. But take my arm, for the steps are un-even.'

As she did so, Mr Ashman turned from thanking his servant, and she saw his face fall. *Oh, dear!* The young man had gone to quite some effort to organise their excursion, and she wondered if perhaps he might have wished to show her the Goblin Ha' himself.

'Mr Ashman,' she said softly, 'Do please lead the way, for you know so much about this place.'

His face brightening, he moved in front, lifting his torch aloft as he entered the darkness. Anna and Will followed, and she could hear the others following behind. Within a couple of steps it was clear they would be forced to descend in single file, so narrow was the staircase. With Mr Ashman's torch in front and Will's behind, Anna focused on each step, being careful not to slip on the well-worn stone steps.

'You may place your hand on my shoulder if you need to, Miss Lennox,' Mr Ashman murmured, and she gratefully did so, wondering at the fact that the warmth of his shoulder through his coat did not make her insides flutter, as they would have done had it been Will.

Then they were at the bottom and took a few steps

inside the chamber. As the others arrived and the number of torches swelled to four, the hall became fairly well illuminated. Anna looked about her with interest at a vaulted ceiling, sturdy walls and some sort of alcove at the far end. It was a good hall, and an impressive feat of engineering, given it was underground. In its day it must have astounded all who saw it.

'What of the people who lived here?'

Will replied. 'The Gifford line eventually died out, and the castle and lands went to the Hay family, who were next in line through marriage. Both families were ever loyal to Scotland. They say the place was destroyed by Robert the Bruce as he retreated.'

'But why?' Rose asked.

'So it would not be of use to the advancing English.'

This set off some raillery between Garvald and his English friend, which Anna watched with a glad heart. Will was clearly a proud Scot, and she loved that about him.

Catching the direction of her own thoughts, she caught her breath.

Love? No.

Immediately, she reassured herself that there were many things she loved about many people: Izzy's energy; Lady Kelgrove's searing wit; Mr Ashman's earnestness. Well, perhaps not *loved*—not in the case of young Mr Ashman. She *liked* him, but not in the way she…

'Can we go? This place is eerie.' Rose's voice shook a little.

'Of course, my love. Follow me.' This time James led the way, with Izzy and her husband falling in behind Rose, leaving Anna and the two bachelors to take up the rear. Bachelors? Now why would she use that word? It was accurate, certainly, but did it need to be said, even in her head? She was also unmarried, and now had no need for a husband, as both her sisters had made stellar marriages. She would never know the pain of poverty or loneliness in old age, for she would always have the company of her sisters, their husbands and any children they might have. She was quite looking forward to being an aunt.

So why did she feel like sighing now?

The following days fell into something of a pattern. Anna would leave her bed early, write in her journal, then walk in the gardens before breakfast. Will, who was also an early riser, would usually join her, and together they would speak of everything and nothing. Anna had a sense of a single long, bright day when they had played together as children, and another now when they were spending time together as adults.

In between there was a dark night of things not known, and she was determined to fill it by discovering everything that Will had experienced after they had left. He seemed equally curious about her time in Elgin, so they spent hours together talking about their childhood and formative years—the people and places that were important to them. They also talked and debated—sometimes fiercely—about books, music, and

politics, and it warmed Anna's heart to discover he had
a well-formed mind, along with his good heart. Well, of
course he would. He could not have differed so greatly
from the child she had known.

On one of their excursions they had ventured into
the woods a little, and had been surprised to find Mr
Thaxby gathering plants.

'Good morning!' he had greeted them, closing his
little sack of botanical samples. 'I had thought to be the
only guest abroad so early.' His gaze darted left and
right, and it struck Anna that his manner was often fur-
tive, as though he did not like to be the focus of attention. In company, she realised now, his wife did most
of the conversing on behalf of them both.

'Oh, we often walk before breakfast,' Will replied.

'Indeed?' Thaxby looked from one to the other, his
eyes gleaming at this information, making Anna set
her jaw. Why should they not walk early? There was
nothing untoward about it. He bowed and left them,
and Will turned to watch him go.

'He is a strange little man, is he not?'

Anna shuddered. 'I cannot like him, no matter how
much I try. And it is not like me to dislike someone so
completely.'

He sent her a warm glance, indicating the path ahead,
and they walked on. 'This does not surprise me in the
least—neither that you dislike him, nor that it is unusual
for you to do so. What I cannot understand however is
that you imply you have found something likeable about
his wife. And Lady Renton, for that matter!'

She acknowledged this with a rueful grimace. 'Lady Renton and Mrs Thaxby are different in their vulgarity. One seems entirely oblivious, or uncaring, about the impact of her barbs. The other lies and dissembles without a qualm. The former is easier to forgive, for Lady Renton's malice is there in plain sight. Plus, Lady Renton's daughter, Lady Mary, is a darling, and so the mother cannot be all bad, I think.'

'I applaud your logic, and admire your generosity. But Mrs Thaxby...?'

'I know, I know. She thinks only of herself.'

'And money.'

'Yes, wealth, or the appearance of wealth, is everything to her, I think.'

'I suspect she would kill her own husband if paid to do so!' The humour in his eyes made it clear he was jesting, but a shudder went through her. 'Although I believe Mr Thaxby is devoted to her.' There was a brief pause. 'So what redeeming feature can you possibly see in her?' he continued quietly.

Anna thought it through. 'I believe that she is deeply unhappy. Pain radiates from her at times.'

He frowned. 'I have not sensed it. Do you recall the time Lady Kelgrove spoke of George and Richard? My impression was that she feigned emotion in order to leave the room.'

'I thought so too. But her brother died many years ago. Perhaps she has recovered from her grief. And you must admit, Lady Kelgrove was being extremely...'

'Pointed?'

'Yes, pointed. Her implication was shocking, and if false I have no doubt Mrs Thaxby's desire to escape was real. I also...'

'Yes?'

'I feel sorry for her. In London I have heard her speak about her regret at not having children. She was not feigning emotion on those occasions.'

He squeezed her hand. 'You have a kind heart, Anna. Much kinder than mine, for I can find no redeeming qualities in Mrs Thaxby, or her husband. Which reminds me—something curious occurred yesterday, and I should like to know what you make of it.'

She was all attention. 'Something to do with the Thaxbys?'

'Yes. Mr Thaxby's man...'

'John.'

'You know his name? Well, naturally you do, for you are keenly observant. I saw him conversing with Lady Kelgrove.'

Anna thought about this, but could come up with no logical reason why the two might interact. 'Was he assisting her with something? But, no, she is a stickler for etiquette. She would know that while your footmen are at her disposal the servant of another guest should never be approached.'

'Exactly.' He paused. 'I wondered if she was seeking information from him.'

'Information? What manner of information?'

'I know not. But I thought it interesting.' He opened

his pocket watch to check the time. 'Shall we turn back?'

There were no answers, only riddles, it seemed. While Anna and Will always had plenty to speak about, she particularly enjoyed trying to unravel the mysteries with him. His mind was good, and they often reached the same conclusions at the same time.

She sighed. Everything else was a muddle. Her sisters were married and she herself was adrift, uncertain of her path. She could dwindle into an aunt, being known for ever as an aunt and sister... There was something different about 'sister' in that context. As the eldest, she was used to leading the others—helping Rose to focus and take action, holding Izzy back from occasional rashness. Now they looked firstly to their husbands, not to her. So where did that leave her? Who exactly was Miss Anna Lennox? Was she more than the sister of Princess Isobel and Lady Ashbourne?

Should she marry, she would gain the status of being a married lady, as well as having her own husband to lean on, to speak to, to hold... Mr Ashman would make someone a very fine husband, but not her. Sadly, Anna's attention was already entirely taken up by another gentleman—a gentleman who was also a dear friend, making it hard to know her own heart or read his.

When he looked at her in *that* way, did he see her as a possible wife, or only his friend? She dared not risk making assumptions. As with the mystery of her parents and the Thaxbys, it would not do to presume. No, she must assume nothing, for to do so in this case risked hurt—a deeper hurt, perhaps, than anything she had ever known.

Returning to the puzzle about Mama, her husband and the Thaxbys, Anna documented everything diligently in her journal, reading over her previous entries at the little desk in her room.

George Fletcher: everything centred around him; she was sure of it. He and Mama's brother Richard had been great friends, and he had spent his summers with the Kelgroves. Was that when he and Maria had come to love one another? Or had that happened following Richard's tragic death, when George had stayed at the Kelgrove country estate for some of his recuperation?

And what should she make of that decision? Had George not felt comfortable in his own home? Or had he simply wished to comfort Richard's family—and take comfort too, from his friend's home, where they had all spent happy times together? George's parents had died when he'd been young, she knew, and the Thaxbys were not warm people. Perhaps Lady Kelgrove had offered him more love than his own family? Anna knew her great-grandmother well enough by now to know that beneath her stiff, blunt demeanour there beat a warm heart.

Her mind moved on, returning to the puzzle involving Thaxby's valet. If John had been with the Thaxbys for a long time it was possible he had known George. Which therefore provided a logical explanation as to why Lady Kelgrove should seek the man out. And a breach of etiquette could be forgiven if the motivation was strong enough.

As to the other riddle, 'the Lady Blue' and the three times three, Anna had at first spent hours staring at the Norie painting, silently begging Mama to show her the answer, to no avail. So they had all agreed to leave it to the back of their minds, hoping that not forcing a solution might be more effective. For ten days now she had stayed away from it, but perhaps her eye would soon be fresh enough for another attempt.

After breakfast the younger members of the party—the triplets and the three young gentlemen—would take to the paddock or the field for riding lessons. Anna, fiercely determined to overcome her fears, was fast catching up with her sisters, and had even ridden a mare around the paddock yesterday. The achievement had delighted her, and of itself would have been enough to ensure that this house party would live long in her memory.

Yet it was the least of the joy she found here—more, the joy of being back in her childhood home, of getting to know Lady Garvald, of spending time with Will.

They were now more than halfway through their stay, and Anna had a sense of time slipping away from her. These were days never to be repeated: walking with Will in the mornings; riding lessons; occasional excursions to beauty spots or simply to visit the shops in Gifford or Haddington; evenings spent enjoying good food and wine, and enjoying the company. The Thaxbys and Rentons were tolerable, Sir Walter and his son were frequent visitors, and of course Will and his mother were a delight.

Anna had taken to spending time with Lady Garvald in the late mornings, when the men would ride out or play their first games of billiards after the daily riding lesson for the ladies. There was to be a full moon in a few days, so Lady Garvald had invited all the local gentry for a soirée.

'Not a ball,' she had assured them firmly, 'For the very notion terrifies me! But we shall have dancing, even if only a dozen couples stand up.'

Anna did not challenge her hostess on this, although privately she felt it would be a ball, if most of those invited decided to attend. There was much to be done, and Lady Garvald was grateful for Anna's assistance with lists, food orders and consultations with Cook, the butler and the housekeeper.

Caterers from Edinburgh who would bring their own footmen had been commissioned, and they would procure fresh fish from Granton and carefully packed elderflower ices from a trader on the Royal Mile on the day. Meanwhile the ballroom was getting a thorough cleaning, along with silverware and crockery. On the day itself, Lady Garvald would cut fresh roses from her garden, and Anna had promised to assist with arranging them.

'Anna, I declare you are a treasure!' Lady Garvald beamed. 'I entertain so infrequently that it is all something of a challenge for me, I must admit.' She grimaced. 'The notion has always filled me with dread.'

'And I have never before assisted with preparations for a soirée. We had a ball in London, but it was my sister Rose who assisted our hostess with the preparations. I declare it is diverting to be involved, and I thank you for including me.'

'Nonsense! Besides, it is a useful skill for any young lady to learn, and so your mother would have said.'

As they worked, Lady Garvald often shared memories of Mama and of the time when they had lived there. Anna had the impression of a strong bond between the two women, and said so.

'Oh, yes! We had much in common, of course, being young mothers and grieving for our husbands. But it was more than that. I believe we should have been firm friends regardless of how similar our situations were. Your mother helped me through some of the darkest times in my life, and I believe I performed the same service for her.' She sighed. 'Of course, I now regret not probing further as to the circumstances that had left her alone and fearful, but at the time I respected her wish not to speak of it.' She smiled. 'But now all is well, for you are returned, and you were always in some sense my daughters.'

She embraced Anna then, and Anna was astounded to find that, while she was naturally delighted that Lady Garvald saw them as her daughters, part of her did not want it at all.

But why?

Was her heart concerned that it might be disrespectful to Mama? But no, for the two ladies had raised their four children together during their years here. Anna had never forgotten the lady who had truly been like a second mother to her. But that would suggest Will was something of a brother. Her mind instantly rejected the notion. He had been a friend, yes; he still was. But she had never seen him as a brother figure, thank goodness. Always as a friend.

Her heart sank as she acknowledged the crux of the matter. Despite having made the assertion that she saw him *only* as a friend, she had slowly come to realise her view of him was entirely different from that of James and Claudio, her actual brothers by marriage, and both now the closest thing she had to male friends. Neither of those gentlemen had ever managed to stir her heart, or her body, in the way that Will did, and so effortlessly. He had only to enter a room for her heart to pound, and when he looked directly at her, or touched her hand, her insides either melted or became infused with pulsating energy.

No, not a friend. Not at all.

Yet he probably saw her as a friend. Apart from a few breathless moments, possibly fuelled by her own imagination, he had been unfailingly and frustratingly friendly towards her, his natural reserve easing in her company in ways more akin to a long-standing friend than a lover. Not that she had ever had a lover. But she saw how James and Claudio looked at their wives, with fire in their eyes. Will had never looked at her like that, not really.

So her sisters, knowing her as they did, had been

partly right. They were right about *her*, but not him—and they had seen the truth before Anna was ready to admit it to herself.

She wanted more than friendship. She wanted everything. It had been there all along. She just had not *seen* it before.

Chapter Thirteen

Anna's head was spinning. How could she have been so blind? Why had it taken her so long to realise something so blatantly true that it thrummed through every nerve and sinew of her being? Thrummed through every heartbeat, every thought, every wish, every dream.

Her sisters were wrong about Will, though. He could not possibly view her the way she viewed him. Naturally, they could not read him as they could their own sister. They saw only the neatness of James's best friend—and now, Claudio's bosom bow—marrying the last remaining sister, the spinster.

She shook herself. Such thoughts were unhelpful. Had she not much for which to be grateful? Once more, she listed them in her head: her sisters and their husbands; her great-grandmother; Lady Garvald; Lammermuir House; Will.

He remained ZanZan, her childhood friend, with whom she had been raised for a time. ZanZan had been her best friend. Will did not need to be, for she had met him again only this year, at the age of one-and-twenty. And yet, her instincts told her the man did not love her, for his manner suggested friendly affection, not the passion of a lover.

Could she do anything to change it, to make him see her differently? She ruminated on this, then rejected the notion. She had no skills in flirtation, no arts with which to attract a gentleman. Having seen young ladies flirt openly all season in London, she shuddered at the very notion. Besides, she could not do anything to risk their friendship. She had only just found him again. She did not wish to lose him.

Suppressing a sigh, she made for the drawing room. The gentlemen had developed the habit of riding out on more adventurous hacks in the afternoon, leaving Anna and her sisters in the company of Lady Garvald, Lady Renton and Mrs Thaxby. Anna now played her part in supporting Lady Garvald, diverting the conversation away from the other two ladies' relentless feud, ably assisted by Izzy and Rose.

Once again, she could not help but wonder why their pleasure had to be spoiled by two ladies who, it seemed, were determined to outdo one another in unpleasantness. There was much talk of Lady Garvald's soirée, the older ladies questioning their hostess on the names and lineage of all those invited to attend.

'And of course,' Lady Garvald concluded, 'Sir Walter and his son, whom you know well.'

'Indeed.' Lady Renton's gaze whipped around to

Anna. 'No doubt the son will wish to stand up with you, Miss Lennox.'

'I...' Anna was unsure how to respond, for on the surface Lady Renton's observation was entirely reasonable. She seemed to hint at something more, though, beneath the obvious meaning.

'Mr Ashman will be pleased to dance with many of the young ladies attending,' Lady Garvald assured her firmly. 'For he is a sensible young man, and may be relied upon to not ignore anyone.'

'Humph,' was Lady Renton's response, but Anna sent Lady Garvald a grateful glance.

'They are returned!' Izzy's excited tone revealed that, as ever, being separated from her new husband for anything longer than an hour was a severe trial to her. Anna knew Rose was equally obsessed with her own handsome husband. Anna, having recently listened to her own heart, now understood her sisters as she had not before.

A few moments later the gentlemen entered, having divested themselves of boots, coats and hats. Unable to help herself, her eyes sought out Will, seeking that thrill of delight that always rippled through her as their eyes met.

There he is! And there it was. Her heart was thumping so loudly she was sure he might hear it from across the room.

His eyes seemed to light up briefly, then he schooled his features into neutrality, greeting the assembly generally and bending to kiss his mother on the cheek.

Meanwhile his two friends sat with their wives, while Lord Renton and Mr Thaxby chose a sofa together at quite some distance from their ladies.

'We were just speaking of the soirée tomorrow night,' Lady Renton informed the gentlemen. 'You must all be sure to do your duty by dancing with all of the ladies. All who wish to dance, that is. I myself shall sit it out.' Her air was of one who was expecting to experience *ennui* at an event that was clearly beneath her. Anna bit her lip, hurt on Lady Garvald's behalf.

'Of course!'

'Naturally!'

The gentlemen all agreed with alacrity, and Anna's heart skipped at the thought of dancing with Will. She had done so in London many times, and had always been aware that her heart behaved differently with him. But, now that she knew who he really was and what he meant to her, it would add another layer of wonder to the experience; she had no doubt of it. Yes, she knew his true identity, and more—she knew her own heart.

'Good morning, miss!' Sally entered Anna's bedchamber but, seeing her still seated at the desk, she stopped. 'Oh! Shall I go away again?'

'Not at all, for I am quite finished!' Anna smiled, placing her journal inside one of the many drawers in the pretty desk. 'I shall have a bath this morning, in preparation for the soirée tonight. For now, I need only a simple day dress for my usual walk in the gardens.'

'Yes, miss. And your blue silk is all ready for tonight. What jewellery should you like with it?'

Anna was in the pleasing situation of owning three pieces of jewellery, for the first time in her life. She had a string of tiny pearls from her great-grandmother, a silver cross on a chain from Rose and her husband and a pretty gold-and-amber necklace from Izzy and Claudio. 'The pearls, I think. They will go nicely with the blue gown.'

'Very well, miss. Now, may I quickly dress your hair? Nothing complicated, it is just…'

Anna laughed. 'Yes, you may. Am I so impatient to be outside that you must persuade me to not appear hoydenish?'

The maid blushed. 'Not at all, miss. It is just that since we came here you have been so animated…' She faltered. 'That is to say, I…'

Anna knew ladies could have no secrets from their maids, no matter how hard they tried. 'You may dress my hair, and thank you.' In truth, she *was* impatient. To begin every day by walking with Will was a joy. 'We shall have time for only a quick turn about the gardens this morning, I think.'

She said as much to Will when she met him in their usual spot, suppressing any temptation to behave differently towards him just because she…

'Today I cannot linger, Will, for I am promised to your mother. There is much to do!'

'Indeed! I too shall be busy, checking on both the menservants and the grooms.'

'How many horses do you expect?'

'Dozens! Too many to house in our stables, should it rain.' He glanced skyward. 'We may pray it remains as dry as this all day and night!'

They parted a little later in perfect harmony. Following breakfast and a quick bath, Anna made herself available to Lady Garvald, who gratefully gave her a list of tasks to complete. Dinner was planned for six, with the first of the guests expected to arrive by eight o'clock. Anna had thought she would have plenty of time to see to the matters on her list—including having her bath—but by four o'clock she had only just completed them. Lady Garvald was still in the rose garden accompanied by two of the gardeners, who were cutting the finest blooms to be displayed in large pots and vases throughout the public rooms.

'Oh, Anna, you are an angel! Did Cook find those other tureens?'

'She did, and the scullery maid is even now washing them. And Will has decided which wines are to be served, so I believe we are almost ready!'

'Thank goodness! Yes, those ones as well, please, and some of the yellow ones.' The gardeners set to, carefully cutting the long stems of the most beautiful blooms.

'These are perfect! Would you still like me to arrange them?'

'Oh, yes please, if you would. I have asked for the table in the library to be covered, so they can be done there.'

The library. A familiar tightness made itself known within her. They had not yet managed to solve Mama's riddle, a source of great frustration to her.

Almost twenty minutes later she made her way inside. The gardeners were bringing the flowers to the kitchen door, as was correct, and upstairs maids would be summoned to bring them to the library. Each had their role, and every one of them worked hard.

As she entered the hallway, Anna caught sight of Will, walking away from her.

'Will!'

Before she had even thought about it, she had called his name. The call had not come from her conscious mind. It had come from her heart, the core of herself. She *needed* to be in his company. Always.

He turned instantly and walked towards her, and she fumbled for an excuse. 'Er, do you happen to know if the footmen have brought the vases to the library?'

He took this at face value, seeming not to notice her consternation. Lord, why did she lose all sense of proportionality around him? Also, she should not have been shouting like a fishwife in the market. *What must he think of me?*

'I do not,' he said, 'But let us go there together and find out. Shall we?'

He offered his arm and she took it gratefully, her heart skipping as usual, but still feeling as though he should not be so kind to a hoyden. By the time they reached the library she was a little calmer, yet was glad to see the maids arriving at the same time with

the many baskets of blooms. As per Lady Garvald's instructions, the large table had been covered with a thick
cloth, and multiple pots and vases containing water had
been placed there in readiness.

'What time is it?' she asked Will, assessing the work.

He checked his pocket watch. 'Twenty-past four.'

'I need to get these done by five o'clock, so I can
dress for dinner.' She squared her shoulders. 'Very
well.'

He was frowning. 'May I be of assistance? Or should
we call upon the servants?'

'I actually want to do this myself, for your mother.
She has been so kind to me…'

'In that case, I repeat my offer of assistance. Might
I do anything to help you in your task?'

'Actually, yes. If you could strip the stems of any
lower leaves and thorns, I would be eternally grateful.'

'Would you?' A gleam of humour lit his eye. Picking
up a creamy-white rose, he began stripping it briskly.
'Now that is worth the effort, I think. And tell me…' he
sent her a wicked glance '…what form will this gratitude take?'

Her jaw dropped. His tone, his words, even that look
he had just sent her, all looked a little like flirtation!
But, no, it could not be, surely?

He was awaiting a response. 'Oh, I shall have to
think about it,' she responded lightly. 'Perhaps I could
resist correcting you when you say something that is
incorrect.'

'Incorrect?' He feigned outrage. 'Never!'

She laughed and began placing the stripped flowers into the first vessel. 'I think I shall make this one all white, since we have so many of those. Some of the other vases can have mixed colours, including these wonderful boughs.' At her request, the gardeners had provided leaf boughs of different types and lengths. 'Ouch!'

'What?' She pressed her hand to her mouth, and he took it. 'Pierced by a thorn?'

She nodded, mesmerised by the sight of his close study of her fingers. There was a small drop of blood forming on the pad of her forefinger, and as she stood immobile he took it into his mouth, sucking it. She caught her breath. She could feel his teeth against the sensitive pad of her finger, and the pressure of his warm lips as he sucked the tiny drop away.

'There!' he declared in a matter-of-fact way, just as though nothing of note had happened. 'All better! But be careful—there are thorns everywhere.'

'I... Yes,' she managed, bending her head to her task. But her pulse was pounding loudly in her ears, her mouth was dry and her insides were caught up in a sensation so sweet it took her breath away. She dared not look at him, for fear he would see her, see what was going on within her.

Heat. Need. Desire.

This, then, was what her sisters shared with their husbands. Never had she experienced anything like it.

On they worked, in a silence that felt different from their usual companionable pauses. Eventually they spoke again—just small comments about their task, he commenting on the wide range of colours, she asking him to prepare a few pink roses for the next vase. Occasionally, she felt him looking at her, but she would not—*could* not—return his gaze, for she was all confusion.

By the time she was adding the last few stems to the last vase, she felt calm enough to ask him the time and to look at him in a natural way as she did so. 'It lacks nine minutes to five,' he answered. 'We managed it!'

His grin was infectious, with no sign of any hidden layers to it, and she smiled back at him with ease. Behind him was the painting of the cattle.

Nine. Three times three.

Her gaze dropped to the gilt number below the painting, and she gasped.

'What? What is it?'

She pointed. '"The key is three and three times three".Three and nine.'

'Yes, twelve.'

'No, thirty-nine—look!'

It was true. Below the painting was the number thirty-nine, plain to see. It had been there all along; she just had not *seen* it before. And somehow Anna *knew* that, this time, she was correct. She had solved the riddle.

Chapter Fourteen

Anna was already moving, sinking to her knees on the thick carpet.

'Three shelves.' She counted from top to bottom 'One, two, three.'

Her hand trailed along the books on the lowest shelf, counting aloud until she had reached the ninth. The shelf contained multiple works by Rousseau, but in the ninth position a slim volume stood out. It was not by Rousseau. Her eyes widened as she read the spine: *Lessons for Children* by Mrs Barbauld.

'Mama had a copy of this book in Elgin! She used it for our early reading lessons.' She reached out a trembling hand then paused, fearing disappointment. 'Has this bookshelf remained unchanged in sixteen years?'

Will shrugged. 'Probably. Now, go on.' He had knelt beside her, close enough that she could sense his warmth. Their eyes met, and she was abruptly glad to share this moment with him. 'Take it!'

Holding her breath, she removed the book carefully.

Opening it, she flicked through, then more carefully flicked through from beginning to end.

The book was empty.

Her shoulders slumped. 'I was so certain! The numbers, the fact it was out of place, the very book Mama used to read to us…' She shook her head. 'It should be here!'

'Let me see.' She handed it to him and he turned it over in his hands before opening it. 'How curious!'

'What?' She eyed him in confusion.

'A word here is carefully underlined in pencil. Nothing more, just the one word—see?'

He pointed and she read it.

'Behind.'

He flicked on. 'Again!' He paused near the middle of the book. Once again the word 'behind' had been underlined. Their eyes met, then as one they turned back to the bookshelf, removing the books that had been to the left and right of the riddle's book.

'Something is there!' His voice was tight with excitement.

'I see it! Let me reach…' Slipping her hand into the space they had created, she reached into the area behind, touching cloth. Carefully, he drew it out. It was velvet, carefully folded and surprisingly heavy. Holding her breath, she undid the first fold, brushing away the dust, then the next.

'Paper! A note, perhaps?'

Will was right. As she undid the final fold, a folded note almost fell out. He caught it, but Anna's attention was captured by the beautiful object now revealed, sparkling and twinkling in the light. It was a necklace, but a necklace so wonderful that Anna could scarcely take it in. The chain and setting was gold, the stones a cluster of diamonds surrounding an enormous sapphire.

'Oh, my!' she whispered. 'How beautiful!' Reverently, she held it up to the light, almost blinking at the brilliance of the stones.

'The Fletcher necklace,' he murmured. 'It can be no other.' Unfolding the note, he handed it to her.

Anna gasped. 'Mama's handwriting!'

In a trembling voice, she read it aloud. *'This necklace is the property of Maria Berkeley Lennox Fletcher. Or, if I am gone, it passes to my eldest daughter, Annabelle Georgina Lennox Fletcher, and to her heirs. This treasure fine is yours and mine, my darling daughter.'*

Mama's signature was below it.

It was too much. His arms enfolded her as she shuddered with emotion. With his arms around her, she felt safe, comforted and cared for.

'Why are you always here when I need you?' she muttered into his handkerchief after a little while. 'I believe I have cried more since coming here than I have in years! I am not normally a watering pot, I swear!'

'So you keep telling me. And I keep replying that you are perfectly entitled to cry in circumstances such as these. As to my being here when you need me, I believe that to be a worthy endeavour, and one which I am happy to take on. Now, if you are feeling a little better, might I suggest you bring this to Lady Kelgrove? For she is our puppeteer, I believe.'

'Yes, indeed! She has our interests at heart, and must know of this immediately!'

Lady Kelgrove was initially cross at being disturbed during her toilette, and made it known in no uncertain terms what she thought of young ladies who called at the *most* inconvenient moments. But once Anna had impressed upon her that she must speak with her privately on a matter of great importance, she sent her maid away.

'Well, what is it, Annabelle?'

For answer, Anna carefully unfolded the cloth. 'Now, that is a necklace I have not seen for many a year,' she murmured. Her tone sharpened. 'Who knows of this?'

'Only Will. We found it together just now, in Mama's hiding place.'

'Good. And is that a note with it?'

'It is.'

On perusing the note, Lady Kelgrove pursed her lips. 'Maria's assertion could not be clearer. She uses the name Fletcher for both of you, and states this necklace is your property. So they must have married.'

Sighing, she refolded the note. 'The difficulty is that I cannot find proof of the wedding, and everything will fall without it. My lawyer and his clerks are searching, but I have had nothing from them as yet to confirm it. I even tried to question one of the former Fletcher servants, to no avail, for he was impressively forgetful.'

She lapsed into a reverie, while the clock on her mantel struck half-past five.

I shall be dreadfully late for dinner!

'What can I do with it, Grandmama?'

Lady Kelgrove held up an imperious hand and Anna subsided. She waited, trying not to fidget, while the clock ticked on remorselessly.

Lady Kelgrove looked at her directly. 'What if you were to wear the necklace to dinner tonight?'

Anna gasped at the audacity of it. 'Perhaps Mrs Thaxby or her husband might be surprised into revealing something.'

Lady Kelgrove frowned. 'But, if what I suspect is true, they may be dangerous, and I should not like to put you in any peril.'

'Stuff!' retorted Anna, her eyes dancing. 'What can they do to me at the dinner table?

'Very well. I see no better plan. But tell no one about it beforehand.' She glanced at the clock. 'Not that there will be any opportunity to do so, for you are shockingly tardy, Anna. Be quick, now!'

Anna needed no second bidding. Dashing to her bedchamber, she found Sally in a high state of agitation. 'Oh, there you are, miss!'

'I know. I was with Lady Kelgrove and I am dreadfully late! Do what you can, please.'

By the time she had donned her stays and stockings, undergown, slippers, and the blue silk gown, it lacked only ten minutes to the hour, so Sally dressed her hair in double-quick time.

'Thank goodness you have natural curls for me to work with, miss. If we had to use the curling iron, there would be no chance of me having you ready in time.'

Anna barely heard her, for her mind had been racing the whole time. George Fletcher was her father. There could now be no doubt. And it looked as though her parents had been legally wed. Which meant...

'Sally, tell me, what do you know of Mr Thaxby's man?' Something about Lady Kelgrove's tone had made Anna wonder if she believed that John did in fact know something.

'John? A good man, and well-liked among the servants. He does not deserve the treatment—' She clamped her lips shut.

'Quite. No, I shall not wear the pearls after all.' Rising, Anna lifted the velvet-covered treasure from her bedside table, where she had placed it on entering her bedchamber.

Sally's eyes grew wide. 'Miss!'

'Isn't it exquisite? It was my mother's, and now it is apparently mine.' She shook her head. 'I cannot imagine a more beautiful necklace.'

'Nor I, miss.' Lifting it with great care, she inspected the clasp, then fastened the jewellery around Anna's neck. 'Ooh, how beautiful! And sapphires are perfect for your blue eyes, miss.'

It felt cool, heavy, and decidedly strange. 'And my gown!' She smiled. 'Now, pass me my gloves and fan, and I shall go.' She thought for a moment. 'Please do not speak of this with anyone.' She should not have told Sally it was her mother's necklace. That was a detail to be revealed at the right moment—by Lady Kelgrove, no doubt.

'Of course not, miss!'

Hurrying along the landing, Anna saw a manservant emerge from one of the other bedchambers, a gentleman's boots in hand. Normally, this would not have earned any particular attention, but she had been thinking about this particular servant just now.

As she walked towards him, making for the top of the stairs, John stood to the side, as was proper.

I must speak with him—but not now. Not when she was already so late. He bowed as she passed, perfectly correctly, but something about him...

Glancing over her shoulder, she saw that the valet had not resumed his progress. Indeed, he was standing as still as a statue, his face ashen and his shoulders stiff. Clearly, he had seen and recognised the necklace. Even now, he would be perhaps recalling Lady Kelgrove's questions, and working out exactly who Anna was. Still, she need not worry that he would tell his master, for she herself was about to reveal the necklace to everyone.

She could not tarry. Glancing at the tall clock in the hall, a sick feeling went through her. Ten past six! To keep the party late for dinner was an unforgivable insult to her hostess.

Yet that was the least of her anxieties as she stepped through the door.

Chapter Fifteen

All eyes turned to Anna and she paused in the doorway, suddenly uncertain. Lady Garvald and Lady Kelgrove had the two chairs beside the fireplace. The Rentons were to the left, the Thaxbys to the right. Her sisters and their husbands were standing by the piano, chatting with Mr Ashman, while Will and Sir Walter were conversing beside the second window.

'Good evening,' she ventured, hearing a tremble in her voice. 'I apologise for keeping you all waiting.'

'Well, since you were assisting me by arranging all of the flowers until very recently, I cannot be critical of you, my dear.' Lady Garvald patted an empty chair beside her and Anna walked forward. 'Both my son and Lady Kelgrove explained that you had left yourself short of time to dress, so I asked Cook to hold dinner for ten minutes.' She nodded to a nearby footman, who bowed and left the room. Dinner would shortly be called.

'What are you wearing around your neck?' Mrs Thaxby's voice was unrecognisable—strangled and strange. Rising from her seat, she advanced towards Anna in an alarming manner. Her eyes were round and almost seemed to protrude, her expression contorted with what looked like rage.

Instinctively, Anna shrank back, one hand going to her throat, then with determination she straightened. Out of the corner of her eye, she saw Will begin to move towards them, then her attention focused back on Mrs Thaxby.

'Mrs Thaxby!' she began, hoping her play-acting was in line with Lady Kelgrove's plans. 'Are you quite well? Why should you want to have my necklace?'

'It belongs to me! Indeed, it was stolen from me twenty-two years ago! I say that necklace is *mine*, and you are a thief!' There was a collective gasp and murmur of disapproval from the assembly.

Anna suspected that Lady Kelgrove's plan was deliberately to shock Mrs Thaxby with the reappearance of the necklace, perhaps in the hope she might say something revealing about Richard or George. So Anna would do her best to play her part.

She managed a light laugh. 'Whatever can you mean? Twenty-two years ago I was not even born! I could not possibly have stolen it!'

Mr Thaxby now came forward, placing a hand on his wife's arm and sending her an intent look.

'My wife is distressed, for that necklace is an heirloom in her family, and was indeed stolen from her twenty-two years ago.'

Will's tone was sharp. 'Mrs Thaxby would do well

to control her words. If she were a gentleman, I should call her out for the insult to Miss Lennox!'

Anna's heart warmed at this display of loyalty, and to her gratification she could hear murmurs of agreement from other male voices Both of her sisters' husbands would see it as their duty to protect the honour and reputation of their sister-in-law. Will had done it too. Why? Because he was the host here, or because he cared?

Briefly, Anna met the gazes of Izzy and Rose, trying to send them a message to let her manage this drama in her own way. While Rose looked puzzled, and Izzy outraged, both remained silent.

Anna turned back to Mrs Thaxby. 'Are you certain, Mrs Thaxby, that it is the same necklace?' The woman's eyes flashed with what looked like pure hatred, and Anna recoiled. But Will was beside her, and so she persisted. 'After all, sapphires and diamonds are not uncommon in the *ton*.'

'Of course I am certain. How dare you suggest otherwise? This is the Fletcher necklace. It belonged to my mother, and her mother before it.'

'So was it worn by the wife of the Fletcher heir, then?' A frown of puzzlement appeared on the other woman's brow. 'I mean to say,' Anna persisted, 'It was not passed from mother to daughter, but from each Fletcher man to his bride?'

'Well, yes, but since George died it had to pass to me. As his only living relative, I inherited everything.'

'How did the necklace come to be lost?' Will had decided to join in, and Anna knew he would tread carefully.

'It was not lost, I tell you! It was stolen!' Her tone was fierce. 'After George's death, I went to look for it. It was gone from the safe.'

Will laughed. 'So it may not have been stolen at all! Perhaps your brother sold it. It seems clear it was his property, not yours.'

'He would never have done that, being raised with foolish notions of loyalty and tradition! He was nauseatingly *good*, and so everyone described him.'

'You find it nauseating that your brother was good, Mrs Thaxby?' Lady Kelgrove had decided to enter the fray.

'Of course not! You are twisting what I say.' Visibly struggling, Mrs Thaxby took a breath, then continued in a calmer tone. 'Nevertheless, I say you are wearing stolen goods and, unless you can show you came by the necklace honestly, it should be returned to me. Is that not so, Sir Walter?'

The magistrate stepped forward, just as a gong sounded in the hallway. 'This is all highly irregular, I must say. And just before dinner too!' He eyed Mrs Thaxby. 'Since the loss of the necklace pre-dates Miss Lennox's birth—which you confirmed yourself by saying it disappeared twenty-two years ago—for now I shall leave the necklace with her.' He turned to Anna. 'You are not planning to leave this place?'

'Oh, no! We are fixed here for at least another ten days.'

'Good.' He rubbed his hands together. 'Then I suggest we dine, for we are already late! I shall address this matter in the coming days.'

Lady Garvald assented and led the way on Claudio's arm, while Will accompanied Izzy—the highest-ranking lady—and Lord Renton offered his arm to Lady Kelgrove. As the party paired up in order of rank, James accompanied Lady Renton, while Sir Walter led Rose to the dining room. That left only Anna, Mr Ashman, and the Thaxbys. As Mr Ashman offered his arm to Mrs Thaxby, he threw a reassuring glance towards Anna.

I am among friends, Anna reminded herself as Mr Thaxby offered his arm with an unctuous smile and a look of pure venom.

'Miss Lennox.'

She could not speak, nor smile at him. Never until this moment had she resented her usual status as the lowest-ranked lady in the room. What did such things matter, after all? But it did matter that she was forced to endure his company as they walked stiffly to the dining room. Yes, and he was likely to be seated next to her too. He might wear the social mask, but she had sensed his anger, seen the fury in his eyes just now.

She was right. Will was of course at the head of the table, with Izzy, James, Lady Kelgrove, Mr Thaxby, Anna and Lord Renton to his right, while on Will's left his mother had assigned Lady Renton, Sir Walter, Mrs

Thaxby, Mr Ashman, Rose and Claudio. That left Anna stuck between Mr Thaxby and Lord Renton.

Lord Renton was perfectly affable, and made no mention of the recent confrontation as they conversed lightly during the first course, allowing Anna's pulse to settle a little. But when the footmen moved in to serve the second course—beefsteak and oyster pie, as well as haricot beans *à la bonne femme*—Lady Garvald turned the table, as was correct, by beginning a conversation with Prince Claudio. The effect rippled through the room, everyone now turning to converse with the person on the other side, and Anna was forced to accept Mr Thaxby's offer to pass her any dish she would like.

With a neutral expression she requested the stuffed cucumbers and a slice of pie, and he complied, serving her with a flourish before asking the footman to refill her wine glass. She drank very little after that, and was relieved when the conversation turned yet again. This time, Lord Renton had less to say, so she was able to observe Mrs Thaxby attempting to use all her dubious charms on Sir Walter, as well as hearing snatches of the conversation between Mr Thaxby and Lady Kelgrove.

'And did you report it as stolen at the time? Hire a thief-taker, or inform the Bow Street Runners or the constables?'

'Well, no, my lady. We were grieving, you must understand. My wife's brother...'

'Strange. Pass me the cucumbers, Mr Thaxby, if you please.'

A bubble of humour at Lady Kelgrove's audacity

threatened to spill out of Anna, and to counter it she asked Lord Renton if he often travelled to Scotland.

'Not as often as I should wish,' was his response, and she laughingly told him he had given exactly the right answer. They then debated why certain among the *ton* despised everything that was not English, and continued in convivial conversation through each subsequent turn. The contrast with Mr Thaxby was noticeable. Anna had seen another side to the Thaxbys tonight—a side that made her shiver. She only hoped she and Lady Kelgrove had made the right decision in provoking such a pair.

Finally, the ordeal was done—at least, the formal dinner part of it. Tonight, instead of the ladies retiring to the drawing room to await the gentlemen, the entire party made their way to the ballroom and hall, where before long Will and his mother began receiving their guests.

Knowing Lady Garvald was entirely occupied, Anna briefly spoke to her sisters, explaining how the necklace had been discovered. They were all excitement, especially given the note, and Mrs Thaxby's confirmation that it was the Fletcher necklace.

'There can be no doubt now as to the identity of our father,' said Izzy. 'I do wish he had not such an unpleasant sister, though.'

On this they all agreed, before the necessities of the soirée separated them. Since Lady Garvald remained occupied with receiving guests, Anna checked all was well with the housekeeper and butler, and helped to solve a last-minute dilemma about whether to place the elaborate silver epergne on the first table or the central one in the supper room. The musicians were already in place on their little dais in the corner of the ballroom, and Anna's flower arrangements had been placed strategically throughout, adding beauty to the already stunning ballroom. While it was still bright outside, hundreds of candles were at the ready, to be lit after sunset.

All is ready.

Before long Will and Lady Garvald came to the ball-room, indicating that all the expected guests had now arrived, and both began making their way around the room, performing more introductions. Apparently everyone invited had attended, and Lady Garvald was at once gratified and worried by it.

'I just hope there are no disasters, Anna!' she confessed. Anna, sensing her disquiet, refrained from telling her that the evening was most definitely more a ball than a soirée, given the numbers of guests. Certainly everyone was dressed for a ball, and once again she was glad of her blue silk gown.

'I am confident that you have planned for every eventuality,' she assured her, and Lady Garvald squeezed her hand.

'Bless you! Now, may I introduce you to…?'

Anna complied, and received with a polite smile the usual astonishment at the fact she and her sisters were identical triplets, and with equanimity various flowery compliments from a number of local gentlemen. Before long, two distinct gatherings had formed—one around Prince Claudio and Princess Isobel, and one around her.

What on earth is going on? She could not account for it. While understanding that she and her sisters were thought of as pretty by the *ton*, never before had she received such attention, and she was not certain she liked it very much.

Thankfully she had already reserved dances for Will, James, Claudio and Mr Ashman, otherwise she might have ended up spending the entire evening dancing with men she had never met before—not a prospect she would have welcomed, for it was so much more comfortable to dance with gentlemen she knew. To her great relief the Thaxbys had taken to a corner of the room and were deep in conversation. Anna shivered just watching them, but just then, during a lull in the general hubbub, she overheard a female voice behind her mention her name.

'Miss Lennox. She is Princess Isobel's sister. My mama has instructed me to make a friend of her, if I can. Imagine! She is related to an *actual* prince and...' The rest was lost as the gentlemen with Anna made some new remark, but suddenly all had become clear. She was not being pursued for her own sake, but for her connection to Prince Claudio. Princes were an uncommon sight here, of course.

With a cynicism that she would not have had a year ago, she understood that even if she had been old, ugly and devoid of teeth, some of those present, men and women, would have tried to court her or befriend her.

Turning briefly, she saw the speaker was a dark-haired young lady in a pale pink gown, before her attention was again reclaimed by her sham admirers.

A little later, Lady Garvald introduced her to the dark-haired young lady. She was part of a group—two older ladies, and two younger. The two older ladies were sisters, it seemed, and they each had a daughter. The dark-haired girl was Miss Hughes and her cousin Miss Newton. Anna curtseyed, smiled and said all that was appropriate.

Then Will and Mr Ashman joined them, and the girls' demeanour underwent an abrupt change. Miss Hughes, who had eyes only for the Earl of Garvald, became at once coquettish and flirtatious in a way that Anna could never imagine replicating, while Miss Newton blushed and stammered in the general direction of Mr Ashman.

How interesting!

Abruptly, and with a sense of relief, Anna found herself on surer ground. The mysteries of her parents and of Richard's death could be forgotten for a little time, while she indulged in a habit developed during her *ton* season—that of watching people, and divining them. So she stayed with the two girls and their mamas, much longer than she had with anyone else, and by the end of fifteen minutes was fairly certain that Miss Newton was head over ears in love with Mr Ashman, and that he was entirely oblivious to it.

Regarding the obvious lures being cast by Miss Hughes in the Earl's direction, Will was either ignoring them or was also remarkably oblivious. Anna saw no evidence of any true affection being shared between them, but then, what did she know of the male heart? And gentlemen often chose brides for reasons of alliances and common sense, not love.

She swallowed, suddenly unsure. Once again she was struck by the preposterous notion that she should do *something*—though she was unsure what, exactly. But *something* that might make him see her not as his childhood playmate, but as an eligible young woman.

The dancing was beginning and Will had arrived to claim her hand for the opening quadrille. They had danced together many times in London, but now things were different. First, he was not just the Earl of Garvald, but Will, ZanZan and the man she now knew she loved.

She loved him! Well, naturally she did. Using the word in her head for the first time was novel, but the feeling itself…that had been growing for a very long time. Pausing for a moment to savour this new knowledge, she returned to the differences between dancing with him in London and dancing with him here.

First, she loved him. That made everything different.

Second, they were in Lammermuir House, her childhood home.

Third, she was wearing Mama's necklace.

And fourth, she and Will were opening the ball together. As he led her to the top of the dance floor, and other couples began falling in around them, it struck her that she should not have had this honour, and she said so.

'Why ever not? Who would you have had me dance with?'

'Izzy is highest in rank, and Rose is next tonight.' Lady Renton—who would have ranked higher than Rose—had informed them she would not dance tonight, Anna recalled. Glancing about, Anna noted Lady Renton was engaged with a group of local dames, holding forth masterfully and seemingly enjoying a new audience.

'Very properly, I asked both your sisters—and, well, see for yourself!' He indicated the dance floor. Sure enough, Izzy and Rose were there, taking to the floor with their own husbands, quite in defiance of tradition. 'They were quite determined that I should dance with you first,' he continued, and Anna felt a wave of mortification rising within her as she imagined the knowing smiles and pointed tone her sisters would likely have adopted.

'I see.' And she did. She just hoped that he did not.

'How do you, Anna?' he asked softly. 'The Thaxbys…'

'Let us not speak of it now, for your mother's ball is about to begin, and I am determined to leave mysteries aside for a few hours.'

'Very well—I approve!' He grinned. 'My lady.' He bowed as the musicians began the opening bars, and she mirrored him with a slow curtsey. As they advanced and retreated in the steps of the dance her gaze met his frequently, and their hands clasped regularly.

This is how it should be—he and I together.

Daringly, she spoke to him about the two young ladies.

'How well do you know them?'

He shrugged. 'As well as any man knows his neighbours. Miss Hughes is a similar age to you; Miss Newton, a little younger.'

'And were you close friends with them after—after I left?'

'Not at all. I wanted no other friends.' He took a breath, then continued. 'I spent more than a year trying to punish my mother for something that was not her doing. I was so *angry*. In vain did she host gatherings with the local children, for I remained aloof. Once I went away to school, I began to make friends with some of the other boys, but I never again had female friends like you and your sisters.'

'I see.' And she did. She truly did. Her curiosity about Miss Hughes remained unabated, however, fuelled by something suspiciously akin to jealousy. *Jealousy!* She had never in her life experienced it, and it was astonishing how intense was the feeling. The next time the dance brought them together, she asked, 'What is your opinion of Miss Hughes and Miss Newton?'

Puzzlement crossed his face briefly. 'I have no strong opinions on either of them. They are both pleasant young ladies. Why do you ask?'

She laughed lightly, mostly in relief. 'Miss Hughes has apparently been instructed to make a friend of me, as I am the sister of Princess Isobel.'

His brow cleared. 'Ah. Yes, Mrs Hughes is ambitious for her daughter, I have no doubt. And for her son.'

'Her son?'

'Mr Hughes. Can you have already forgotten him? Is he lost in the throng of your cicisbeos?'

'My *what*?'

'Your admirers.'

She sniffed. 'I understood only married women may have such gallants. And I am unmarried.'

'Yes.' He said. 'Yes, you are.' A strange expression crossed his face. 'But you certainly have admirers. I could barely get close enough to speak to you earlier, and had to ask my mother to extricate you and introduce you to some of the ladies.'

'You…you asked her?'

Why should he intervene in such a manner?

'I did.' He frowned. 'Was that wrong of me? I thought you looked a little uncomfortable.'

'I am perfectly capable of looking after myself, Will! Including fending off *faux* admirers, if needed.'

High-handed. Yes, he had been decidedly high-handed.

Naturally, he focused on one word in particular. '*Faux*? Do you think their admiration of you is not genuine?'

She grimaced. 'I think my most attractive feature tonight is my relationship by marriage with royalty. Or possibly Mama's necklace, which may suggest I am wealthy.'

'If you are the true Fletcher heir, then you are indeed

enormously wealthy. And it is true that your sister is now a princess. But it should not change you.' He gave a wry smile. 'Such cynicism in one so young!'

'Yet you do not deny it.'

'I most emphatically do deny it! Yes, being Claudio's sister-in-law will bring you to their notice, but your character and your beauty will keep them with you. I know many of these young men, and they have a healthy dislike for young ladies who are vapid, vulgar or vain, let me tell you! This is Scotland, after all!'

'While I can only admire your skill for alliterative epithets, I am not sure I share your opinion.' She eyed him curiously. 'So have you not found these flaws in me?'

'Not at all, although doubtless you have others yet to be discovered!'

She tossed her head at this, strangely enjoying their verbal fencing, while still remaining cross at his earlier interference.

'A gentleman should not comment on any flaws a lady may have. He should see only her good qualities.'

'I do not think that rule applies to close friends such as you and I.'

Close. She liked that word. *Friends*, not so much.

'And so,' he continued, 'I may say with impunity that you have a tendency to brood, a leaning towards anxiety and a desire to manage everyone around you.' The glint in his eye told her he was being deliberately provocative. 'These may be considered flaws by some.'

'With impunity? I think not!' Impulsively, she threw

caution to the wind. 'If we are being frank, as only friends can, in that case dare I say you are excessively reserved to the point of rudeness at times?'

He recoiled. 'Rudeness? *Never* have I been rude! My mother has raised me to know how to behave.'

'Well, if you can caricature me, I must be offered the same privilege!'

'Touché!' He twirled her around, perhaps a little more forcefully than required, then caught her before she should lose her balance. 'But I know you, as those *admirers* never shall!' His expression was grim.

'And I know *you*, Will, better perhaps than anyone save your own mother!'

The anger abruptly went from his eyes, replaced by something thoughtful, rueful. 'And perhaps even better than that.'

The dance had ended. They stood, simply looking at one another, until a hum of conversation around them brought them back to attention. After completing the formal end-bow and curtsey, he asked if she wished him to procure her a glass of wine or ratafia. When she declined, he bowed again and marched off, a stiffness to his gait that she knew denoted vexation.

He talked with Miss Hughes and her mother next. Anna, conversing with Sir Walter, had to turn away from the sight of their shared smiles and easy conversation. Being at outs with him was disturbing to her equilibrium, yet she remained cross, frustrated and in no mood to reconcile.

What should have been a perfectly wonderful dance together to open the ball had turned into a falling out that, in her mind, seemed enormous.

Chapter Sixteen

Will was entirely confused.

Just when he thought he was making progress, the road had turned sharply and unexpectedly, leaving him feeling as though he was no longer on solid ground. While it was probably inevitable that he and Anna would have a falling out at some point, tonight's disagreement had been unanticipated. Equally unexpected was how affected he was by it. To be out of harmony with her was insupportable. As he watched her talking with Ashman, once more doubts flooded his mind. What was between them, exactly? And how did it compare with the connection between Anna and himself?

The way she looked at him sometimes was so intense, the air seemed to thrum between them. Could she really be confusing such passion for *friendship* still? His friends had strongly urged him to take care, for they said Anna saw him only as ZanZan, not Will. But something within him refused to believe it.

Yet, he reminded himself, she had no experience of such matters, no way of knowing how rare such a connection was. Indeed, Ashman might seem to her a safer option, for Will's passion was too strong ever to be called *safe*. Had she been deliberately provocative earlier, seeking to push him away?

No matter, his challenge now was to observe her with Ashman, then workout how the hell to restore the intimacy between them. He stifled a sigh. He still had their shared mission to uncover the truth, although she had said she did not wish to speak of it earlier. But Mr Thaxby was clearly angry, and his lady had spent the evening sending dagger-like glances in the direction of the Lennox triplets, between copious glasses of wine. He sighed. He needed to stay alert. If the Thaxbys really had committed murder, then who knew what they might do to cover it up?

The musicians struck up the opening bars to the Boulanger, and he recalled he needed to make his way to Princess Isobel.

As Mr Ashman approached to claim her hand for the next dance, the Boulanger, Anna reflected on Will's description of her flaws, and reluctantly acknowledged his words, while delivered far too harshly in her opinion, were not strictly unjust. Ruminating and making herself worried were two of her habits, her pattern of wishing to manage situations as much a response to anxiety as anything else. He probably understood that. But to hear one's imperfections announced so plainly had felt…harsh. Too harsh.

Yet she had been equally harsh in return, calling him

rude. A man of such consequence as him would never have been described that way by the *ton*. He was never discourteous, nor disdainful. He was simply…reserved, aloof, composed.

What was worse, she now understood his reserve and the reasons behind it, and she had been unkind to use the word rude. Guilt now mingled with her ongoing outrage at his frankness, both compounded by distress at not being in harmony with him.

Besides, she concluded with a hint of defiance, *it will do him no harm to think on how he appears to others.*

'Splendid evening, is it not?'

Lord, she was making a habit of being less than attentive to Mr Ashman. And she had dared to call Will rude! With determination, she smiled at her partner, and before long she was quizzing him on Miss Hughes and Miss Newton. He knew both well, naturally, having been playmates with them when they had all been children.

'Miss Newton was a little younger than the rest of us, and as I recall we used to chase her away when she tried to tag after us!'

'The gentlemen are not chasing her away now,' Anna noted dryly.

'Excuse me? I do not understand your meaning.'

Lord, even clever men could be surprisingly obtuse!

'I mean to say that she is remarkably pretty and, inasmuch as I can judge anyone's character on first meeting, I would say of all the new people I have met tonight she is the one I liked best.'

He smiled broadly, a hint of pride in his tone as he said, 'Well, naturally. Hetty is a great sport altogether! Never any drama from her!'

'I do hope you have managed to secure her hand for a dance, for I fear her card must be almost full.'

At this, he twisted round, his jaw dropping as he observed the throng around her. 'Well, just look at that! Hetty! Who would have thought…and she is in remarkable good looks tonight. I never thought to…'

'Go! Quickly,' she urged, 'For the musicians are nearly ready to start our Boulanger. I shall wait here.'

He needed no further encouragement, and she watched with a satisfied smile as he cut through the group of young gentlemen to speak to Hetty, and how she nodded with a shy smile. They spoke briefly, then he returned, a decided air of relief about him.

'Thank you, Miss Lennox. I got my request in just in the nick of time.' He flushed. 'I have not been to a ball in an age, although we stood up in the Assembly Rooms in Haddington many times last winter. Hetty was away at school,' he added. 'She is different now.'

Stifling a smile, Anna asked him if he needed to reserve dances with any other young ladies. 'Oh, no!' he declared. 'I am quite content to dance only with you and Hetty, for you are quite the prettiest girls in the room!' This last was said with a gallant flourish, and Anna reflected how music, a ballroom and some punch could change the demeanour of even the most reserved of gentlemen.

Apart from Will, of course.

Ever the Earl, he had returned to his mother's side, clearly checking on her contentment, and as Anna watched he made his way to Izzy, whose hand he had clearly secured for the Boulanger.

'Well, by that definition, you must include my sisters, surely?' Anna's tone was teasing.

'Ha!' He acknowledged her hit. 'But they are married, and I prefer to dance with single ladies.' He bowed, as the dance was about to begin, and she responded with a curtsey.

She was still thinking of Hetty. 'And is prettiness the only factor you are considering in unmarried ladies tonight, Mr Ashman? For I think there are other ladies here who may be considered as pretty as Miss Newton.' She paused. 'Miss Hughes, for example.' The dance took her away from him then, but not before she had seen the faintest of frowns mar his brow.

Good. Let him think about why he prefers Hetty.

She was to be disappointed. By the time the dance brought them together again he had an air of resolution about him. 'You are correct, Miss Lennox. I shall ask Miss Hughes to dance as soon as I may. It would not do to slight an old friend by seeming to favour another.'

And so ends my brief career as a matchmaker.

'Very proper, Mr Ashman—although I was not suggesting you were slighting anyone. Miss Hughes is not short of partners, I think, and there are plenty of gentlemen dancing tonight. Lady Garvald need not have worried there would be a shortage of dance partners for the ladies.'

Her meddling had had exactly the opposite effect to what she had intended for, rather than focusing on Hetty, Mr Ashman would now be dancing with both ladies.

But perhaps that might serve to help him see the difference between them.

Still, her probing had reinforced her impression that Miss Hughes was not as likeable as Miss Newton—a notion she found deeply satisfying.

Ha! Let the Earl dance with her all night, then, for I care not!

So she smiled and kept to pleasantries for the remainder of the dance—and for the next four dances, as the young men of the district did their best to flatter her. Thankfully, it was then supper time, and Will came to her as they made their way to the supper room.

'How do you now, Anna?' There was some intent in his voice which left her feeling strange inside.

His question goes deep. It is not superficial.

'I am perfectly fine, my lord.'

He raised an eyebrow. 'I am taking you to mean the exact opposite, Miss Lennox.' His formality matched hers, and she felt a stab of hurt inside at his demeanour—even though she herself had caused it.

His expression turned serious. 'Mrs Thaxby seems certain that your mother's necklace is the Fletcher heirloom.' He had clearly been ruminating himself. Now here was common ground.

'I thought I had indicated I did not wish to speak of

these matters tonight!' She arched a brow, letting him know she was half-jesting.

'I apologise.' He bowed. 'It is consuming my attention, I am afraid.'

'Mine too.' This was only half a lie. Both he and the Thaxby mystery were consuming her.

'You are right. She knew the necklace straight away.' She glanced around to make certain no one could overhear them. 'It will not be long, I think, before she realises we may be her nieces.'

He frowned. 'It may take longer than you might expect. Despite her cunning, she is not the cleverest of women, I think. Besides, if she had no notion of George and Maria as a couple, why should she not think the necklace was stolen? There is an old saying: "a thief sees a world full of thieves".'

Anna gasped. 'You think her a thief?'

'I make no accusations, for I cannot be certain. I know only that how people *see* the world reveals much of what they *do* in the world. You, for example, see always good in people. Is it not so?'

She shrugged. 'Does not everyone?'

'No, and that is exactly the point I am making.' He glanced in her direction again. 'Was Mr Thaxby discourteous towards you during dinner?'

'Not discourteous, no. Stiff, perhaps—on his dignity.' She frowned. 'He is rightly loyal to his wife. It must be difficult for both of them to see me wear the Fletcher necklace.'

'You are much too generous, do you know that? Little

wonder, for you were raised by my mother as well as your own, and what I know of Maria tells me she was every bit as kind-hearted as my own mother.'

Her inner glow intensified at this praise of darling Mama, and at the way he was looking at her now—as though she *mattered* to him. She caught the direction of her own thoughts. Well, of course she knew she mattered to him. She was just unsure exactly in which *way* she mattered.

'How is Lady Garvald now?' she managed. 'I have not had the chance to speak with her for the past couple of hours.'

'Yes, your hand has been engaged for every dance.' Was there an edge to his voice? She glanced in his direction, but his face was expressionless. 'My mother is finally beginning to settle,' he continued, 'Understanding that her soirée—which everyone is calling a ball—is going extremely well. Once the supper has been successfully endured, I suspect she might even allow herself to enjoy it a little.'

'I am glad to hear it. And it is a ball, it is clear. But calling it a soirée made it easier for her, I think.'

They had reached the supper room, and Anna's gaze immediately sought out Lady Garvald. 'There she is, talking with that footman. I shall go to her.'

'She is ever anxious about being a hostess—which is why she entertains so infrequently.' His eyes softened. 'Your assistance and kindness has meant the world to her, Anna.'

There it was again, that breathlessness that only he

could cause. 'It is the least I can do for her, after everything she has done for us.'

'Garvald!' It was one of the guests, a portly gentleman with a ruddy face. Anna could not recall his name. 'Capital evening, my lord! And I must compliment you on your excellent wines!'

Murmuring an excuse, Anna moved away, reflecting that the gentleman in question had clearly imbibed copious amounts of said wines.

'Lady Garvald, how do you?'

'Oh, Anna! It is going well, I think, is it not?'

Anna laid a hand on her arm briefly. 'It is going *very* well! Everywhere I go I hear nothing but praise. And just look at the faces of the guests—they are all enjoying the evening, and so should you!'

She gave a wan smile. 'I cannot. I am just so worried that something will go wrong.' Her gaze roved over the food tables. 'Do we have enough pork cutlets? Lord, what if there is not enough meat?'

'There is plenty of meat,' Anna replied firmly. 'I have attended many balls and soirées this season, and if anything your table is more generous than that typically provided in London.'

'Truly? So you believe we have adequate provisions?'

'I know it.'

She exhaled, shaking her head. 'What you must think of me, Anna!' She grimaced. 'The truth is, I have always had a dread of being a hostess. I know it is expected of me—I am, after all, a countess—but there are so many ways to fail tonight!'

'Dare I say your neighbours are universally supportive? If you are subject to any criticism, it would be more likely from certain of your houseguests who make it their business to be perpetually displeased. And you manage them with aplomb!'

'That is true. Although it is difficult, I feel much more sure of myself in my own drawing room, rather than standing in a ballroom as hostess. Oh!'

'What? What is it?'

Lady Garvald was staring at nothing, her face a picture of shock. 'It is you.' Her eyes were suddenly suspiciously bright. 'You are so like her.'

Instantly, Anna knew whom she meant. 'My mother?'

Lady Garvald nodded, swallowing. 'Maria was forever encouraging me, supporting me, taking the extravagance from my fears until they were small enough to manage.' She smiled mistily. 'You have the same gift.'

Anna's heart swelled. They were all thinking of Mama tonight, it seemed—the ball, the Fletcher necklace… 'I am honoured you should think so. But now—' she indicated the merry throng '—you are at a successful ball—yes, a *ball*—and I should like you to enjoy it. Will you take some supper?'

'Perhaps a little something, for my stomach is not as sick as it has been all evening.'

'Good.' Together they joined the queue of people perusing the food tables, asking the footmen to add their favourites to their plates. 'I should warn you,' said Anna, 'That after supper soirées and balls in London sometimes became a little…boisterous.'

'That I do remember.' Lady Garvald gave a wry smile. 'Some of the gentlemen are becoming a little… bosky, are they not?'

'And some of the ladies too, if you look closely.'

'No! Who?'

Anna dimpled at her. 'I shall not tell you, for it is quite entertaining trying to divine who is drunk and who is merely half-sprung.'

Her eyes widened at Anna's daring language. 'Well, I would say that Mrs Hughes may have over-indulged a little, for look at how she is hanging off Sir Walter Ashman. Poor man!'

'I agree. Now, who else?'

Her brow furrowed. 'Mrs Thaxby. I suspect she has a fondness for wine in general, which her husband is well aware of.'

'Have you noticed how he often serves drinks to the ladies? A kind service, but it enables him to disguise the amount his wife is taking, by also serving another lady at the same time. But we are perfectly capable of counting!' she added wryly.

Lady Garvald sighed. 'I have seen it. I think he also tries to manage her pace of drinking, for otherwise she would simply signal the footmen to constantly refill her glass—which is what she does when he is not present.'

They shared a glance, then Anna searched out Mrs Thaxby. 'She is unhappy. And troubled.'

And she may have done a very, very bad thing.

She tilted her head towards Mrs Thaxby's table.

'Look, she is alone. No doubt her husband is procuring food and drink for her.'

'We should sit with her.'

Stifling a sigh, Anna nodded agreement, and together they made their way to a small table near the back of the room. 'Mrs Thaxby! May we join you?'

Raising her eyes to them, eyes dulled by alcohol, Mrs Thaxby nodded and they sat, the footmen bringing Lady Garvald's and Anna's plates and serving all three of them with wine. Mrs Thaxby drank deeply then confirmed in answer to Lady Garvald's query that her husband was indeed reviewing the available dishes on her behalf.

'He knows my preferences, you see,' she informed them, her speech decidedly slurred.

'You are fortunate to have such an attentive husband,' offered Lady Garvald, biting into a morsel of beef.

Mrs Thaxby shrugged. 'Fortunate? On the contrary. I am the most unfortunate soul in England, I have no doubt.'

Oh, dear. The wine is making her maudlin.

'Oh, come now, Mrs Thaxby.' Lady Garvald's tone was brisk. 'You have wealth, security and a devoted husband. There are many who would welcome such blessings.'

'Indeed I am cursed,' muttered Mrs Thaxby, lifting her glass again. 'Cursed from birth.'

'From birth?' Anna was confused. 'Whatever can you mean?'

Mrs Thaxby eyed her malevolently. 'You are young

and green, Miss Lennox. You have not yet understood how limited life is for we females.' She shook her head. 'Had I been born a boy, everything would have been different.'

'How? How so?' Anna's bewilderment made her struggle to understand Mrs Thaxby. 'Although we have fewer freedoms than gentlemen, I do love being a woman. Do you not?'

'It is not about being a woman. Naturally I cannot change that, and have no wish to. It is about the *privileges* afforded to men.' Her gaze became unfocused and she murmured, almost to herself, 'Everything I have ever done has been to rectify the injustices I have suffered. Yet still I suffer. Even now, certain people have the arrogance to question, to insinuate... I have often wondered what happened to the girl. If there was a girl.' She threw a look at Anna—a look so venomous that Anna recoiled a little. 'How came you by my necklace?'

Anna touched it instinctively, while nervousness rose within her.

What should I say?

'I inherited it.'

'From Lady Kelgrove, I presume?' She almost spat as she said the name. 'And where did she come by it? He stayed there, that year. Was it stolen from him then?'

'My dear, I have brought all your favourites.' It was Mr Thaxby, and there was a definite air of disquiet about him.

Had he heard what his wife was saying?

Resisting the urge to exchange a glance with Lady

Garvald, Anna pretended to listen as Mr Thaxby expounded in quite some detail about his wife's preferences in food. Mrs Thaxby herself had slunk into sullen silence, and barely picked at it.

Frankly, Anna was relieved when she and her hostess were able to leave the couple, as the next round of dances was shortly to begin. Still, Mrs Thaxby's comment about Lady Kelgrove was reassuring in that she clearly had not yet worked out exactly how Anna had come by the necklace, and why. The comment about a girl was concerning, though. Anna could only imagine the woman's rage when she discovered George and Maria had had three daughters. Shuddering, she realised she could do nothing about it now, so went back to the dancing.

It was after midnight, and the ball was over. Anna stood on the terrace, only half-hearing the bustle behind her as the servants began clearing away empty glasses and scraping at spilled candle wax. Tomorrow the entire ballroom would receive a thorough clean, but for tonight there was a decided air of satisfaction among the staff, who knew the ball had gone well, partly thanks to their contribution.

Anna had been surprised to discover her simple upbringing in Elgin had made her more aware of the needs and aspirations of servants, but she could not regret it, no matter how many times she heard similar transgressions being decried by some members of the *ton* as a 'vulgar' affinity. Even Lady Kelgrove, raised a lady, tended to call all footmen 'John', Anna had noticed. Yet, as far as Anna knew, there was currently only one John in this household—Mr Thaxby's long-suffering valet.

It could never be vulgar to consider the needs of others. So Mama had taught her, and Anna and her sisters had been grateful for every ounce of assistance they'd received from Mr Marnoch's staff as they had been growing up. So she made a point of seeking out both the housekeeper and butler just now, to thank them for all the efforts that they and their fellow servants had made to ensure Lady Garvald's first ball had been a raging success.

Will's mother had retired not five minutes ago, declaring herself exhausted, but Anna had lingered, knowing that if she went to bed now she would not sleep. There was too much going on inside her head, and her heart: the Thaxbys; Lady Kelgrove; the necklace; Mama's note. And, most of all, Will.

A sudden need for silence gripped her. Impulsively, she stepped off the terrace, discarding her evening gloves and leaving them on a nearby table. Moving away from the bustle of activity in the ballroom, she walked slowly and deliberately into the blessed darkness of the garden.

The stars came into view overhead as her eyes adjusted to the gloom. The moon had risen, giving light to the carriages currently on their way home from the Garvald ball, and bathing the gardens in silver-white beauty. She swayed a little, realising that she too was not unaffected by all the wine and punch she had consumed tonight. Even when one did not wish to be half-sprung, it was difficult to avoid a certain degree of boskiness on nights when footmen assiduously refilled one's glass at every turn, and when the exertion of dancing left you thirsty.

There was a stone bench nearby a little to the left, she recalled. Walking carefully, she managed to find it and sat down with a sigh, raising her eyes to the heavens. Somehow, all of her other thoughts and worries had faded in less than a minute, leaving only one person in her mind.

Will. She loved him entirely, completely, with everything she was, and knowing everything he was. Her mind returned to their little falling out earlier, which now seemed meaningless. They truly *knew* each other—surely the perfect recipe for a successful marriage?

Her heart skipped as she acknowledged the direction of her own thoughts.

Marriage?

Yes. She would marry him in an instant if he loved her. But only if he loved her. If he did not, then she would be doomed to a lifetime of unhappiness.

Her mind flicked briefly to Lord and Lady Renton, then to her sisters and their husbands. Yes, a love match was the only way.

Oh, why can he not see?

But it seemed likely he thought of her only as Zan-Zan's friend, and the three Lennox girls as his long-lost sisters. At least, she had no evidence he thought of her in any other way, and dared not hope too much, for fear her heart would be crushed by disappointment.

If he were to marry—and she had no notion if he was even considering the matter—he would be more likely to choose a woman who knew how to flirt, how to make him notice her in that way. Although he criticised 'vapid' young ladies, she had heard many times how even sensible men might fall foul of a fetching young miss who was entirely unsuitable for them. Recalling Miss Hughes's coquetry earlier, she briefly wondered if she could ape it.

Instantly, her spirit shrank inside with mortification, giving her a clear answer to *that* conundrum. In London, many young ladies had flirted with the eligible gentlemen, much to Anna's bewilderment, who had thought them remarkably silly. Yet now, when she needed to break through the barrier of assumptions Will had made about her, about their friendship, she found she had no way of doing so.

Why can I not flirt with him in the way other young ladies seem to find so easy?

The closest she had come to it was friendly raillery and teasing, such as they had enjoyed earlier when he had asked her what form her gratitude might take. Another young lady might have made more of the opportunity, using coquettish looks and allowing a touch to linger for a little longer than necessary.

But I am me, and can be no one else. But could she try? If given the opportunity, could she be brave? She knew not.

'Are you well, Anna?'

It was Will. Lost in thought, she had not heard him approach. Dumbstruck, she did not answer for a moment, feeling as though she had conjured him up through the sheer force of her love for him.

'Anna?' Now he sounded genuinely uneasy. 'Has something occurred? The Thaxbys…have they said something to upset you?' He sat beside her, and she drank in his beloved features in the dim light. The moon and stars above were painting him in silver, and now that she knew her own heart she wanted only to stay in the moment forever. He was there, just next to her, looking more handsome than any man had the right to, his brow furrowed with concern for her. Her heart swelled in her chest—or, at least, that was how it felt.

'N-no. I am well, thank you.' Her tongue felt sluggish. Was her speech a little slurred? Lord, she hoped not! Briefly recalling her earlier conversation with Lady Garvald regarding the various stages of inebriation of the ladies present, she idly wondered if she herself was full drunk or simply a little bosky.

'My mother's ball was a great success, was it not?' Now there was a hint of humour in his voice, or was she imagining it? Her brain seemed slow, fuzzy.

'It was! Everyone enjoyed it, I think—well, *almost* everyone,' she amended, recalling the Thaxbys and Lady Renton.

'And you enjoyed it, I trust? I know you were concerned about my mother, but you were still able to?'

'Oh, yes.' She breathed. 'It was wonderful. But I

may have had too much wine. I declare my head is spinning.' Daringly, she reached out with both hands, resting them on his chest. 'There is only one thing left that would make tonight perfect.'

'And what is that?' His voice was tight, his expression hooded.

She leaned towards him, her voice a whisper. 'Will you not kiss me, my lord?'

Chapter Seventeen

Having seen Anna step into the garden, Will immediately followed. Events from earlier had greatly disturbed him, and he refused to seek his bed until all those in his care had safely retired.

Having the Thaxbys under his roof was not something he welcomed—even more so now that long-held secrets were beginning to emerge. While he still found it difficult to believe that they had murdered George Fletcher—and Richard Berkeley too—he knew he must treat the possibility with seriousness, and that meant remaining alert and doing all he could to keep his loved ones safe.

Lady Kelgrove, while clearly having affection for the Lennox girls, was driven by the desire to know the truth of her grandson's death. And why should she not be? Yet, if the Thaxbys truly were cold-blooded murderers, then provoking them would involve significant risk.

Anna's earlier entrance wearing the Fletcher necklace had caused great consternation yet, even under the shock of discovery, the Thaxbys had said nothing compromising. He was determined to speak with Lady Kelgrove tomorrow. And in the coming days he would need to speak to Sir Walter, too, about the true owner-ship of the necklace. The last thing he would wish was for any stain on Anna's good name.

He sat beside her, concerned as to why she had gone outside by herself. Had something occurred to distress her? When she replied in the negative, and with a voice thickened by his best wines, he had to suppress a smile. Miss Anna Lennox—the sensible one of the triplets—was decidedly and deliciously foxed.

He deliberately encouraged her to speak further, ask-ing an innocuous question about the ball. Who knew when such an opportunity would come again? For Anna liked having her wits about her, and so usually drank sparingly. Yet he had entirely underestimated the im-pact on her sensible restraint, for a moment later she placed both hands on him and asked for a kiss.

She followed it up by stretching towards him, press-ing her lips to his. Instantly he was lost. His arms slid around her and he kissed her back, thoroughly and ex-pertly.

Finally! It was, naturally, he who came to his senses first. He froze, shock warring with the need to kiss her a hundred times as he had so often dreamed of doing. *Not like this.*

He wrenched his mouth from hers then slid back, ensuring there was no contact between them save her hands, which still rested on his chest. Her eyes were closed and she was swaying slightly, sending shame rocketing through him. He should never have taken advantage of her inebriated state. He desperately managed to control the urge to take her in his arms and once again explore every corner of her sweet mouth with his tongue.

No; when he kissed her again he wanted her to be clear-headed and fully aware of her actions. To continue to kiss an inebriated maiden would make him the worst of philanderers, and he was no rake. He should not have done it in the first place! And so, despite every nerve in his body screaming at him to do otherwise, he covered her gloveless hands with his own and gently removed them from his chest.

The sensation of skin on skin was too much for him so, quite without thought, he bent his head and pressed his lips to the inside of her wrist, allowing himself to linger and closing his eyes to better enjoy the moment.

Ah, Anna!

Opening his eyes, his gaze met hers and he caught his breath, for her eyes were filled with slumberous desire. To see her like this was the realisation of a thousand dreams yet frustratingly, as a gentleman, he could not act on them. What if he were to kiss her and more, and she regretted it? He could not risk such an outcome, particularly since it might lose him her friendship too.

'I cannot,' he managed in a gentle tone. 'You are foxed, my Anna, and you do not know what you are doing.'

She frowned in puzzlement, as if he were speaking in a foreign language. Taking advantage of her sluggish brain, he rose, drawing her to her feet. 'The ball is over and it is time to retire. Will you walk with me?'

She nodded, and it crossed his mind to wish for a ring on her finger, and he leading her to his own bed-chamber.

Soon, my love.

Tucking her hand into his arm, he accompanied her back to the terrace, through the ballroom and up the wide staircase where they had played together so frequently as children.

'I shall leave you here, Anna. Sleep well.' Raising her hand, he kissed it then turned it over and kissed her palm, daringly touching the sensitive skin for an instant with the tip of his tongue. He was rewarded by a sharp intake of breath, followed by a shaky, 'Goodnight.'

Ah! He knew what it was for one's speech to reveal one's inner turmoil. Anna had no stammer, but the events of the past few minutes had changed everything. Her request for a kiss, the tremble in her voice, the desire in her eyes… A woman did not look at a *friend* with such eyes, after all. Exhilaration rushed through him. Maybe, just maybe, his friends had it wrong. And maybe his dearest wish could be realised after all.

Anna opened her eyes, stretched and turned over. Her head felt heavy, her mouth foul and there was a slight ache when she moved her eyes.

What on earth…?

Memories came flooding back: the ball; the garden;

the wonderful kiss; Will's words, when he had refused to keep kissing her.

You are foxed…

Groaning loudly, she rolled onto her stomach, burying her head in her pillow. Mortification such as she had never known flooded through her. Had she really done such a dreadful thing? And had his rejection of her been just as unspeakable as she recalled?

Yes, and yes.

She groaned again. This, surely, had to be the absolute worst day of her entire life. He had taken the kiss she offered, yet on coming to his senses he had rejected her.

Mortification soon turned to distress and she made liberal use of her handkerchief as she cried for her loss: loss of his friendship; loss of that easiness between them… Her foolishness last night had surely ruined everything. The loss of her dearest friend as well as the possibility he might come to love her some day. Loss surrounded her in this place.

Sally came and, like the coward she was, Anna told her to go away. No, she would not be getting up, for she was unwell. Breakfast? *No.* The very thought made her feel sick. Despite knowing she was being self-indulgent, Anna was too unhappy to care. So she cried again and curled up into a ball, until a gentle scratching at the door made her quickly wipe away her tears.

'Come in!' she called, having a fair idea who was there.

'They told me you are ill!' Lady Garvald was all

concern, and Anna's heart warmed at Milady's evident affection for her.

'Oh, no!' she denied as Lady Garvald closed the door and walked towards her. 'I believe I am suffering from nothing worse than a surfeit of wine.'

Lady Garvald's brow cleared as she sat on the edge of Anna's bed. 'Oh, dear! Well, at least there is an explanation.' She gave a grin that was half-concern, half-mischief. 'My head felt decidedly muddy when I woke, I must admit. And to think we were busy assessing the other ladies' levels of intoxication at supper!'

Anna had to smile weakly at that, and the next few moments were spent talking about the ball and how successful it had been.

'Such a relief!' declared Lady Garvald. 'And so much easier, knowing you were assisting me.' She pressed her lips together before adding, 'It was quite like having Maria with us, I think.'

Exhaling slowly in a clear attempt not to give way to her emotions, she glanced around Anna's room. 'This was her bedchamber, you know. That is why I asked the housekeeper to put her eldest daughter in here.' Her gaze became distant. 'She always said it was too generous, putting her in a guest room when she was a paid companion. I disagreed, saying that as well as being my highly valued paid companion she was also my dear friend, and this chamber befitted our friendship.'

'Truly?' Anna looked around the room. 'I had not remembered this was her room. She was so often in the nursery...'

'Yes, she insisted on caring for you herself as much as possible. I recall, when you were babies, the wet nurse was astonished by how infrequently she was required. Your mother had a—a *vigour* that made me throw away my own listlessness and truly live again.' Her brow furrowed. 'She had experienced such adversity yet never allowed it to deter her. She was indomitable.'

'Like Lady Kelgrove.'

Lady Garvald nodded. 'And like you and your sisters.'

Anna shook her head as memories of last night washed over her.

How can I ever face him again?

'Not like me. I am weak. I am cowardly. I am nothing like Mama in that regard.'

Lady Garvald took her hand. 'Now, then, what is all this about?' When Anna shook her head, she continued, 'Are you not Miss Annabelle Lennox? Queen's diamond, well-regarded in the *ton*, able to walk into a drawing room wearing a priceless heirloom even though some of those present may wish you harm? Are you not the Miss Lennox who led and cared for her sisters for many years after your mother's death? The Miss Lennox who *notices* and helps and makes it her business to look after others?'

Anna eyed her blankly.

'I shall tell you what your mother told me many times: every failure, every moment of adversity, only serves to strengthen women. We are forged in fire. We are steel. We are iron.' Her gaze grew distant. 'We endure what we must. The pains of our bodies. The vagaries of fate. The slights and humiliations of unhappy people.' Now she focused on Anna again. 'Nothing will break us, for at our heart we *are* the fire. Do you not feel it, burning within you—the fire of hope, of possibility, of powerfulness?'

Anna gasped. Lady Garvald's stirring words were indeed bringing a flame to life within her. 'Yes. Yes! I had not thought of it in such a way before. They call us the weaker sex. They seek to—to manage us, or cosset us. But we are perfectly capable. I mean…' She faltered, lost in her own confusing thoughts.

'We may not be able to heft a heavy weight or control a fiery stallion, yet we are strong in other ways— all of us, including you.'

'Yes.' Anna felt it beneath all the thoughts, all the conflicting emotions. Deep within her was an endless well of herself—of Anna. She dimly felt that connection to other women: the women of her family; her sisters; her mother; her great-grandmother—to all of the other women of her line. And to Lady Garvald.

'You were like a second mother to us,' she said softly. 'We missed you terribly.'

'And I you.' They embraced, then by mutual unspoken agreement began to speak of other things, including the various neighbours Anna had met at the ball. 'I particularly liked Miss Newton,' Anna offered, causing Lady Garvald to beam at her.

'Your discernment is evident, for she is quite my

favourite too.' She leaned forward, adding in a confidential tone, 'Until recently, it had occurred to me to wonder if she and my son might make a match of it one day—not because I thought there was any particular attraction between them, you understand. It was more that I wish him to be happy and settled, with the right sort of wife. But it is clear to me now there can be nothing between them. One only has to see someone in the company of the person they *do* prefer to understand that. And I am delighted to say I know now with certainty they would not suit. Not at all.'

Anna did not know what to make of this at all. Was Lady Garvald referring to Mr Ashman or…?

'And what is your opinion of her cousin, Miss Hughes?' There was a knowing look in Lady Garvald's eye.

Anna focused on the question, setting aside all other notions for now. 'I thought her a perfectly amiable young lady,' she replied carefully.

Lady Garvald laughed. 'Ouch! Well said, Anna—faint praise indeed!'

'Oh, but I do not mean to offer her insult. I barely know her.'

'You have divined both of them, I think. But I shall say no more, for I see you are uncomfortable.' Her tone turned brisk. 'Now, I shall send you a tisane, which is even now being prepared by my cook for Mrs Thaxby. She and her husband have a great interest in herbs, you know, and he has recommended this particular tisane for the day after a party.' She gave a mischievous grin.

'I have no doubt it is meant to counter the effects of too much wine, and so may be efficacious for you also.'

She left soon afterwards, exhorting Anna to rest, but Anna could not. While she still felt severe mortification about her dreadful actions the night before, and had no idea how she was ever to face Will again, she had lost the urge to cry about it.

Sally brought the tisane and she drank it, enjoying the warmth and the taste of the fresh herbs within. Restlessness rose within her afterwards, and she knew not what to do with it. *I shall write, then*. Her journal had been of great assistance to her on previous occasions when she had been worrying about something. Writing about her problems or anxieties in her journal often served to reduce them to a manageable size.

This, though, was the most private, most mortifying experience she had ever committed to paper. With determination, she outlined every detail: her shocking forwardness; the divine kiss; his gentleman-like rejection of her advances; her worries about what it might mean for their friendship; her understanding that he clearly did not feel the same way about her as she felt about him. This last was particularly difficult, as it meant the abandonment of long-held dreams.

Finally, it was done, and it truly felt as though some of the awfulness of her mortification had gone out of her body and onto the page. Putting away her pen and closing her journal, she slid open the drawer as usual, then paused. While she had no reason to think anyone might read her honest words, she still wished there was somewhere more private she could stow her journal. Glancing around the desk, a thought occurred to her. Desks often had additional drawers and spaces, not obvious at first glance. Her gaze roved around the expertly crafted bureau-style desk, noticing for the first time a line of beautifully carved flowers on the lower edge of the upper shelves.

Flowers... Mama's chamber...

The hairs on her arms and at the back of her neck abruptly stood to attention and her heart raced furiously. With a shaking hand, she trailed her finger along the line of flowers, then pressed the third flower from the left. Nothing happened. She pressed harder, and this time there was a slight feeling of pressure—a little give that should not be there in a piece of solid wood. Holding her breath, she used her thumb and pressed with great force.

All at once it gave way, as a long-dormant mechanism was sprung. Anna jumped as a hidden drawer popped open on the side of the desk. Mama's secret drawer—she remembered it!

Wasting no time, she pulled it open. It was both deep and wide, and Anna briefly wondered at the craftsmanship that had enabled it to be so well designed that it had not occurred to her to wonder whether the space on the left-hand side of the desk could be accessed.

Inside was a bundle of leather-bound books, as well

as a number of loose papers. Ignoring the dust, Anna
lifted out the first book and opened it to the first page.

There, in Mama's handwriting, she saw what was
clearly a diary entry.

Wednesday, 6 July 1796
The dry weather continues, so the children played
all day in the gardens. Anna and Rose dutifully
kept their bonnets in place, but my rebellious Izzy
made hard work of it. In the end, Anna and Xander
cleverly made it part of their game, so she went
along with it. I was glad, for I should have hated
to bring them inside on such a glorious day. Mar-
garet, meanwhile, is hiding some secret. When I
ask her about it, she will only look mischievous
and tell me she is certain I shall be proud of her.
It made me recall how diffident she was when I
first knew her. Together we have overcome grief
and loss, and now we share much joy in life—par-
ticularly through the eyes of our beloved children.

That was all but, flicking through the book, she saw
that Mama had made entries almost every day. Most
of the book was empty. Holding her breath, she navi-
gated to the last entry.

Monday, 25 July 1796
And so I end my habit of near-daily musings, for
we depart on the morrow. My heart is breaking at
the notion we must leave our home and those we

*love so dearly, but I must keep my girls safe. I shall
take with us only the most important items, and so
I shall leave behind my little journals. All of it is
preserved in my memories anyway, and will not
be lost. This house... Margaret and little Xander...
I pray I might return some day, though I cannot
imagine how it would be safe to do so. And I am
truly delighted that Margaret is once again making connections with the* ton. *It is a sign that her
healing is complete, I think. Wrenching the girls
away from their ZanZan is the most heinous thing
imaginable, and I am filled with horror at my own
cruelty. But it must be done, for those who killed
my husband and my brother have no compunc-
tion and, I believe, no remorse. I only hope I can
find another home where we all might be safe, and
where my daughters can grow and thrive.*
Maria Fletcher

Mama had signed it simply, using only her given
name and her surname. Wiping away tears, Anna simply sat for a moment, trying to take it in.

...those who killed my husband and my brother...

That was plain. If both George and Richard had been
killed, and by the same evil people, then surely it had
to have been the Thaxbys? But why—why would anyone do such a thing?

Turning to the other books and papers, she began

flicking through them, realising they covered Mama's entire time at Lammermuir House—the early entries being made on loose sheets before Mama had bought, or perhaps been gifted, her first leather-bound tome.

Anna resisted the temptation to delve more deeply, knowing her sisters had to be here when she did so. So, with a great deal of composure and restraint, she set them aside and rang for Sally, who passed on the message that the princess and the viscountess were to come to Miss Lennox's room as soon as they were able. Sally then dressed her hair and helped her don a simple day dress of white muslin trimmed with embroidered bluebells.

Rose arrived first, a concerned crease on her bow. 'Anna! Whatever is the matter? Are you unwell?'

Anna walked towards her and took both her hands. 'Not at all. Oh, Rose, I have found Mama's journals!'

Rose's eyes widened. 'Her journals? I did not even know she kept a diary!'

'Nor did I. Though she always encouraged us to keep little journals, if you recall. But look—here they are!' Leading Rose to the side table, Anna indicated the books and papers that she had gently dusted with one of her best handkerchiefs after Sally had gone. 'And just look!' Picking up the relevant diary, she turned to the last entry, then waited while Rose read it.

'Oh, poor Mama! How terrible for her!'

'I know.' Anna shook her head slowly. 'She had so many troubles to bear. But she was brave, and strong, and she always did the right thing, even when it was difficult. I can do no less.'

'What troubles do you bear, Anna?' Rose asked gently.

Anna shrugged, dismissing the mortifying memories that once again threatened to consume her. 'I was tasked by our guardian to discover why Mama ran with us to Elgin. We already have most of the answers. The rest, I suspect, are in these pages.'

'How much have you read?'

'Almost nothing. I wanted to wait for you two.'

Thankfully, Izzy arrived soon afterwards, and once she understood what Anna had unearthed she immediately took a journal to Anna's bed, sat down and began to read. Exchanging a knowing glance, Anna and Rose chose a volume each and joined her.

The following hours were a mix of silent reading, exclamation and discussion. Discovery after discovery was exclaimed upon—most of them small details of their quiet life here, but details that were precious in the finding.

Sally brought tea and sweetmeats, but the triplets barely touched them. They uncovered much about themselves, their mother, Milady and ZanZan and their lives as children here in Lammermuir House. There were also multiple references to Mama's dear husband, George, her brother, Richard and her grandparents.

'Mama missed them all, it is clear,' said Anna, thinking about it. 'She lost so much—her closest family either dead or estranged.'

'But she found a new family here,' Rose observed.

'She did. And then lost them too.'

'But she had us!' insisted Izzy fiercely.

'She did. And we had each other.'

'We still do.'

Izzy had been reading on. 'Oh, listen to this!' She read aloud. '"I still find it difficult to understand how George's sister and her husband came to hate him so much. I know he would have happily given them every penny he had to be allowed to live. But, once he began speaking of marrying, they murdered him".'

Anna exhaled. 'So there it is once again, in plain English—Mrs Thaxby and her husband murdered him. She was his only sibling.'

Rose was still thinking about the other aspect of Mama's words. 'She just wanted him to have lived. Unfortunately for our papa, the law does not work in that way. He was still under-age, remember.'

'So he could not gift his estate to his trustees or anyone else.'

'And, if he married, he might have had an heir.'

'So they killed him.'

'Because wealth was more important to them than George's life!' Rising, Izzy paced about the room. 'Oh, if I could I would fight a duel with them—with them both!'

Inwardly, Anna was feeling the same anger. Mr and Mrs Thaxby were received everywhere, and no one knew about their heinous acts other than some of the people here in this house.

'They have killed twice already.' Rose's thoughts seemed to mirror Anna's.

'Yes! We must be careful. If they realise we know, or that we are George's children, they could kill again.'

Just then there was a knock at the door. All three of them hastily closed their books, but it was only Sally, returned once again.

'Beg pardon, Miss, but I've come to dress you for dinner. If you are well again, that is to say.'

'Dinner?' Anna was astonished. 'What is the time?'

Even as she spoke she realised that she had slept late, then spent quite some time feeling sorry for herself before Lady Garvald had called. Then she had been writing, and then...

'Lord, James will be wondering where I am!' Rose scrambled off the bed.

Izzy sniffed. 'I dearly *hope* Claudio is wondering where I am!'

Sally bobbed a curtsey. 'Beg pardon, my ladies, and I do not mean to speak out of turn, but the gentlemen have been riding all afternoon.'

'Thank you, Sally. Please leave us for a few moments.'

Once the maid had gone, Anna carefully placed the papers and books back in the secret drawer. 'We must say nothing of this in public, for I believe there is real danger.' She bit her lip. 'I only wish our great-grandmother could be more discreet. Knowing what we know now, I fear she is putting herself in harm's way.'

'Agreed.' Izzy made for the door. 'I shall tell her

after dinner, for it is too late to call with her now. And Anna?'

'Yes?'

'Probably best *not* to wear the Fletcher necklace to-night.'

Chapter Eighteen

Dinner was largely uneventful, mainly because Anna had covered herself in an invisible suit of armour. After the astounding discoveries today, last night's events seemed far away—almost as if they had happened to someone else, or to her, but long ago.

The first time she saw Will, though—when they'd greeted one another in the drawing room just before the gong—she had been unable to hold his gaze and had covered her consternation by crossing the room to speak with Lord Renton.

The evening was warm, and the ladies were making good use of their fans. There was a temptation to drink more through simple thirst, but Anna resisted it. Lady Kelgrove complimented her hostess on the wine, and Mrs Thaxby promptly indicated with a nod to a footman that he should refill her glass. And this after they had only been seated for less than five minutes.

Will, of course, seemed to be completely natural in his manner, showing no sign of uneasiness because of events from the night before. Perhaps, then, he was accustomed to half-sprung ladies making advances to him? Her innards tightened at the very notion. But, no, she would not allow her thoughts to continue to veer in that direction, for that way led to mortification, regret, and utter sadness.

Thankfully, as usual she was not seated near him, being placed once again with Mr Thaxby. He was polite enough, and the only time she saw anything of the undercurrents was when Lady Kelgrove made a pointed comment about her dear son Richard and how his life had been cut short by what she described as, 'Evil people who will soon, I trust, be brought to justice.'

Oh, dear! was Anna's immediate thought. *My great-grandmother is either deliberately provoking them or is slowly losing patience.*

Either way, there were risks.

Under normal circumstances Anna's gaze would have met Will's, but given the recent happenings between them she dropped her gaze to her plate—which was why, from the corner of her eye, she was able to see the whiteness of Mr Thaxby's knuckles as he gripped his knife and fork tightly in response to Lady Kelgrove's comment. A hit, then! Despite the Thaxbys' seeming nonchalance, Lady Kelgrove's barbs were clearly penetrating whatever armour the Thaxbys had built around themselves.

Afterwards the ladies retired to the drawing room in the traditional manner, leaving the gentlemen to their port. Making a show of hanging her fan on her arm, Anna was careful not to catch anyone's eye as she rose from the table. As they took their seats in the drawing room, Izzy sent Anna a long look before making her way to Lady Kelgrove. Understanding entirely, Anna joined Mrs Thaxby on the satin settee, distracting her with a series of idle questions and comments about last night's soirée.

A brief glance showed that Rose had engaged Lady Renton and Lady Garvald in conversation, allowing Izzy to apprise their great-grandmother of the afternoon's discoveries without being overheard. Sometimes it was good to be a triplet, for they understood one another precisely in such moments.

Their great-grandmother seemed utterly determined to expose the Thaxbys, but had until now only her own conviction that they had killed Richard. Surely Mama's writings formed the proof that Lady Kelgrove sought? Even now, Izzy was apprising her about what they had read today. And, daringly, she was doing so in the same room as the Thaxbys themselves!

'Indeed?' Lady Kelgrove queried sharply at one stage, and Anna hurriedly covered the brief silence with a comment about Mrs Thaxby's tisane. 'I was very grateful for it, for I must admit I felt unwell this morning.'

Mrs Thaxby's eyes lit up. 'Good wine is essential to a happy life, I believe,' she declared, signalling to the footman to bring her yet another glass. 'And having the right tisane to counter its after-effects can help. But there is a better solution.'

'Is there?' Anna looked into her blue eyes, suppressing a shudder at the emptiness she saw there... Emptiness, or maybe just coldness.

She is my aunt. But she murdered my father, and my uncle.

'Yes. I shall tell you what it is, but lean closer, for I do not wish anyone to hear us.'

Anna complied, getting a strong trace of alcohol from Mrs Thaxby's breath. Suppressing an instinct to recoil, it briefly occurred to her that in this moment she was being more judgmental about Mrs Thaxby's drunkenness than the fact that she had committed murder. The latter still felt impossible, even though she knew in her mind that it was true. The former was all too real.

Besides, Mrs Thaxby could say the same of me today, for we both drank with our dinner, and we were both foxed last night.

Anna, however, had had only one glass of wine with her meal this evening as, following last night's events, she was wary of not noticing how much she had.

'More wine!'

'What? More wine? I do not under—'

Mrs Thaxby tutted. 'Must I make myself plain? Wine *before* breakfast. I find it to be the absolute best cure for the morning effects.'

'Oh, I see.' Anna did not, not really, but supposed that remaining perpetually bosky might prevent the symptoms of sobriety.

'Indeed,' Mrs Thaxby continued, 'One might say that more wine is the cure for most of life's ills.' Her gaze became unfocused. 'Lord knows I have suffered, with all manner of sicknesses and aches and ills these long years.'

To Anna's relief, the door opened just then, admitting the gentlemen, who had decided to join the ladies with rather more haste than was usual. The fact that two of the gentlemen were newly married might account for it, but Anna wondered if, having heard from Rose and Izzy confirmation that the Thaxbys were indeed murderers, James and Claudio wished to be by their wives' sides even more than they usually did.

'Leave all to me,' Anna heard Lady Kelgrove order Izzy. Resisting the urge to swing her head towards them, she felt another pang of anxiety. Lady Kelgrove would no doubt be enraged once again, and Anna hoped the new information would not make her reckless.

The gentlemen's arrival triggered the usual adjustments in the seating arrangements. Tonight they were *en famille*, so Sir Walter and his son were not present. Claudio and James sat with Izzy and Rose while, to Anna's astonishment, Lady Kelgrove crossed the room towards Anna's chair—as if she wished to sit with Mrs Thaxby. Lady Kelgrove was clearly up to something, and Anna was helpless to know what to do for the best.

'You may take my armchair, Anna,' Lady Kelgrove instructed regally.

Anna complied—well, there was nothing else for it— rising and making her way to Lady Kelgrove's empty seat. At the same time, Will walked towards the upright chair beside it.

Oh, Lord! I am to converse with him!

Strange to think that conversing with Will had been the high point of every day since their arrival in his home. *But now?* Now all was changed.

'Are you well, Anna?' he began. 'My mother tells me you required a tisane earlier.'

Anna could feel her colour rising. 'Oh, yes, quite well.'

'But you kept to your room all day.'

She eyed him levelly. 'Females need to do so, from time to time.'

Now it was his turn to flush. 'I apologise, Anna! I did not mean to pry. Lord, I am a clumsy fool!'

Anna could not persist in the face of this honest concern. 'It is I who must apologise. For so much—not least the fact that my words just now may have given you a false impression of my reasons for not coming downstairs today.'

Glancing about briefly to ensure no one was watching or listening, she added in a low voice, 'I found my mother's journals in the desk in my chamber. My sisters and I spent quite a few hours reading them.'

'Really? I am delighted to hear it—for many reasons. And what have you learned from the diaries? For, by your manner, I deduce there must be something of significance.'

She nodded. 'The…suspicions we share, about past events, have been confirmed.'

His brow furrowed. 'All of it—George? And Richard?'

She confirmed it, trying to ignore the painful lump in her throat.

Have I lost our friendship through my dreadful behaviour last night?

Having Will as her friend was vital to her happiness, and to lose him again would be unthinkable. They had only just found one another again, and she had risked all by importuning him so dreadfully. She might never have his love, but she hoped she had not lost his affection.

'I must speak with Sir Walter.' Will's brow was furrowed. 'We know them to be ruthless, and you and your sisters may be in danger as soon as they discover your connection to that family. And Lady Kelgrove too, for she has no fear of stirring this hornet's nest.'

'Actually, I suspect the Thaxbys have no idea that Mama married and had children. Until they realise that, then we are just three random young ladies, and no threat to them.'

He raised an eyebrow. 'Young ladies who are now in possession of the Fletcher necklace.'

'Hush!' Glancing about to see who might be listening, she was relieved to see that Mrs Thaxby was currently being distracted by her own husband, who had brought two glasses of wine for his wife and Lady Kelgrove.

He is probably unaware of the three glasses his wife managed to imbibe during the brief period before the gentlemen rejoined us.

She chastised herself inwardly. *Lord, I am becoming obsessed with Mrs Thaxby's drinking!*

They all spoke together and then Lady Kelgrove,

normally composed, let her fan slip from her fingers as she looked up at Mr Thaxby.

Oh, dear! What had he said to discompose her? Oh, how she wished Lady Kelgrove would be careful. To be fair to the elderly lady, the Thaxbys had murdered her grandson—something she was perfectly entitled to be angry about.

And my great-grandmother has recently had confirmation of it.

Lady Kelgrove tried to catch the fan but it slipped to the floor, and both Thaxbys retrieved it for her, Mr Thaxby presenting it to her with what was clearly a false smile. Anna shivered. Frowning, she met Izzy's gaze, and instantly Izzy rose, making for Lady Kelgrove and the Thaxbys.

Izzy will not allow them to intimidate her. Not that Lady Kelgrove was prone to being intimidated, but yet…their great-grandmother was only one woman, after all. And, despite her indomitable nature, sometimes her frailty showed through.

Turning back towards Will, Anna was taken aback to see humour in his gaze. He seemed to have kept his eyes on her, and had missed the brief exchange between Lady Kelgrove and the Thaxbys.

'You are telling me to hush? Ah, that is the Anna I remember from all those years ago. You always were something of a managing female—even at five years old!'

He meant to tease. She knew it, yet all she could

think about was last night and her inappropriate advances.

A managing female.

This, then, was why her teachers had constantly reminded her to be more self-effacing, more obedient, more ladylike. Because being more self-assured and emphatic led her into situations where she might make an error of judgement—such as last night.

Her thoughts flicked to her sisters. Rose was the most compliant of the three, yet had been seen kissing the viscount in a public park as a debutante—emphatic action indeed. Izzy could be confident to the point of rashness, yet as far as Anna knew she had not done anything as foolish as trying to kiss a gentleman who did not wish to be kissed.

Anna had always seen herself as the leader of the trio—unafraid to be bold when needed, urging caution when needed. Until... Ah, last night's wine had much to answer for!

Realising she was gaping like a fool, she knew she needed to respond. Unfortunately, the words which bubbled out of her were, 'Oh? And you think it a bad thing for a female to have her own opinions, then?'

He flinched—the tiniest of reactions, but she saw it. Then his expression hardened. 'Not at all, and I should have thought you know me better than to ask such a question.'

I have pierced him!

After a full London season, Anna had come to know something about the frailties of male pride, And, of course, Will was correct—she did know him, very well indeed. So this could be more than pride. Might she have hurt him? Abandoning all her inner worries for a moment, she squared her shoulders, declaring, 'Sometimes I am not sure I know you at all!'

The words erupted from her, fuelled by the swirl of confusion inside. What had he been thinking last night when he had rejected her?

He eyed her levelly. 'At all? That seems rather strong.' He frowned. 'There are certainly things you do not know—important things. You did not know me in London, certainly. You did not even recognise me.' Was there a hint of accusation in his eyes? 'But you know me now.' He paused. 'And I know you.'

'Somewhat.' It was almost a whisper. She almost became lost for a moment, drowning in the beauty and power of his gaze and words. Then reality asserted itself. He must not think her actions last night meant anything in particular. 'And we are still friends, I hope?'

Was there a hint of…*something* in his eyes? Something inscrutable and puzzling?

'Why would we not be?' He seemed to hold his breath for an instant. 'You can trust me, you know.'

'Thank you.'

What does he mean by that?

'We must speak more of these matters. We missed our usual walk this morning, but will you be there on the morrow?'

'Er… I shall, yes.' Lord, why had she not thought of some excuse? Mortification mingled with fear of having lost him. Yet the thought that she might have to forgo these walks had felt like bearing a wound deep inside. And he wished to speak about serious matters!

Lord, if he mentions the kiss I shall die of mortification!

'Miss Lennox!' It was Lord Renton. 'Will you play for us?'

She rose instantly, with a polite nod of farewell to Will.

'Naturally! Something gentle, I think, after our lively exertions last night!'

Seating herself at the piano, she found the sheets she wanted and arranged them in front of her. Taking a breath, she paused, then began to play the *andante* from Mozart's *Sonata in A Minor*. Yes, a minor key was right for tonight.

Playing calmed her as nothing else could. Thoughts of her parents, of the evil done by the Thaxbys, even of her mortifying advances towards Will, all evaporated for the moment as she lost herself in the sound of the music and the sensation of her fingers pressing the keys at exactly the right instant, her eyes running ahead on the sheet music.

Someone moved the sheets so she could see the final page properly, which was helpful, for this was not a piece she knew by heart. The movement ended, and her playing was received with acclaim by some, politeness by others.

'Brava!' murmured Will, for of course it was he who had come to assist her. As their eyes met she felt a smile come into hers—for who could not look into Will's warm gaze and not feel her heart swell fit to burst from her chest? *Stop!* She reminded herself such notions had made her behave in a most inappropriate manner. She could not risk such a thing happening again.

No more wine, no more foolish notions!

'But you must play on, my dear!' Lord Renton was insistent.

So she gave them the *menuetto*, then the Turkish *rondo*—as lively a piece as was possible, and one which required the utmost concentration, for the intricacies and speed required could easily be her undoing.

Will turned the pages for her; he could read music, though he had previously confessed to her that a lack of diligence had prevented him from mastering the piano. His preference had been for riding, fencing and, more recently, boxing. But she must not think of him at such a moment, for Mozart demanded all her attention.

Finally done, her shoulders slumped in what felt like exhaustion. Accepting the accolades of the party, including a quiet, 'Well done!' from Will, she waited for a few moments until their attentions quietened, then left the drawing room.

The retiring room used by the ladies was along the same corridor, and on entering she was relieved to find it empty. Sinking down into a soft armchair, she closed her eyes and allowed the remaining peace of the music to wash over her.

Just a moment later the door opened, but somehow

she could not find the vigour to look and see who was there.

'Beg pardon, miss. I just need to leave some clean pots and bordaloues here. I shall return with towels,' murmured a serving girl.

Anna lifted her hand but did not open her eyes, and was relieved when the girl left. She would enjoy this blessed peace for a little longer. All too soon, though, she heard the door open again, then close. A swish of skirts told her she was not alone, but something was not quite right. The serving maid's simple linen dress and apron would not rustle so. Opening her eyes, she turned her head to see Mrs Thaxby advancing on her.

'Well, and look at who is here, all alone.' Her eyes glittered, and Anna's insides abruptly clenched in fear. She was suddenly fully alert.

'Ah, Mrs Thaxby.' Using every iota of inner strength, Anna managed to sound self-assured. 'I am afraid I am still feeling the effects of last night's wine.' She knew Mrs Thaxby liked to advise, and wine was clearly her favourite topic. Perhaps that distraction might defuse the rage she now saw in the older woman's eyes. 'A full twenty-four hours since I drank so much, and my brain is still befuddled.'

'Is it? Then perhaps this is a good time for me to pose some questions to you.'

'Questions?' Anna heard the tremor in her own voice. So did Mrs Thaxby, it was clear, for she gave a small smile of satisfaction.

'Your great-grandmother seems remarkably unclear

as to how she acquired my necklace.' She tilted her head, as if in sympathy. 'The elderly often become forgetful. But perhaps she told you where she found it, or bought it, perhaps?' Her tone became cajoling. 'You are the eldest, after all, which is why she gave it to you, I conjecture.'

'I am certainly the eldest. But you must ask my great-grandmother, for I cannot say anything on this matter.'

'*Can*not, or *will* not, hmm?' Mrs Thaxby was now uncomfortably close, looming over Anna.

She has murdered twice before. Gathering all her inner strength, Anna rose, as if unaware that Mrs Thaxby was uncomfortably close. Crossing to the mirror, she made a show of checking her side curls. 'It is a beautiful necklace. Did you ever wear it?'

This new diversion seemed to work. Pouting, Mrs Thaxby shook her head. 'Never! The injustice of it rankles with me, as I am sure you can understand.' She sighed mournfully. 'I distinctly recall my mother wearing it before she died.'

'When did you last see it?' Anna asked, genuinely curious.

'Let me think…' She frowned, then her eyes widened. 'George was showing it to his friend Richard the night of…the night they were attacked. Perhaps those brigands took it!' Anger flashed in her eyes. 'I might have known we could not…'She broke off, as if recalling where she was. Her face was pale and she looked genuinely disturbed.

We could not trust them... Was that what she had been going to say? So the brigands who had killed Richard and left George for dead had been hired by the Thaxbys. It had been obvious, but to hear Mrs Thaxby almost say it was shocking.

Suppressing a shudder, Anna made for the door. 'I shall return to the drawing room now. Goodbye, Mrs Thaxby.'

Lost in thought, Mrs Thaxby did not reply, so Anna slipped out, a decided sense of relief running through her. On returning to the drawing room, she saw there had been a further change in the seating arrangements. Lady Kelgrove had reclaimed her usual armchair and was now chatting with Will, while Izzy was now sitting with her husband. Mr Thaxby...

Anna stilled briefly. Something about him was peculiar, and she was not sure why. He seemed agitated, and was currently mopping the back of his neck with a handkerchief, despite the fact that the heat of the day was rapidly cooling. She saw with a quick glance that none of the ladies were using their fans. For a man who was generally implacable and inscrutable, it struck her that Mr Thaxby was behaving in an odd and unexpected way.

'Are you unwell, Mr Thaxby?' she heard Lord Renton ask, even as Lady Kelgrove beckoned her to join them.

'Never better, my lord,' declared Mr Thaxby—a clear falsehood, or so it seemed to Anna.

'Why are you looking at Mr Thaxby so, Anna?'

Never one to mince her words, Lady Kelgrove asked the question even as Anna was taking her seat. Thankfully, her volume was low enough that the others had not heard her.

With a nod to Will, Anna thought about it. 'He is acting strangely. Something has disturbed him.' She looked directly at her great-grandmother. 'He heard you—at dinner.'

Lady Kelgrove leaned back in her chair. 'My comment about those who commit evil receiving justice? I hoped he might. How did he react?'

In a low voice, Anna related having observed Mr Thaxby gripping tight his cutlery, and also apprised them of her conversation with Mrs Thaxby in the retiring room.

Lady Kelgrove nodded approvingly. 'Good girl. I believe my barbs have prompted him to take action, but I cannot know for certain.'

'What do you mean? Has he said something?' Will's tone was sharp. 'I will tolerate no risk or discomfort to my guests, my lady.'

She eyed him evenly. 'As to that, none of us can know the lengths they will go to—or may already have gone to. Princess Isobel has told me about Maria's journals. I should like to read them on the morrow, but for tonight I simply continued my current strategy of letting them know in plainer and plainer language that I know them to have murdered my son. What she said to you just now is even further confirmation of two things—that I have the right about it, and that they know, or suspect, that their deadly secret is known—at least by me.'

'But that might place you in danger!' Anna kept her voice low, despite fear for her great-grandmother's safety rising within her. 'If they believe you are the only person who knows, then they might attempt to—to silence you.'

'And that is exactly my plan, child.' Lady Kelgrove remained inscrutable. 'We must bring this to a head—lance this pestilence once and for all.'

Lord, what a foolish plan!

'Even if it costs your life?'

'Even then.' Lady Kelgrove patted her arm. 'I have lived long and achieved much. I shall die satisfied if I can expose the killers of my grandson and his friend.'

Anna exchanged a concerned glance with Will, but Lady Kelgrove was not done.

'They hired the men who attacked the carriage, but George was said to have died of illness, so I suspect they may have done that deed themselves.'

'He was said to have died of some kind of flux, is that correct?'

'Yes.' Lady Kelgrove's tone was clipped.

'Poison? Mr Thaxby is something of a botanist…'

'Precisely.'

Anna was piecing it together. 'When he spoke to you earlier—when you were sitting with his wife—did he threaten you?' She recalled the dropped fan—a highly unusual show of vulnerability from Lady Kelgrove.

Her great-grandmother's eyes danced with merriment. 'Perhaps, perhaps not. But say no more, for here comes his lady.'

Sure enough, Mrs Thaxby had returned. Anna noticed her face remained pale.

It is all coming back to them after twenty-one years of secrecy.

With a brief glance towards Lady Kelgrove, Mrs Thaxby sat with her husband and Lord Renton.

Lady Kelgrove continued, 'All the pieces of this little riddle are beginning to emerge. But one thing we still need is proof of your parents' wedding. All will fall without it, for only a legitimate heir or heirs can disinherit George's sister. Can you and your sisters search for that as you read the journals?'

'Of course. She uses the name Maria Fletcher in them, so I do believe they were properly married.'

Will looked from one to the other, his expression one of admiration. 'I know not why some people insist that females are weaker or less quick-witted than men.' He sent Anna a mischievous glance as he referenced their earlier conversation. 'You two ladies are astonishing.'

At his words, a wave of pride and warmth rushed through Anna. Meeting his eye, she clearly saw there what he had expressed with words: admiration for both of them, an elderly lady and his friend.

Lady Kelgrove sniffed. 'You are only just realising this?'

'Well, no, I believe I have known it for a long time. But I see it now before me.'

'Hrmph. Can you ask Lady Garvald to invite Sir

Walter tomorrow? Indeed, I think we may need him to reside here for a little time.'

'Of course. I had already determined to do so, but I shall speak to my mother this instant. One of the grooms can bring a message tonight, for there is still plenty of moonlight.' Rising, he bowed, then made for Lady Garvald, who was currently seated with Lady Renton and Rose.

'A good man, I think,' mused Lady Kelgrove. 'He will do very well.' She nodded firmly. 'It will give me great satisfaction to see you all settled.'

Her meaning could not have been plainer. 'Oh no, but we are *friends!* I mean, there cannot be anything of…of that nature between us.'

Lady Kelgrove snorted. 'What a foolish statement. Were Lord Garvald to hear it, I suspect he may revise his recently stated opinion with regard to your quick-wittedness.'

'But—'

'Child, listen to me. Friendship is the best foundation for marriage, believe me.'

Anna eyed her dubiously. 'But he only wants friendship.'

Her great-grandmother tutted in exasperation. 'What on earth makes you think so? Have you not seen the admiration in his eyes when he looks at you?'

'Well, yes, but that is simply admiration for his friend. Why, he gave you the same look!'

'Lord save us! If you cannot tell the difference between the way he looked at me and the way he looked at you just now, then I despair for the propagation of the species! Now, hush, before you say anything equally bird-witted, and reflect on what I have told you.'

Chapter Nineteen

Anna hushed and reflected. She reflected until it was time for bed, then tossed and turned for hours, still reflecting. When the birds announced the approach of dawn, she sat in the window seat, reflecting until her head hurt.

In the end she gave up. In truth, she could understand that, if she looked at the situation from the perspective of common sense with a dash of pessimism, then Will saw her only as a friend and wished her to remain that way—his rejection of her advances being a case in point. But then there were the other hints which, if she took them and put them together, created a veritable *symphony* of admiration that was distinct, intent and... and everything she could wish for.

It was safer to believe in friendship, for to hope for more and be disappointed would cause her untold pain. Round and round she went in her mind, until she could no longer think clearly at all.

Finally, it was morning proper, and she rang for Sally.

'Will you be walking in the gardens this morning,

miss?' the maid asked, hovering around the various day gowns and walking dresses in Anna's wardrobe.

'I shall, yes,' Anna replied, turning away briefly to hide the heat in her face. 'I shall wear my new gown, please—the one with the lace trim. And the blue silk spencer.'

'Very well, miss. There is, I believe, a pretty silk shawl which will set it off to perfection, if it pleases you? And the bonnet with the blue ribbon, perhaps?'

'Oh, yes! A capital suggestion.'

If I am to walk out with him this morning, and if there is even the possibility that he...that he... I shall try to look my best.

Half an hour later, and with palms decidedly warm inside her thin gloves, Anna made her way downstairs and out to the rose garden. Instead of tying her bonnet under the chin as usual, Sally had tied it to one side, under Anna's right ear. It gave her a rakish look that was decidedly pleasing.

The morning was cool and dry, with only a few puffy white clouds against the cerulean sky. Despite the fact that dozens of roses had been harvested for Lady Garvald's soirée, the garden remained replete with riotous colour and heady scents. Best of all, there was Will, seated on a stone bench, watching her walk towards him. His jacket was blue, his waistcoat gold and white, offset by a perfectly arranged cravat. Buckskins and highly polished boots completed his costume. He looked every inch the gentleman—and the most handsome gentleman she had ever seen.

As she went closer, with each step her dilemma asserted itself. *He likes me. He likes me not. He sees me as a woman. He sees me as a friend.*

One thing was certain—she had to know. Could she be brave and simply ask him? Would it spoil things?

He rose.

'Good morning, my lord.'

Instead of bowing in response to her curtsey, he took her hand. 'Good morning, Miss Lennox. Are we to be very proper this morning?'

Seeing the opening, she took it. *I must know.* 'That I shall leave to you, my lord.'

His brow creased. 'Why so?' Tucking her hand into the crook of his arm, he led her away, down the rose-dappled pathway.

She took a breath. 'While I value our friendship, my mind keeps returning to my dreadful actions on the night of the soirée. I must apologise for any discomfort I caused you.'

'Well, you did cause me discomfort, that is for certain. Great d-discomfort.'

Her heart sank.

So I have my answer.

'You see,' he continued, 'I had wanted to k-kiss you for the longest time, but I had no idea whether you saw me as a man or simply...'

His voice tailed off, but she knew what he was thinking. 'As a friend?' Astonishment rippled through her as the rest of his words sank in. 'You *wished* to kiss me?'

Now there was a glint of humour in his eye. They

had come to the end of the path. Without hesitation, he led her to the left, towards the woods. Well, why would he not? They often walked there.

'I did. I do. I have wanted to kiss you since the day I danced with you in St James's Palace.'

'When we were presented to the Queen—last *March*?' Her heart was pounding so loudly, she could hardly speak.

He likes me!

'I knew instantly who you were—the Lennox triplets. I knew Izzy's liveliness, Rose's dreaminess, and you…'

'Yes?' She could hardly breathe.

'You were the Anna I remembered—*my* Anna—except now you were a beautiful woman. I believe I was lost during that dance.' He grimaced. 'Yet I was clearly a stranger to you.'

'Oh, Will! I am sincerely sorry. I had no idea who you were.' *Nor what you were feeling.* Bewilderment was making it difficult to think clearly.

He gave a rueful smile. 'I came to no harm, I assure you. In fact, it was a useful lesson. I had been a target for the matchmaking mamas ever since my first season. But you treated me with *friendliness*.' He emphasised the word. 'A lowering experience, but one I doubtless fully deserved. And I knew I had to tell you who I was, but agonised about how to do so.'

She nodded thoughtfully. 'Hence the house party, for all of us.'

'Yes. Regardless of anything that might develop between you and I, all three of you deserved to know the truth.'

'I shall never forget the moment I realised you were ZanZan. It was…overwhelming.' He had held her then, and since, with the affection of…a friend? No, with more; her heart was pounding, her brain struggling to take it all in.

'Yes,' he said simply. 'But by then I had confused matters somewhat by making a friend of you.'

'Then why…?'

'Why did I not continue to kiss you?'

She nodded.

'I told you why at the time.'

'Because I was…' She could not bring herself to say it.

Seeing her consternation, he smiled. 'You were foxed. And you might have regretted it. I told myself that the next time I kissed you, your mind must be clear. But tell me, why did my friends believe you wished only friendship from me?'

She grimaced. 'I did not understand what I was feeling. I thought that I must have half-recognised you all along—my friend ZanZan—and *that* was why…'

'That was why…?'

'That was why I was drawn to you.' She sent him a shy smile. 'But I was—I am—*entirely* drawn to you.'

There! She had said it. Not in so many words, but clearly enough that he must understand she loved him.

'Anna!'

He understood, and the fire in his eyes made a different sort of excitement kindle within her. They were nearly at the woods, and as they took the final few steps Anna had a brief moment to notice everything: how close together they were walking; the warmth of his arm beneath her thin glove; the way they walked in step with each other—just as though this were a dance and they the two most attuned dancers in the world. She noticed the excitement pulsing through her—body, mind and heart entirely focused on him and on the revelations of the past few moments. She deliberately noticed the birdsong, the breeze whispering through the trees and the colours of the woods—greens, browns and yellows.

Now they were among the trees, and, finally, out of sight of the many windows of Lammermuir House.

'Anna,' he said again, and his deep voice reverberated through her. They had stopped, and he turned to face her. 'May I kiss you?'

This is the best moment of my entire life.

'Yes. Please.' She pulled on the ribbon of her bonnet, undoing it, and he made a sound deep in his throat as he watched her.

'Anna,' he said again, lifting both hands to touch her face. He gently stroked the sensitive skin of her cheeks, and she felt as though she might die from the sheer sensation.

And he has not yet even kissed me!

He leaned closer, so close that she could feel the warmth of his breath on her face. His face was a blur this close, so she closed her eyes. An instant later, his lips were on hers—warm, wonderful and moving, moving from side to side—just a little, but it was enough for her to feel as though she had been struck by lightning—small strikes, repeated and giving only pleasure. Now he slanted to fit his lips perfectly on hers, and instinctively she moved too, tilting her head to help the alignment.

When they had kissed before, she'd known that it was wonderful, but she had been unable to clearly remember the details. This time...

Oh, my goodness!

Never had she felt anything like it. Her insides felt as though they had turned to liquid, and the same affliction now affected her bones, for she distinctively felt a weakness at her knees. But there was more to come, for now he parted his lips to explore hers gently with his tongue.

Anna thought she might die from the sensation, so delightful was it. She gasped and instantly his tongue was in her mouth, flicking across her parted lips and leading to a strange moaning sound which she realised she herself was making. She tentatively reciprocated, lifting her tongue to meet his, and his groan of desire was surely the most delicious sound she had ever heard.

After some time, the kiss changed. Now he was demanding, using greater force and more movement, and she met him at every turn, enjoying the new thrill from the passion they were sharing. His hands left her face, sweeping around her back to haul her close, and she gasped at the sensation of his body against hers. Following her instincts, she braced against him and he groaned again, pressing his hips against her midriff even as his hands swept down her back to her bottom. Now he pushed hard against her and she moaned again, not understanding what was happening to her but knowing that she liked it very, very much.

Abruptly he was gone, stepping back and sliding his hands onto her arms to steady her. Opening her eyes, she saw the desire in his and again her insides clenched. Her breathing was disordered, her heart racing, and it occurred to her that surely no one had ever felt like this before? Her body was a pillar of flaming desire, her heart exploding with love for him, and her mind... Her mind soared in the heavens somewhere—absent, but contentedly so.

Their eyes held, and held. As her body's combustion began to cool, the love in her heart seemed to strengthen the longer they held one another's gaze.

'Will...' she managed.

'Anna.' Sliding his hands down her arms, he took both her hands to his mouth and kissed them. Even through her gloves Anna felt the sensation. What would it be like without glove, without any clothing? Little wonder that her sisters spent so much time in their husband's beds. She had had exactly two kisses in her life, but she wanted more. She wanted all of him, all the time—forever.

Bending, he picked up her bonnet and handed it to her. As she carefully re-tied the ribbon next to her right ear, he watched her intently. When she was ready he placed her hand in the crook of his arm again and they walked on—just as though they had not just engaged in passionate love-making in the midst of a Scottish woodland.

They talked then about her advances towards him, and how it had encouraged him to hope. Reassuringly, he had not been put out in the least. 'And I am glad that I did not continue to kiss you then—despite the effort it took not to do so.' He sent her a warm glance. 'Instead, our kiss just now was perfect. We had privacy and sunshine—and neither of us is in any way bosky!'

Happiness bubbled out of her. 'It was indeed perfect. I could not be happier.'

Stopping, he turned to face her again. 'There is but one thing that could complete my happiness, Anna. I—'

'My lord! My lord!'

They turned their heads. A young page was running towards them at full tilt, his little face red from exertion.

'You are to come quickly, my lord!'

Chapter Twenty

Anna's heart sank. Abruptly, all of the realities came rushing back as her mind regained dominance over her body and her heart. Fear coursed through her.

'What has happened?' Will's tone was clipped; he too was concerned.

Is it Lady Kelgrove? My sisters? Have the Thaxbys done something?

The page bowed, still out of breath. 'Her ladyship has sent me to fetch you. I know one of the grooms is being sent for the doctor too, sir.'

A sick feeling rushed through Anna and she exchanged a glance with Will. 'Very well,' he said. 'Tell my mother I shall come directly. Where shall I find her?'

'She was in the breakfast room, sir.'

The page dashed off again, and Anna and Will hurried after him. Neither spoke, but he covered her hand with his, squeezing it gently, and she took some comfort from it. As they neared the house, a horseman passed them, heading towards the gate—the rider one of the grooms whom Anna had met during her riding lessons.

Who is sick? And how bad?

Pausing only to exchange boots for slippers, and for Anna to hand her bonnet to a maid, they made their way directly to the breakfast room. It was still early, and therefore not unusual for the room to be half-empty. Glancing about, Anna saw Lady Garvald, the Rentons and the Thaxbys, but her sisters and their husbands were absent, as was...

'Oh, my dear Anna.' Lady Garvald rose to greet them. 'Lady Kelgrove's maid says she is dreadfully unwell. She has apparently asked for the doctor to be sent for.'

Without considering why, Anna's gaze immediately flicked to the Thaxbys. Mrs Thaxby seemed unconcerned—but then, other people's troubles rarely seemed to concern her. Mr Thaxby, on the other hand... Anna's eyes widened. He was showing the same restlessness as he had the night before, but was there a hint of satisfaction glinting in his eye?

What has he done?

Oh, Anna knew she was leaping to conclusions. He was no friend to Lady Kelgrove, and news that she was unwell might simply have pleased him. It did not necessarily mean that he...

'Are my sisters still abed?'

Lady Garvald nodded. 'I have sent servants to inform them, so they will be up and dressed before long.' She made a helpless gesture. 'Lady Kelgrove would not allow me into her chamber—her abigail, Hill, was most insistent. She wishes to see only the doctor and her great-granddaughters.'

'I shall go at once.'

With a glance towards Will, and a curtsey to all, Anna hurried out of the breakfast room. As she climbed the stairs, she noticed the sick feeling in her stomach was increasing. Lady Kelgrove was dear to her, and the notion she was unwell was deeply concerning. Worse, the notion that her sickness might not be natural was terrifying.

Knocking on the door, Anna tried to compose herself. It would never do to let Lady Kelgrove know her suspicions. The door opened a crack, then more widely.

'Miss Lennox!' Hill bobbed a curtsey. 'I hope you can help me, for I do not understand what ails my lady!' She lowered her voice. 'She has had a—a *digestive* upset during the night, but is much more affected by it than she should be.' Wringing her hands, she then took a corner of her apron and dabbed at her eyes.

They were already walking towards the large bed. The curtains had been drawn around it and, as she lifted a hand to draw them back, Anna braced herself for what she might see.

Lady Kelgrove looked tiny against her pillows, her long grey hair in a simple braid and a thin linen nightgown exposing her neck and collarbones. Her eyes were closed, her arms lying over the covers, and Anna was struck by how aged and frail she looked. Fully dressed, with her hair dressed and her indomitable spirit, one could easily forget that she was eighty-four. Just now, it was all too apparent.

Anna swallowed, bending over to speak softly to her.

'Great-Grandmother! I am here. It is Anna.'

Her eyes opened and one thin hand clutched at Anna's arm. 'Anna!' Her voice was thready, faint. 'I must speak with you alone.'

'Of course!' Anna glanced towards Hill, who nodded and left the room, quietly weeping. She would be just outside the door, Anna knew, ready to tend to her beloved mistress in whatever way she could.

'Is she gone? Are we alone?' Never had Anna seen the strong, stubborn Lady Kelgrove exhibit such uncertainty, such...was it fear?

'Yes, all alone, I guarantee it.' Anna sat on the edge of the bed. 'Now, what do you need to speak with me about?'

As she gazed anxiously at her great-grandmother's face, a change came over the old lady's expression. The fear in her eyes was replaced with mischief, and she released the hand clutching Anna's arm.

'Ah, good to see my play-acting has fooled even you, Anna, for you and Hill are both quick-witted and discerning—most of the time, leastways.

Anna's jaw dropped. 'Play-acting? Are you not ill?'

'Not a bit of it!' Lady Kelgrove declared cheerfully, just as there was a knock at the door. 'I had nausea and flux during the night, as may happen to anyone from time to time. But I am already recovering.' She gestured in the general direction of the door. 'If that

is one of your sisters, bring her in. Anyone else must
be sent away.'

What on earth is she up to?

Anna's mind was reeling, but her heart felt only relief that her great-grandmother was not, after all, at
death's door.

It was both her sisters. 'We met on the landing just
now,' said Rose, her brow furrowed with anxiety. Izzy
just looked fierce—which Izzy always did when troubled.

'How is she?'

For answer, Anna waved them in, unsure what she
was supposed to say. Sure enough, Lady Kelgrove sub-
jected Izzy and Rose to more of her 'play-acting', then
broke into laughter that had more than a hint of a cackle
about it.

Bemused, they looked at one another. Anna raised
a wry brow. 'Play-acting, apparently. She has been unwell but, she says, is now recovered.'

'What? But why would you do such a thing?' Rose
was clearly as bewildered as Anna.

Izzy laughed along. 'Ah, infamous! You fooled us
all. I salute you, Great-Grandmother!'

'I used to lead your great-grandfather a merry dance
when we were young, you know.' Her black eyes danced
with glee. 'He could never tell when I was jesting—a
useful deficiency which I fully exploited.'

Anna was determined not to be distracted. 'There is
a reason for this, is there not? This is no jest.'

Sobering, Lady Kelgrove looked at Anna. 'Aye.' She

sighed. 'Yesterday you told me that we were correct, and that those wicked, wicked people killed Richard.'

'Yes. And George.'

'The first murder,' Lady Kelgrove continued, 'Was simple in its execution—they simply hired ruffians to stage a murder by way of a staged robbery. But the hired men made a mull of it. They killed the wrong man—the intention was to kill George, not Richard.'

She pursed her lips. 'Richard was of no interest to them. Their intention was fratricide, and he was less than nothing to them. But George survived.' She eyed them keenly. 'George's inheritance was their aim. The Fletcher lands and properties are not entailed, so everything passed to the sister, as the closest relative— the closest *known* relative, that is. But I wondered, time and again, how did they kill George?'

Izzy frowned. 'He was said to have died of some sort of flux—not uncommon, even in young and healthy people.'

'Exactly. Yet I know it was murder. And, judging from the Thaxbys' reactions to my barbs, they know it too.'

Anna knew exactly what she was suggesting. 'Mr Thaxby's tisanes! And his interest in all things botanical!'

Lady Kelgrove nodded. 'Precisely.' She took a breath. 'I have reason to believe that yesterday evening Mr Thaxby attempted to poison me.'

There were collective gasps, then the questions began. 'But how?'

'When?'

Anna took a breath. 'You say "attempted"—was he not, then, successful?'

Lady Kelgrove grimaced. 'I hope not, but I cannot be certain. I took a hand in things, and can only pray that I did the right thing.' She looked up at them. 'I must admit, girls, that I did not sleep very well, for even after my physical discomfort eased I was constantly wondering if I would begin to feel ill again at any moment. That was how the idea came to me to pretend to be so.' She grimaced. 'Of course, if he has used something slow-acting, I may yet become ill. But this way I can set my affairs in order before I go.'

'Do not even say that, Great-Grandmother!' Rose took Lady Kelgrove's hand. 'You will be here to keep us in order for a long time yet!'

Lady Kelgrove sniffed. 'Maybe, maybe not. But we must observe them carefully today. And, much as I hate to say it, I must not be left alone with either of them. It would not take much for them to snuff out my life— one of my own pillows would be enough.'

'I did think,' Anna said slowly, 'That Mrs Thaxby seemed untroubled by the news you were unwell. Mr Thaxby, however...'

'Well? Spit it out, girl!'

'He seemed pleased. And also agitated.' She shrugged. 'I may be imagining it, of course, but...'

'Good girl, Anna. Precisely as I imagined! Now, here is what I need you to do...'

They listened carefully. Hill was to be encouraged

to go to the servants' hall, where she would undoubtedly reinforce the belief that Lady Kelgrove was deathly ill. Anna was to spread concern among the guests, and also seek Will's assistance, for Lady Kelgrove wished to speak to Mr Thaxby's valet without his master knowing. Rose and Izzy were to bring Maria's journals to Lady Kelgrove's room, where collectively they would assemble the evidence to be shown to Sir Walter. And later, when all was ready, Sir Walter himself was discreetly to be brought to Lady Kelgrove.

'Anna, where is the Fletcher necklace?'

'It is in Will's safe. I thought it best, for Mrs Thaxby is quite fixated on it.'

'Good. Leave it there until all of this is over—unless I need you to incite Mrs Thaxby once again. But, if I am right, all will be clear by the end of the day. Oh, and Anna?'

'Yes?'

'What took place between you and Mrs Thaxby after you played the piano last night?'

Anna shook her head admiringly. 'You miss nothing! I found myself alone in the retiring room with her, and she spoke of the necklace again.' Anna briefly recounted the conversation.

'Hmm. He may be the one to commit the evil deeds, but she is clearly party to it. Now go, Anna. Your sisters will remain with me for now.'

Anna went, firstly sympathetically instructing Hill to go to the housekeeper for tea, and promising to call for her as soon as the doctor came. Hill went—unhappily, it had to be said—and Anna's heart warmed at the abigail's regard for her employer. It struck her that, whether it was soon or a few years in the future, Lady Kelgrove would indeed die one day, and when that happened Hill should be given a safe retirement and a comfortable pension.

As Hill made for the servants' staircase, Anna returned to the breakfast room, where she hoped to find Will and his mother. Bracing herself before going in, she knew that she did not need to play-act, for Lady Kelgrove's words had not been reassuring. If the elderly lady had indeed been given a slow-acting poison, then they might well lose her in the coming days.

All eyes turned to her as she entered, the gentlemen rising from their repast to acknowledge her. Following a round of formal greetings, Anna sat, accepting a cup of tea from the footman and wondering idly how they were all supposed to keep themselves safe from hidden poisons.

'How is Lady Kelgrove, my dear?' Lady Garvald was all sympathy.

Anna answered carefully. 'She has suffered in the night. We must await the doctor's opinion, but I must say I have never known her to take to her bed.'

'That is concerning indeed. Please let me know what I or my staff can do to assist.'

'Of course. My sisters are with her just now, and I shall rejoin them shortly. We plan to take turns for breakfast.'

In reality they could easily have asked for rolls and

chocolate to be brought to Lady Kelgrove's bedchamber, but it was important that Anna complete the tasks set for her—including her responsibility to ensure the household genuinely believed Lady Kelgrove to be unwell.

All present asked for their good wishes to be sent to Lady Kelgrove, whether sincerely or just politely. Anna took them all with equanimity, thanking everyone while privately acknowledging that Mr Thaxby looked and sounded entirely genuine. If he had indeed tried to poison Lady Kelgrove, this then represented a level of deception and coldness that Anna could simply not fathom. She shivered.

'It might be this sultry weather,' remarked Mrs Thaxby, setting down her fork to mop her brow. 'I declare it is making me feel decidedly colicky.'

'Perhaps,' Anna murmured, though privately thinking the morning was still pleasantly cool. Mrs Thaxby continually needed to be at the centre of people's attention, which was wearing.

Does she know what her husband has done? Anna could not imagine so.

'The doctor should be here shortly,' said Will, and Anna looked at him properly for the first time. It all came back instantly—the magical kisses and magical words they had shared on this morning's walk. It felt as though a lamp was lit inside her—a lamp that burned with the power of a hundred suns.

He is Will! And he is my *Will!*

'That is good news indeed.' Her words could not have

been any more neutral, yet speaking to him, meeting his gaze, made love, hope and passion rise within her. But Lady Garvald gave her a curious look, so she busied herself by taking a sip of tea.

The sound of a carriage outside made all heads turn to the window. 'The doctor, I presume,' observed Lady Renford.

'No! Look, there is a crest!' Mrs Thaxby's tone had a gleeful edge and Anna was wearily reminded of the ongoing battle of wits between the two ladies. They loved to contradict one another—on principle, it seemed.

'It is probably Sir Walter. I invited him for the day. He is impressively early.'

Mrs Thaxby, craning her neck, was moved to pout. 'His handsome son does not accompany him today. What a disappointment that must be for you, Miss Lennox!'

Anna flushed, but could find nothing to say. On her right, Will asked Lord Renton about their planned ride after breakfast, and the moment passed.

The door opened, a footman announcing Sir Walter, who entered with a great deal of bustling and joviality. Despite telling them he had already broken his fast, he accepted Lady Garvald's invitation to join them, and was soon tucking in to beef and eggs, washed down with tea. Claudio arrived shortly afterwards, followed by James, and the gentlemen then dominated the gathering, engaging in a lively conversation about horseflesh and horseracing, to which Anna could contribute exactly nothing. But she did not mind, for it gave her the opportunity to observe the others.

The Rentons, sitting at opposite sides of the table. The Thaxbys, together but saying little. Lady Garvald, gracious and diligent in her care for her guests. Twice Anna saw her beckon the footmen, who would return shortly afterwards with more food, as the gentlemen could clear a board with great efficiency. Claudio and James, with easy jesting and a great deal of wit, were engaging Will and Lord Renton in raillery, and it occurred to Anna once again that both her sisters had chosen well.

This led her thoughts to places where they probably should not go. What had Will been about to say earlier when the page had interrupted them? But *no*, she told herself sternly. Such matters would have to wait, for even now Lady Kelgrove was abed, possibly having been poisoned. And Anna had further tasks to complete—important tasks.

She tried to catch Will's eye discreetly, for she needed to talk to him about Mr Thaxby's valet. Unfortunately, the gentlemen were currently discussing their planned ride immediately after breakfast, following a route of Will's suggestion which he said would guarantee them some fine fences. Sir Walter would go too, Will having offered him what he described as a 'good-hearted' mount. Even Mr Thaxby, who did not join in their levity, could not forgo the enticement of such sport. Anna could almost see in his eyes the moment when he engaged with the idea and agreed to go.

Their meal complete, the gentlemen rose, bidding farewell to the ladies and exiting with a great deal of clatter and noise. Anna could do nothing about it, but she had failed in the final task set for her by Lady Kelgrove—to seek Will's help in discreetly sending Mr Thaxby's valet to Lady Kelgrove. The departure of the gentlemen left a silence, broken by the ticking of the clock and the gentle sound of Lady Renton stirring her tea with a silver spoon.

'Well,' she began, 'Thank goodness for that! Now we shall have some peace.'

Mainly addressing Lady Garvald, she then proceeded to dominate the conversation, filling it with her observations about the weather, her new gown and other such nothings, while Anna became increasingly restless within. Mrs Thaxby concentrated on her wine, with which a footman had helpfully presented her almost as soon as Mr Thaxby had left the room. Anna had not even seen the woman's signal to the servants, but it seemed they were well aware of her habits.

Another carriage arrived soon afterwards—this one plain and crest-free. With a great deal of relief, Anna accompanied Lady Garvald to greet Dr West, a kindly-looking man in his middle years. As they climbed the stairs, he asked for more information about his patient, having been given only the sketchiest of details by the lady's groom, he said.

'Miss Lennox is Lady Kelgrove's great-granddaughter and has been tending to her,' Lady Garvald explained.

'I see.' He turned to Anna as they walked. 'What can you tell me, Miss Lennox?'

What may I tell him?

Lady Kelgrove would likely not wish her speculation about poisoning to be known. Yet, if she had been poisoned, surely the doctor should be informed of it?

'She was sick and also experienced…er…flux during the night.'

'I see. And is she generally in good health?'

Now they were on safer ground. 'Indeed she is—in fact, she is resoundingly healthy for a lady of her age.'

'And…er…' he coughed discreetly '…might I ask how old she is? It is helpful to know in my profession.'

Anna told him, and a moment later they reached Lady Kelgrove's bedchamber. 'This is Dr West,' she said when Izzy opened the door. 'This is my sister, Princess Isobel, and my other sister, Lady Ashbourne.'

Following the greetings, and the usual comment about how alike they were, Dr West proceeded into the room, followed by Lady Garvald. Although their great-grandmother had previously forbidden entry to all but the triplets, Anna hoped she would not mind their kind hostess being present.

As the doctor introduced himself to Lady Kelgrove and began questioning her about her illness, Anna exchanged glances with her sisters. Thankfully they seemed serene, signalling that their great-grandmother had remained in fine spirits since her absence, she hoped.

Now, of course, Lady Kelgrove was play-acting for

the doctor—as good a show of weakness and feebleness as Anna had ever witnessed.

She is an absolute wretch!

With her permission, Dr West gently pressed on her stomach and looked inside her mouth, as well as placing his hand on her head to check for fever. His examination complete, he advised bed rest, a tisane of mint leaves and ginger root and an avoidance of rich foods in the coming days. Lady Garvald undertook to ensure everything would be provided for Lady Kelgrove as per his instructions, sending her bedridden guest a look of warm sympathy and concern.

Dr West was just preparing to go when there was an urgent knock at the door. Rose, who was closest, opened it—to reveal a young serving maid who looked extremely agitated.

'My lady!' She curtseyed to Lady Garvald. 'It's Mrs Thaxby. She has just cast up her accounts and is moaning and carrying on like she is in agony! Her abigail has taken her to her chamber and the girls are cleaning the breakfast room, my lady.'

'Oh, dear!' Lady Garvald turned to the doctor. 'It seems you have another patient, Dr West. If you will be so good as to follow me?' With a brisk farewell to Lady Kelgrove and the triplets, Lady Garvald escorted the doctor from the room.

The door closed behind him and Anna took a breath. 'And to think I thought Mrs Thaxby was merely seeking attention when she said she felt unwell earlier. I am

chastened, for my thoughts were decidedly unchari-
table!'

Lady Kelgrove shuffled into a sitting position. 'You
need not feel sorry for either of them, for I believe they
both are truly wicked. Now, is the valet coming to speak
with me? And what of Sir Walter? Rose saw him arrive
nearly an hour ago. Will he stay long enough for us to
complete our work here?' She indicated the small pile
of journals on her bedside table. One of Anna's sisters
must have fetched them. There were no papers, though,
and the height of the pile suggested that not all of Mama's diaries and papers had been brought to Lady Kelgrove's chamber.

'Never mind that for a moment,' Anna dismissed
firmly. 'Firstly I wish to know how you are. Any further discomfort?'

'Nary a bit! I am well, as I told you earlier.'

'But Mrs Thaxby is unwell,' said Rose with a frown.
'Might she be afflicted by the same illness that struck
you in the night? Perhaps it is just a common malady,
rather than anything sinister.'

'If it is *not* the same illness then I shall be astonished!' declared Lady Kelgrove. 'But we must be quick,
for Sir Walter will wish to speak to you about the necklace, Anna, and we are not yet ready. Bring me the rest
of those journals and papers, and be quick about it!'

Izzy came with her, and together they emptied the
secret drawer of all its remaining treasures, carefully
closing it again.

'What do you think ails Mrs Thaxby?' Izzy asked, her brow furrowed.

Anna shrugged. 'Stomach complaints are not uncommon, and can sometimes spread through a household. We know this.'

'Yes but...' Izzy bit her lip but said nothing further. *Poison.* The unspoken suspicion hung between them. What had Lady Kelgrove meant? And was the possibility now gone, since Mrs Thaxby was also ill? The woman would not have poisoned herself, and Mr Thaxby's devotion to her was indisputable.

As they hurried along the landing back towards Lady Kelgrove's bedchamber, an idea came to Anna. 'Take these!' Handing Izzy her share of Mama's papers, she turned as if to go back. 'I shall join you shortly.'

Why should I wait for Will?

Normally only gentlemen interacted with valets, but the gentlemen were out riding. *All* the gentlemen, including Mr Thaxby. Which meant Anna might be able to speak to his valet without being caught. As she passed Mrs Thaxby's door, she heard agonised wailing from within, and winced. Mrs Thaxby certainly sounded as though she was in severe pain.

The next chamber belonged to Mr Thaxby. Holding her breath, she opened the door without knocking and walked inside. As she had hoped, the valet was there alone. Seeing her, he leapt to his feet, abandoning the garment he seemed to be in the process of mending. He bowed, then stood, waiting. For just a moment Anna stood frozen, sensing the enormity of the moment. If this man knew things, would he tell her? And, despite the abuse he received, was he loyal to his master, as all good servants were trained to be?

'Your name is John, is it not?'

He dipped his head. 'It is.'

'And how long have you been in service to Mr Thaxby?'

A gleam of approval lit his eye. 'More than twenty years, miss. And I served the Fletchers before that.'

This was encouraging. 'Did you?'

'Aye. I was valet to the young master—Mr George, that is. And me only a handful of years older than him.'

Anna's heart was now decidedly faster than it ought to be, and her palms prickled with excitement. *He knew my father!*

'Was Mr Fletcher…that is to say, do you know if he…?' How to word things delicately? Despite his open demeanour, the man might wish her ill as much as his master did. 'Was he good to you?'

'He was the best of gentlemen,' John replied, his eyes softening. He thought for a moment, then added very deliberately, 'And a great favourite with the ladies, despite being so young. But he only ever had eyes for one lady, if I may say so.'

We understand one another.

'Miss Maria Berkeley…' Anna breathed. 'My mother.'

He nodded. 'The very same.' He shook his head. 'I only put it all together very recently when I saw the Fletcher necklace, and then the Lammermuir servants told me that Lady Kelgrove's granddaughter had lived here with her children—you and your sisters, miss. Mr George... We both assumed she was carrying a single baby.'

He knows!

Anna ginned. 'Not Mama! She did not do anything by halves!'

'A formidable young lady, if I may say so, miss.'

'You may certainly say so, and I thank you.' She nodded firmly. 'Lady Kelgrove wishes to speak to you, if it pleases you?'

He straightened his shoulders. 'I always believed this day would come, and I am happy to speak to her again. She asked me some questions before, but I had to feign ignorance. My master...' He grimaced. 'I must warn you, miss, if my master learns the truth...' He swallowed. 'He might seem civilised, but a monster dwells within him.'

Chapter Twenty-One

Nausea roiled through Anna's stomach. Each time she was reminded of the Thaxbys' evil acts, each time there was further confirmation that their suspicions were correct, it made her feel sick, frightened, and perfectly furious.

'I shall do my best to protect you, John,' she said quietly. 'And I believe I can guarantee you a new position, should you need one.' Through Will, James or Claudio, she would make certain of it. Being cast off without a reference was the worst thing that could happen to a servant.

Monster.

She managed a nod. 'Come, now.' Turning, she led the way, allowing him to walk a few paces behind her. Any servants that saw them would hopefully think nothing of it and assume that John was on some legitimate errand. Reaching her great-grandmother's door, she poked her head inside to check who was present. The bed was strewn with papers and journals, her sisters and Lady Kelgrove engrossed in reading. On hearing the door open, they lifted their heads.

'Mr Thaxby's valet is here,' Anna told them softly.

Lady Kelgrove inclined her head regally. 'You may admit him.'

In he came, looking extremely discomfited at finding himself in my lady's bedchamber. He bowed deeply.

Lady Kelgrove came straight to the point. 'Tell me of my granddaughter's relationship with Mr George Fletcher.'

'They loved one another deeply, my lady. It happened after the attack on the heath, when he went to your country estate for his recuperation. I was with him there, and I saw how Miss Maria nursed him, how they came to care for one another.'

'Was his sister aware of their connection?'

'No. Nor her husband. They resented your influence over him, my lady, and at the same time seemed grateful not to have the responsibility of caring for him.'

Lady Kelgrove's eyes grew distant. 'He was like a second grandson to me, particularly after Richard was killed.' She eyed the valet sharply. 'What do you know of that incident?'

'I know very little. As to what I *suspect*, I have not voiced it in a very long time. It would have been dangerous to do so.'

'Will you speak of it now—tell me of your suspicions?'

He squared his shoulders. 'I believe that Mr Thaxby had hired someone to attack the coach that night. I was not there, so I cannot say. But, afterwards, too much seemed strange.'

'The level of violence upon the occupants of a crested coach?'

'Yes. It made no sense, for highwaymen are not normally so ruthless. It was only after the falling out with Mr Fletcher that I began to wonder if there was some connection between the events.'

'Falling out?' Her tone was sharp. 'Due to what cause?'

'His desire to marry, my lady.'

'He told them of it? Lord, his own naivety was his downfall?'

'He was only twenty years old, my lady.' John spoke softly, but it warmed Anna's heart to see how he defended George, even now. 'Thankfully, he had been out and about around town for a short time before he resolved to tell them.'

'Why "thankfully"?'

'He told them only of his desire to marry, without mentioning the name of his lady. They assumed he had developed a sudden *tendre* for one of the young ladies who had lately arrived for the season and, perhaps understandably, were not best pleased with the notion.'

He shrugged. 'At the time it seemed reasonable. He was very young and if, as they assumed, he had become suddenly enamoured of someone, then as responsible trustees it was right for them to dissuade him.'

'True. Had Maria come to me, I should also have dissuaded her. She was at the time almost eighteen, and with a single season behind her. While I should have been pleased to see her settled, I might have worried that George would eventually stray. Young men can be very volatile, you know.'

'Not my master.' John's tone was firm. 'As steady a young man as ever there was. And he adored Miss Maria.'

'You assisted them to run away?'

'I obeyed my master's orders.' He held her gaze and after a moment she gave the slightest of nods, accepting his perspective.

'Continue.'

He exhaled. 'He did not take me with him, so I had no idea where he was or what he was doing. I only hoped he and his lady were well.'

Anna could hardly breathe. Finally, they were hearing the whole story. *If only Will were here!*

But she would save everything in her memory to recount to him later, for she was certain he would be interested in every detail.

They talked on, Lady Kelgrove asking John to provide more details of the elopement. It had been arranged by letter, John having sent it to Maria's serving maid. 'Young Ellen!' Lady Kelgrove gasped. 'So she knew!'

'What happened to her?' Izzy asked.

Lady Kelgrove shrugged. 'She got a position as a lady's maid in another household. And she never breathed a word, even though she knew I was grieving for my "dead" granddaughter.'

'I suppose,' suggested Rose, 'She could not say anything, since it was Lord Kelgrove himself who put it about that Maria had died.'

Lady Kelgrove pursed her lips. 'True. My husband has much to answer for—and so I shall tell him when I join him after this life is done.'

Anna had to laugh. 'The poor man will be dreading your arrival in heaven, Great-Grandmother!'

This earned a twinkle. 'Poor man nothing! I shall have strong words for him, I assure you! But do continue, John. Where did they go when they eloped?'

'I know not. As I said, Mr George disappeared for many months, and I heard that Miss Maria had died of the smallpox. I assumed him to be distressed at losing her, and was dreadfully worried about him. And then one day he turned up in the Fletchers' country house, bold as brass, and wishing me a good day! To say I was flabbergasted is an understatement.'

'What was his demeanour?' asked Rose.

'He was in alt. "I am a married man," he told me, sending me a wink. "And I mean to inform my sister of it!" So I told him that Miss Maria Berkeley was said to have died, and that sobered him.'

'How had the Thaxbys reacted to his disappearance?'

He sighed. 'They were furious at his disobedience, but at the same time enjoyed the freedom to spend his money as they wished.' He thought for a moment. 'I think his presence had inhibited them to some extent before then.'

He grimaced. 'By that time I had been assigned to the service of Mr Thaxby and came to know him rather better.' He shook his head. 'Doubts had been sown in my mind about the attack on the heath when his friend had been murdered. It seemed a preposterous notion, but I wondered if Mr George had been the one meant to die that night.'

'I came to the same conclusion, but I have no proof.'

'Nor I.'

There was silence, then Lady Kelgrove continued, 'And what of George's death?'

John shook his head. 'That was a bad business, and no mistake. As I say, Mr George had been gone for many months, and came back because he wanted them to approve of his marriage. But after speaking to them he kept saying how he had seen a different side to them, and how they would not approve of his marriage, ever.'

He shrugged. 'I made my own disapproval plain, for I thought him mistaken—the heat of a fervent mind. Afterwards, though...' He sighed. 'Mr George was right and I was wrong. If I had only seen it earlier, recognised the danger...but I thought it was the eternal tale of young lovers eloping from the justified disapproval of their families.

'I did counsel him to refrain from telling them he was already married, and to whom. I advised him to say only that he *intended* to marry, as he had done previously. "I shall come into my majority in a matter of months anyway, John," he said to me.' John sighed. 'In reality I believe Mr and Mrs Thaxby were already focused on that fact.'

He shook his head. 'For three or four days there were

constant arguments, which ended with Mr George warning them that he would shortly be holding the purse strings and that they would do well to remember it.' His lips tightened. 'I happened to be present during that exchange, and I honestly believe that was the moment when Mr Thaxby decided he must be murdered soon.'

'And they clearly did not know it was our mother whom he loved.' Izzy's expression was thoughtful.

'That is correct, Your Highness. Indeed, at one point Mr George hinted to them that he was enamoured of a serving maid. The mistress was filled with rage at the very notion, and made as if to strike him, but Mr Thaxby held her back. "Not like this, my love," he said to her, and something about it made me shudder at the time.' He frowned. 'It still does.'

Anna understood, for his tale was extremely disturbing. Mr Thaxby had coldly planned to murder George and had then carried out his evil plan—presumably, with the full support of his wife.

'What happened then?'

'Mr George got sick…that very night.' He closed his eyes briefly. 'It took three days for him to die.'

Anna found her voice. 'Did he know?' John looked at her. 'That Mr Thaxby had done it?'

John nodded grimly. 'Mr and Mrs Thaxby came to see him when he was sick and, when they left, Mr George was distraught. He told me then that his brother-in-law had admitted to poisoning him, but that it could not be proven, and no one would ever believe him. He wrote to her.'

Rose said, 'Anna,' and something in her voice drew Anna's attention away from John's tale. 'We found this just now, among Mama's papers.' She was holding out a letter.

Anna's eyes roved over it, noting that it was simply signed '*George*'. Taking a breath, she read it.

My Darling Maria,
Our hopes are dashed for ever.

 My sister and her husband have poisoned me, and I may have only hours left in this world. They refuse to send for the doctor, and laughed when I suggested it. My love, they believe themselves to be safe and, while I told them I wished to marry, they believe I am enamoured of a serving maid, so they do not suspect the truth. But we cannot be certain they will never find out, for there are more than a few people—including servants—who know about us.

 Once I am gone John, my steadfast valet, will deliver this letter, and when you get it, you must not return to our little hideaway. Find somewhere new, somewhere safe. That way, my murderous sister and her evil husband cannot find you, nor our precious child.

 They killed Richard too—she admitted it to me today. That was their first attempt to murder me, and your dear brother was accidentally caught in their scheme. I must trust John and believe him when he says he remains loyal to me. He says he will stay in their service and attempt to seek justice for me, and for Richard. He will take care of my inheritance so long as he lives. However, he cannot tell what he does not know, and so I recommend you do not even tell John where you are going.

The money I left you will not last long, but I fear if you return to your family my sister may discover that you are my wife and may try to harm you and our child. Your grandparents, I am sorry to say, have apparently put it about that you died of smallpox. Therefore, I urge you to go where you cannot be found, and where you may be safe.

I am most heartily sorry. I have failed in my duty to protect you and our child. I know of nowhere in society that can withstand their enmity and the reach of their wealth. My wealth, indeed, but their aim all along has been to take it for themselves.

My eyes grow dim and my hand weak. I must stop soon. It remains only for me to assure you of my ever-lasting love and devotion. Some day, my darling wife, we shall be reunited in heaven. I urge you to be safe, and be happy. Remarry if it pleases you, and know that my only desire is— and ever was—your happiness.

George

Lord! Overcome, Anna reached for the back of a nearby chair for support. Then Rose was there, placing an arm around her and murmuring words of comfort.

'They *laughed*.' Anna felt a shudder ripple through her. 'I do not know why that detail in particular is so striking, but it is sending a chill through me. When he asked for the doctor, they *laughed*.'

Rose shook her head sadly. 'Yes, they did. And for over twenty years they have lived off the benefits of their wicked actions, while our father was dead, and Richard was dead, and Mama...'

'Mama endured struggles she should never have had to endure,' Izzy finished fiercely, her hands bunched into fists and her voice tight with emotion. Rounding on John, she asked, 'Why did you never tell anyone? Why did you work for them all these years?'

He dropped his head.

'Isobel, you forget yourself!' Lady Kelgrove spoke sharply. 'You know his position as a servant means he cannot answer such demands.'

'You are correct.' Izzy took a breath. 'I am sorry, John. Please forgive me.'

'Thank you, Your Highness. If I may be permitted to speak...?'

'Please do.'

'I stayed because of you—all three of you. Course, I did not know there were three, but I knew that Maria lived, that she was with child, and hoped that she was hopefully safe. The last orders I got from Mr George were this: "Deliver the letter into my wife's hand then return and protect my inheritance. Some day Maria will come, or our child will.'"

John looked at each of them in turn. 'That day has finally come. And I am pleased to tell you that the old Fletcher servants who remained all worked for *you*, not them. For more than twenty years we hoped. We never stopped hoping.'

'That is laudable indeed. But...' Anna could not understand it. 'What can servants do that would make a difference?'

'You might be surprised, miss. The butler, cook, housekeeper and steward all visited Mr George's sickroom before his death, without Mr and Mrs Thaxby's knowledge. And, for all Mr Thaxby's cunning, he never knew that the steward has been diverting the greater part of the Fletcher wealth into government bonds and gold—to protect it, you understand.

'And Mrs Thaxby could never comprehend just why the chimneys always smoked when she received distinguished guests, nor why we never seemed to have as much silverware as she recalled from her childhood. She had a fondness for expensive jewellery, you see, while he is something of a gamester in secret. So together we have done as our true master requested, awaiting the day when his wife and child came to claim their rightful inheritance.'

Lady Kelgrove chuckled. 'I am glad to hear you were

working *for* him and not against him. I should not like to come up against such efficient opposition.'

'And are those servants still in senior positions in the Thaxby household?' Rose asked curiously.

'Mr Baker, the steward, remains, as does the butler and housekeeper. They are currently in the Edinburgh house, for Mr and Mrs Thaxby intend to return there after this house party. There is a new cook, for my mother died some years ago.'

'Your mother? I am sorry, John.' Rose's voice was gentle.

He nodded briskly. 'She would be so happy to know Mr and Mrs Fletcher's children are alive and well.'

They all stilled, for there was a knock on the door. Instantly, John retreated to stand by the wall by the fireplace, his face a mask of impassivity. Rose admitted the callers—Lady Garvald and the doctor. Dr West's expression was grim—a strong contrast to the benign confidence with which he had spoken to Lady Kelgrove earlier.

'My lady,' he began, 'I must inform you that Mrs Thaxby is gravely ill, and that concerns me in respect of your own health.' He approached Lady Kelgrove's canopied bed. 'I know of only two possibilities as to why you have both experienced the same symptoms in the same few hours. One, that there is a gastric infection present in this house, or two, that you have both eaten something disagreeable. I have therefore asked

Lady Garvald to review with her cook everything that you both have eaten and to dispose of it instantly.'

'Which of course I shall do,' added Lady Garvald, 'Although Cook is in high dudgeon at the very notion that her cooking may be to blame.'

'Fear not, Lady Garvald. Your cook is entirely innocent.' Lady Kelgrove sent the doctor a keen glance. 'Is there not a third possibility, Dr West?'

He stilled. 'Well, yes, but I discounted it instantly.'

'Why? Because we are of the *ton*? Evil may live among us as much as it does in the meanest hovel.'

'I...see,' he said, his eyes wide. 'I see. And you believe...?'

Lady Garvald was looking from one to the other. 'Surely you cannot be suggesting...?' Her hand flew to her mouth. 'Oh, my lord!'

'Quite,' stated Lady Kelgrove, her tone clipped. 'Yes, Dr West, I do believe it.'

'But how?' Lady Garvald looked horrified.

'When the gentlemen return, I shall speak to Sir Walter. In the meantime, what is my prognosis?'

The doctor looked gravely troubled. 'Given that your symptoms have already eased, I would be hopeful... although there are some substances whose symptoms come back a second time following a brief respite. I urge you to take caution.'

She gave a bark of laughter. 'How, may I ask? My fate is already set, I think.' Her eyes became unfocused. 'As is that of Mrs Thaxby.' She straightened. 'Anna!'

'Yes?'

'Go to Mrs Thaxby. You need to be there when... You understand me, I think.'

When Mr Thaxby realises his wife has somehow taken some of the poison?

'Of course.' She moved towards the door.

'One moment.' The doctor raised a hand and she paused. 'Lady Kelgrove, when do you believe this... event...took place?'

'Last evening.'

'Ah.' He grimaced, then turned to Anna. 'It may be of limited benefit, but you should encourage Mrs Thaxby to empty her stomach. An unpleasant experience, of course, but better out than in!'

Anna nodded, inwardly feeling pessimistic. If Mrs Thaxby had taken the poison yesterday evening and she was only now casting up her accounts, then the substance had had twelve hours and more to work through her body. Lady Kelgrove, on the other hand, genuinely looked well, so had hopefully been purged of whatever noxious substance Mr Thaxby had administered.

As she passed the top of the staircase, a commotion below caught her attention. The gentlemen had lately returned, it seemed, and were currently divesting themselves of cloaks, hats and boots with the assistance of the footmen. Her eyes sought Will, and her heart skipped as she spied his familiar dark hair. As if sensing her presence, he looked up, his face instantly breaking into a wide smile.

Despite her heart lifting, she found she could not

return his smile—not with all the talk of murder, and with the scent of death in the house.

I need him by my side.

Without hesitation, she began descending the staircase.

Chapter Twenty-Two

Will had enjoyed riding out—clean air in his lungs, feeling nothing but the thrill of each fence, his mind needing to focus entirely on directing his stallion. If he was honest, it had been the perfect distraction from the sense of menace he had felt earlier. Was it because Lady Kelgrove was ill? No, it was more than that—although, like most of the others, he was deeply concerned about Lady Kelgrove.

Most, but not all of the others. Lady Renton had only a limited ability to consider other people's perspectives and feelings, and the Thaxbys seemed entirely devoid of such sensibilities. As he divested himself of boots and cloak, he fleetingly wondered if that was why Lady Renton and Mrs Thaxby enjoyed their endless verbal battles.

A movement above caught his eye and he raised his eyes. There was Anna, standing at the top of the stairs, and his heart swelled at how divine she looked. Surely no goddess could rival her? His eyes swept over her beautiful face and perfect form, and now his loins recalled their ferocious and tender kisses just hours ago. Had it not been for that interruption by the page, he would already have secured her hand—or so he hoped. A man could never know for certain until his chosen lady had said yes.

Inwardly, he had little doubt, for this was Anna, the other part of himself. ZanZan had lost her and Will had found her again. While they disagreed heartily and healthily at times, at a deeper level he knew that they were destined to be together, and he sensed that Anna knew it too. As he watched, she began to descend, but something in her demeanour made the hairs on the back of his neck stand to attention.

Something is amiss—something more than earlier.

Her expression was serious, her air one of disquiet.

'Anna! What is it?'

The other gentlemen quietened, as if sensing his concern, one by one turning to look towards her as she descended.

'Lady Kelgrove…?' His breath caught in his throat. The elderly lady was dear to him.

She shook her head, the tiniest of movements. 'She remains unwell, but now another is also sick.'

Out of the corner of his eye, he saw Mr Thaxby lift his head sharply.

'Who?'

She had reached the hallway, and now turned to Thaxby. 'It is Mrs Thaxby. I am sorry to bring you these tidings, sir, but the doctor says your wife is gravely ill.'

The man crumpled. There was no other word for it.

His hands went to his head, and a strange wailing sound emerged from him. His knees then buckled, and Will was just in time to catch him, Sir Walter grabbing him by the other arm. They exchanged a grim glance above Thaxby's head before leading him to a nearby bench.

'Now then, Thaxby, rest here a moment.' Will gently pushed the man's head down between his knees in an attempt to prevent a full faint. 'You have received a shock.' Looking around, he caught the eye of the nearest footman and mouthed the word, 'Brandy.'

'Impossible!' Thaxby was muttering. 'But how? I took such care...'

Will saw that Sir Walter had heard him, for the look he gave Will was both puzzled and incredulous. Despite wishing it were otherwise, Will could put only one interpretation on Thaxby's reaction: that he believed he had somehow inadvertently caused his wife's sickness. Which meant...

'How is Lady Kelgrove?'

'The doctor thinks she is suffering from the same ailment as Mrs Thaxby.' Anna's words were uttered in a neutral fashion, but the look she threw him held reassurance. She glanced at Thaxby, whose head was still buried between his knees, then back at Will, her eyes holding a clear warning.

'I must go to my wife.' Thaxby rose quickly, then reeled a little. 'Where is she?' His eyes were wild, his hands trembling.

'I shall take you,' Anna murmured. 'She is in her bedchamber.'

He set off towards the stairs, and Will rushed to assist him, for he remained unsteady. Together they climbed the stairs, Will vaguely aware of the stunned silence among the gentlemen in the hallway below.

The door opened, and Will's gaze was immediately drawn to the woman in the bed. Mrs Thaxby looked deathly pale, her eyes closed. A serving maid was engaged in wiping her brow with a damp cloth. Her fingertips were blue, Will noticed, and her skin held a strange yellowish tinge. Mr Thaxby ran directly to her, flinging himself upon her chest and wailing incoherent apologies.

'Oh, my dear,' Will made out. 'How could this have occurred…? I am sorry, my love… My dear, my dear…'

Anna exchanged a shocked look with Will, and he responded with a wry grimace. Whatever Thaxby had done, it was clear that he genuinely cared for his wife. Shaking her head, Anna went to the window and opened it wide. The maid sent her a concerned look, and Will was reminded that it was generally recommended to keep closed the windows in a sickroom. But Anna had the right of it, for surely fresh air was better than this stuffiness? It was not as if Mrs Thaxby had caught some airborne disease…

Anna rejoined him and together they stood watching the scene unfold. Mrs Thaxby patted her husband's shoulder, but seemed unable to speak, while he seemed unable to stop crying and muttering. It was mostly unintelligible, but the gist remained clear: there was something about angels too, angels destroying… No, Will could not make sense of it.

'All is lost,' Thaxby said clearly then. 'All is lost.'

He rested his head on the bed, finally silent, and remained that way for a few moments. He then rose wordlessly, walked straight past Will and Anna without so much as glancing in their direction, and left the room.

With an exchanged glance they hurried after him, but he went only as far as his own bedchamber, next to his wife's, entering and firmly shutting the door. A footman hovered on the landing, a bottle of brandy and a glass in his hand. Will nodded in approval.

'Bring it to him,' he instructed the man. 'Tell him I sent it.'

'Very good, sir,' said the footman, and knocked on Thaxby's door. He knocked again, then looked at Will. There had been no reply from within. Walking forward, Will opened the door. Thaxby was simply standing there, in the centre of the empty chamber, his eyes unfocused.

'Here is brandy for you, Thaxby,' Will offered.

'A kindness,' Thaxby said, nodding to the footman who poured him a glass. 'It is not what I deserve, but I shall take it nonetheless, and use it well.'

Taking the glass, he set it on a side table, fumbled briefly with something in his watch pocket, then bent over the glass of brandy. Before Will could even take in what he was observing, Thaxby lifted it and drank.

'No! You must not!' Springing forward, Will tried

to knock the glass away, but it was too late. Thaxby had drunk it all.

The man gave a self-satisfied smile. 'My last victory. An unwelcome one, but a victory nonetheless. Now, I shall need the services of my valet in the coming hours and days.' He looked at the footman. 'Can you send him to me?'

Clearly relieved to have an excuse to leave the room, the footman backed out with alacrity. Will's stern glance signalled that he should not speak of this, and the footman nodded.

'Thaxby,' he said, and he heard the emotion in his own voice. He cleared his throat, then tried again. 'Will you speak to Sir Walter?'

'A confession? How quaint!' Thaxby thought for a moment. 'Very well, if only so others may appreciate my cleverness, right to the last.' A flash of anger crossed his face. 'Or almost the last. I still cannot understand how my wife came to be affected.'

Will could bear it no longer. 'I shall fetch Sir Walter.' He did not bow as he left, for such a man did not deserve even a hint of *politesse*.

Anna was still there, on the landing.

'Oh, my love!' Uncaring about any servants who might be passing, he pulled her into his arms, taking solace and comfort from the warmth of her body curved into his. Her arms tightened about him and they stood like that for what seemed like an age, until he felt replenished enough to return to reality. He kissed her then, the briefest moment of his lips brushing hers, and she smoothed his hair back from his brow.

'I am here, Will.' Her voice was soft, and his chest swelled with love and pride at the notion that this woman—this fierce, gentle, steadfast woman—loved him. For she loved him, as he loved her. He knew it as well as he knew his own name.

'Tell me honestly, how is Lady Kelgrove?'

'She is well, and has seemed to recover.'

'Then perhaps Mrs Thaxby might also…?'

She shook her head. 'Mrs Thaxby appears to be suffering from a much more severe version than Lady Kelgrove experienced. Why, my great-grandmother is even now sitting up in bed and directing matters!'

He had to smile at this a little, but he quickly sobered as he recalled Thaxby's latest actions. 'Thaxby took something just now. He added it to his drink.'

She gasped. 'Deliberately? Knowingly?'

'Aye.' He shrugged. 'His choice.' He grimaced. 'He has sent for his valet. Unpleasant tasks lie ahead.'

Anna raised her eyes to heaven. 'Poor John! As if he has not suffered enough!'

He sent her a quizzical look. 'You seem to know a lot about the man.'

'I know more now than I did yesterday, that is for certain. He is with Lady Kelgrove.' Briefly, she apprised him of John's tale.

He whistled. 'Sir Walter will need to hear of this.'

Mischief danced briefly in her eyes. 'Lady Kelgrove has everything in hand, I assure you.' Taking his hand, she led him along the landing towards her great-grand-mother's chamber.

'Great-Grandmother? Will is with me, and has news. May we enter?'

A chuckle emerged from the canopied bed. 'Enter, and welcome.' In they went, and Will saw that the doctor was there, with Lady Garvald, Anna's sisters, and John.

My!' Lady Kelgrove declared. 'This bedchamber is as busy as a ballroom today!' She thought for a moment. 'I believe I shall get up. My play-acting has served its purpose, and now I need to be in the midst of events again.'

Anna and Will exchanged a glance.

'What is it? There is something more to be said, is there not?'

Will told them about Mr Thaxby and the brandy, finishing by turning to the doctor. 'He spoke of "destroying angels", if that is of any use?'

'Oh, lord!' exclaimed the doctor. 'That is the colloquial name for a type of toadstool—the Amanita—that grows in these parts. Pure white, looks angelic, but it is, I am afraid, deadly.'

Will felt his innards clench. 'Is there a cure?'

For answer, Dr West turned back to Lady Kelgrove. 'How much did you take? Do you know?'

'Only the tiniest sip. The wine Mr Thaxby gave me tasted strange—I am something of an expert on good wine.'

'And so you dropped your fan, did you not?' Anna

had clearly deduced something from the incident the night before.

Lady Kelgrove nodded. 'He saw me take the sip and I was careful not to show anything on my face. I deliberately said something provoking, then pretended to be wounded by his vicious reply. *That* was when I made a show of dropping my fan.'

Izzy's jaw dropped. 'What did you say?'

She shrugged. 'I cannot recall exactly. It was about Richard, and how I remain determined to bring his murderers to justice, I think.'

Rose clapped a hand to her mouth. 'You did not! Oh, Great-Grandmother, you are formidable indeed!'

Will could just imagine it. 'And his reply?' His tone was clipped, reflecting his need to manage the maelstrom of emotion within him.

'It was as clear a threat as he has ever given. He said that some matters are best left in the past, as otherwise they might cause harm in the present.'

There was a collective gasp.

'And he had just handed me a glass of wine containing the poison. I imagine he believes himself to be clever.' She sniffed. 'While they were picking up my fan, I set my glass down and took another… I believed myself to be in deadly danger and it was all I could think to do. She then took mine. It all happened very, very quickly.' She frowned. 'Afterwards I told myself I was perhaps being over-imaginative when that tiny sip had tasted wrong to me. But then I became ill.'

Dr West was still pondering this. 'So you had a sip,

but Mrs Thaxby must have taken your glass. If she drank a full glass...' He sighed. 'I shall have to consult my medical texts, but I believe that the Amanita affects the liver and kidneys as well as the heart. Lady Kelgrove, you may become ill again in the coming days, I am sorry to say.'

'I see.' She squared her shoulders. 'But I am well now, and if some pestilence is currently attacking my innards I am not aware of it. So I shall ask you all to go away now, and send Hill to me. I shall see you in the drawing room shortly. Isobel, you may take the books and papers we have selected. I wish you and the prince to assemble them into a logical order, for I mean to speak to Sir Walter next.'

Thus dismissed, they all trooped out. Izzy and Rose hurried to find their husbands, while Dr West and John headed for the Thaxbys' chambers. Lady Garvald, stopping for a moment on the landing with Will and Anna, said, 'I must tell the staff we are about to have another guest afflicted by what Mrs Lowe calls "two-bucket disease".'

She shook her head. 'I know that I ought not to be considering such matters at a time like this, but it pains me to anticipate what the servants are enduring, and will endure in the coming days.' She sent them a keen look. 'It would be most helpful if you could both perhaps smooth things over with Sir Walter and the Rentons. I have sadly abandoned them today.'

Confirming they would, they watched as she hurried off, then turned to one another, Will taking Anna's hands in his. They kissed then—ferociously and passionately, as though to assure themselves that here was love, life and harmony. It was brief, and wonderfully disturbing, but it settled Will to know that, in the midst of hate, loss, and even murder there was love.

By the time they moved on, Hill was bustling towards her mistress's bedchamber, and Will was able to reassure her that Lady Kelgrove seemed much improved.

He frowned as they descended the staircase. 'While I admire and respect Lady Kelgrove's determination, I believe I must now take a hand in matters. I am head of this house, and it is my duty and right to speak to Sir Walter.'

Anna saw the sense in this, and so they parted—Anna to give a brief version of the story to the Rentons, while Will took Sir Walter to his library. When Claudio and Izzy arrived with a smaller pile of books and papers, Will used these to corroborate such parts of the tale as they were able, then left Sir Walter to speak with others of his choosing.

By evening time, Sir Walter was ready to make his pronouncements. They had endured a sober dinner, where no one had eaten very much, and conversation had been minimal. Lady Garvald had rearranged the table, but the absence of the Thaxbys was felt by all. Lady Kelgrove had appeared dressed all in black, and with a fierceness in her expression that Will had only rarely seen.

Afterwards the entire party made their way directly

to the drawing room, where Sir Walter stood by the fireplace to address them all at once. Will awaited the magistrate's judgement with a great deal of uneasiness, hoping he had done enough to prove not one but two heinous murders.

Chapter Twenty-Three

The drawing room crackled with tension, akin to the sensation before a thunderstorm. Anna's heart was racing as Sir Walter made his way to the fireplace. What would he say? Had he been convinced? She knew that after speaking with Will in the library the magistrate had spoken to Lady Kelgrove, then John, as well as Mr Thaxby himself. Had the man admitted it?

'As magistrate,' Sir Walter began, his expression serious, 'I could never have anticipated such a to-do in my own vicinity, but this has come to me, and so I have considered the matter carefully. I have spoken to Lord Garvald and Lady Garvald, to Lady Kelgrove, to Mr Thaxby's valet and to Mr Thaxby. His lady is not well enough for questions, but I am satisfied she can have little to add.

'I have also,' he continued, 'been given access to the private diaries and journals of…let us call her Mrs Lennox. These appear to corroborate much of the account I have been given.'

Mrs Lennox? Anna's heart sank. *Why did he not say Mrs Fletcher?*

'I have therefore come to clear conclusions on three of the four matters placed before me. That is to say...' he enunciated on his fingers '...first, the death of the Honourable Richard Berkeley, grandson to Lady Kelgrove. Second, the death of George Fletcher. Third, the illness affecting Lady Kelgrove, Mrs Thaxby and now Mr Thaxby. And fourth, the matter of the Fletcher estate, as symbolised by the necklace currently in the possession of Miss Lennox. I shall refer to each in turn.

'With regard to the death of Lady Kelgrove's grandson Richard Berkeley, on Hampstead Heath in the year 1789, I find that he was killed by brigands hired by Mr Thaxby. Thaxby has admitted it to me this afternoon, although he states the men were told to murder Mr Fletcher, not Mr Berkeley. Nevertheless, he reports he paid them afterwards, and has never heard from them since.' He bowed to Lady Kelgrove. 'I am sorry for your loss, my lady, and I hope that this information may help you find some peace.'

'I thank you, Sir Walter,' she said, her voice trembling only a little. 'It does.'

Anna felt tears prick her eyes. But Sir Walter was continuing, so she brought her attention back to him. It all seemed like a play suddenly—something that must be happening to someone else.

'Regarding the death of Mr George Fletcher in the year 1790, Mr Thaxby has admitted to poisoning him. When asked why, he stated that Mr Fletcher was making plans to marry, that he was due to reach his majority shortly afterwards and that he had threatened to cut Mrs Thaxby off. Mr Thaxby contends that Mr Fletcher was behaving unreasonably, and that he and his wife were simply being good trustees when they challenged the young man.

'When reminded of the failed previous attempt to murder Mr Fletcher, Mr Thaxby could not then account for it. When asked about Mr Fletcher's marriage, Mr Thaxby was adamant that he had not married, that he could not have legally married as he was underage, and that he had reported being enamoured with a serving girl. He was most clear on this point—that Mr Fletcher was unmarried upon his death.'

'But…' Izzy made as if to speak, but a stern look from Lady Kelgrove silenced her.

Sir Walter continued as though she had not spoken. 'On the third matter—that of the illness affecting three members of this gathering—Mr Thaxby has admitted to having a poisonous toadstool known as Amanita in his possession. He states he attempted to administer this to Lady Kelgrove, as he understood she suspected him of arranging the attack on Hampstead Heath in which the Honourable Richard Berkeley died. He states he cannot account for how his own wife also came to be affected, and swears he never intended to harm her. He also…er… With regard to his own sickness, I shall remain discreet, for regardless of what he may have done I am sure we would all agree the man warrants a proper burial.'

He eyed them all fiercely, and no one contested this. A person who died by their own hand could not be buried in holy ground, and such an event would bring unwelcome scandal to the Garvalds and their guests.

'Under normal circumstances I should be referring this matter for a murder trial—two of 'em, in fact! But if Dr West is correct, and neither Mr Thaxby nor his wife will survive this, then I believe the best outcome for all concerned is to put it down to a virulent illness.

'On the matter of the heirs to the Fletcher estate, I cannot rule, for no clear evidence has been presented to me that George Fletcher and Maria Berkeley were legally married. His trustee Mr Thaxby was adamant on that point, and given his candour on matters carrying more weight and significance I have no reason to doubt him.'

Anna's heart sank. She and her sisters needed no more wealth, but surely Mama's dignity and reputation mattered? Surely George's behaviour towards Mama as a gentleman mattered? For Mama to have been with child meant that they had lived together as man and wife. If Sir Walter believed there was no evidence of a marriage, then all their reputations might be forever sullied. Including Mama's. The magistrate was prepared to use sleight of hand about murder, but not about Mama's marriage. That was so unfair!

But Will was rising, walking towards Sir Walter.

'I thank you, sir,' he said, 'For your diligence and thoroughness. But you must know, after I left the library to prepare for dinner, I continued to search through some of Mrs Fletcher's journals, looking for some hint regarding the marriage—which you had highlighted to me as being unresolved. I know her daughters have not yet had the opportunity to read all of them, but I was searching for some clue as to the marriage, given that was your outstanding concern.'

'And? Did you find something?'

'I did.' Will walked to a side table where he lifted a small book—one of Mama's diaries. A sliver of paper had been tucked inside it as a placemark, so he opened it and began to read.

'Mrs Fletcher writes:

'"How strange it is that I am returned to the vicinity of Haddington, where George and I were so happy! I shall never forget the tiny inn near Ballencrieff where I stayed while the banns were read, while George made all ready in our little cottage. We returned to England once I knew I was with child, in the hope that his sister and her husband would accept our marriage, and so that George could begin to take over the reins of his affairs in preparation for his majority. I was more than six months gone, and George wished for security for our child. So he went to stay with them, while I waited in a nearby inn, praying every day for good news. When his servant came to the inn where I was staying, I opened his letter in great haste and with great hope. Instead, I received the worst news possible. I still have that letter in my possession, and have cried many tears over it.

'"When George bade me run, I ran—and where else should I go but Scotland, where I was so happy? It took a few days, but I managed to book a ticket on the stage to Edinburgh. Unfortunately, the Thaxbys were travelling too, and I was unfortunate enough to see them at the inn in Haddington, so I had to run again, leaving behind my trunk and most of my possessions. But I had my reticule, with his letter, the necklace and the earrings I received from my dear grandmother.

'"I can only assume the Thaxbys left their home before he died in order to distance themselves from any accusations. The Fletcher townhouse in Edinburgh was always George's favourite dwelling, and he had asked me to consider if we might settle there and raise our child in Scotland. But, since the Thaxbys were clearly on their way to Edinburgh, I could not go there. I walked the roads until I found Lammermuir House, and my dear friend Margaret took me in. And so I have seen both good and evil in this life. And I choose always to do good, and to raise my daughters to do the same."'

He lifted his head.

'You will note, Sir Walter, the reference to the banns, and the words she uses—namely "our marriage". It seems clear that they married here in Scotland, where their marriage would have been legitimate, even though she was eighteen and he was not yet one-and-twenty.'

He handed Sir Walter the book and allowed him to see for himself.

'Hrmph!' was his verdict. 'I should need to see a copy of the register, but it does seem possible that this may have been one of the Reverend Buchanan's weddings. I know he would marry runaways, but only if they agreed to have the banns read for four weeks in the regular way.'

Anna's heart was racing. 'They married *here*? Where is the Reverend Buchanan's church?'

Will answered immediately. 'It is the Episcopalian Chapel in Haddington—the Church of the Holy Trinity.'

'Episcopalian… That would make sense, for both George and Maria were raised Anglican.' Lady Kelgrove's expression was thoughtful. 'You girls and your husbands may go to Haddington in the morning to find confirmation of the marriage.'

'May I also go, Great-Grandmother?' Anna asked, her tone teasing. 'I have no husband, but I should dearly like to be part of this.'

Lady Kelgrove waved this away. '*Tsk!* You know I meant to include you and Lord Garvald, although you have not yet made any official announcement. I do wish you would, though, for I think we all deserve some good news today.'

All eyes were on Anna, and she felt a slow flush spreading across her face and neck. 'I… But…'

Will bowed to Lady Kelgrove. 'While I appreciate your frustration, I should much have preferred to m-manage matters in my own way. Nevertheless, I recognise that the moment is upon me.'

At this, Izzy clapped her hands. 'I knew it! Did I not say so, Claudio?'

'You did,' replied the prince indulgently.

Anna's gaze flicked to the others. Rose and James were beaming, as was Lady Garvald. Lady Kelgrove had an air of smugness about her, Sir Walter and Lord Renton looked mildly interested—though not displeased—and even Lady Renton looked as though she approved.

Crossing to where Anna sat on a red satin settee, Will knelt before her. 'Annabelle Georgina Lennox Fletcher—you see, I give you your f-full name—will you do me the great honour of being my wife?'

'Oh, Will! Are you certain?'

'More certain than I have ever been of anything in my life. You and I belong together, and you know it as well as I.'

She did, and any worries about him being bounced into a declaration by Lady Kelgrove dissipated like mist. 'Yes!' she accepted, half-laughing. 'Yes, I shall marry you!'

He kissed her then, in full view of everyone, then drew her to her feet and kissed her again. 'I love you,' he murmured against her mouth as the others applauded. Anna even heard a couple of whistles. *How delightfully undignified!* was her fleeting thought.

'I love you too, Will. And I shall love being your wife.'

Together they turned to receive the congratulations of their family, friends and fellow guests. After a frenzy of hugs from the ladies and kisses on the cheek from the gentlemen, they joined hands and sat together.

The evening lasted at least another two hours, but

Anna could not have said afterwards what was discussed. There was sparkling wine, toasts to their future happiness and, eventually, supper. Throughout, Anna remained in an alt, the warmth of his hand in hers anchoring her to the fact that her dearest wish had come true. She was to marry Will, and that was all that mattered.

Chapter Twenty-Four

William Alexander Edward Henderson, Earl of Garvald, married Annabelle Georgina Lennox Fletcher in the pretty chapel in the grounds of Lammermuir House on a warm day in September. The bride was attended by her two sisters, the groom by Prince Claudio and the Viscount Ashbourne.

In attendance was the bride's great-grandmother, who had lately been ill, it was said, but who had made a full recovery. Locals whispered about the dreadful illness that had carried off two of the Lammermuir House guests a few weeks before, and their gratitude that it had not spread more widely.

Also present was the groom's mother—a well-liked lady in the district. Other notables had travelled to be there, including the Dowager Viscountess Ashbourne and a Mr Marnoch from Elgin, said to be the bride's guardian. There was, it was rumoured, even a message of goodwill from the Queen herself!

The bride wore a blue silk gown, a diamond bracelet, and a sapphire-and-diamond necklace said to be worth a king's ransom, while the groom was attired in a Weston jacket, an embroidered waistcoat, and boots by Hoby, and he carried a fine hat said to have been procured from Lock's of London.

Afterwards the newly married couple celebrated with a wedding breakfast at the groom's home, before travelling to the Fletcher townhouse in Edinburgh, where they would spend their honeymoon. The Lammermuir servants were to have their own celebration at the behest of the groom and his mother, once the breakfast had been cleared away. So it could safely be said that the entire household was guaranteed to have a good day, and that it would live long in the memory.

'We have arrived!' Having spent the journey from Haddington via the coastal road to Edinburgh enjoying the fact that she and her husband were finally alone, Anna had been distracted by the realisation they had now reached Edinburgh. As the coach pulled up outside the Fletcher house, she was acutely conscious of the significance of the moment.

Once the details of her parents' marriage had been confirmed in the wedding register in the Haddington chapel, the lawyers had set to work, and just yesterday Anna and her sisters had received confirmation that they were now the owners of the Fletcher assets. As the eldest, Anna had been awarded both the Fletcher necklace and the various properties, as well as cash in the bank, and the government bonds and gold that had lately been discovered in the ledgers. Izzy and Rose had been given substantial awards as belated dowries, their guardian Mr Marnoch having worked diligently with solicitors from Edinburgh and London these past weeks to ensure all legal processes were completed correctly.

This, though, was the first time Anna and Will had seen the house, Anna having felt strongly that they should not visit until all the legalities had been final-ised. From the outside, it was beautiful—warm stone, multiple windows across four storeys and a decided air of elegance.

Will exited the carriage first then handed her out, kissing her hand as he did so. The promise in his eyes left her breathless. With the benefit of the increased privacy afforded to betrothed couples these past weeks, Anna had enjoyed hundreds of kisses from him, and now considered herself quite accomplished in the art. Soon, though, they would be alone, and Anna's en-tire body thrummed in anticipation of the delights of the marriage bed. Her sisters had told her astonishing things about what would occur, and she was determined to enter the experience with an open mind and a great deal of curiosity.

But first, she had more sober duties to fulfil. As she stepped inside the house and saw the staff lined up to greet their new mistress, Anna could almost sense the presence of her mother in step with her. Maria, as George's wife, should have entered the house as its mis-tress more than twenty years ago. Anna's heart ached for both of them—their time together cut short, her fa-ther's life ended prematurely.

As the butler introduced the senior staff to them, and they in turn introduced footmen, maids, grooms and stableboys, Anna felt the responsibility of it all settle on her shoulders. Just a few short months ago she'd been still at school. Now she was a countess, and responsible for the smooth running of multiple houses and the welfare of the servants working within them. There was a hint of anxiety on some of the faces before her, which she could understand. Mr Thaxby had not treated his servants well and, despite the assurances they might have been given, some might have worried that Lord and Lady Garvald would be equally abusive.

One man knew better.

John had been kept on as some-time valet to Lord Garvald. The Earl had his own man, naturally, but John had been assured he would have work for as long as he wished it, and a comfortable retirement afterwards. And he had earned every moment of it.

'John!' They both greeted him warmly, and his beaming expression displayed his delight.

'Can you please assemble those senior servants you spoke about?' Will asked him. 'We should like to speak to them in private.'

So, before having a tour of the house or even accepting refreshments, the Earl and Countess took the time to thank those who had remained loyal to George Fletcher's memory for more than twenty years, hoping that some day his wife or child might come forward. They listened too, asking sympathetic questions and taking the time to understand how difficult it had been for them all. They were left with a strong sense of the servants' integrity and loyalty, as well as their relief that the matter had now been resolved. The Thaxbys—and their unpleasant demise—were not mentioned by name.

Some hours later, having completed all of their (entirely pleasant) duties, Lord and Lady Garvald retired to their sumptuous suite on the third floor of the house. Darkness was falling, and Sally—who was still reeling from her unanticipated rise in station in becoming personal maid to a countess—had worked with John to make all ready.

The chamber was spotlessly clean, the bed turned down and there were two branches of candles—one on the bedside table, another on the small mirrored table near the window. Suddenly nervous, Anna allowed Sally to remove her gown, undo her stays and unpin her hair—all the while conscious that John was removing Will's boots at the far side of the room. Shaking her head when Sally signalled towards the nightgown she had laid out, she murmured, 'Thank you, Sally, I shall manage the rest.'

'Very good, my lady.' Startled at not being called 'miss', Anna reflected wryly that having a title would take some getting used to. Her sisters had certainly managed. From being simply the three Misses Lennox in Elgin at the beginning of the year, they were now all married—a countess, a princess, and a viscountess. But, much as she held her brothers-in-law in high esteem, Anna knew that she had married the best of men.

Surely there was no one more handsome, more generous, more kind-hearted than her own darling Will?

John and Sally went, the valet gently closing the door
behind him. As she heard Will walking towards her,
Anna held her breath. Keeping her eyes on the gilded
mirror before her, she saw him behind her, saw their
faces together, and she could not prevent a smile.

'My lady.' Reverentially, he bent and kissed the back
of her neck, her ear and her collar bone, sending delicious shivers through her.

'My lord.' She could wait no longer, and turned towards him. Instantly his lips were on hers, their arms
moving to hold one another close, closer yet...

The nightgown proved to be unnecessary, and lay in
a heap on the floor along with their clothing until Anna,
waking with a start, saw that daylight was peeping
through the edges of the curtains. Stirring, she turned
in her husband's arms, enjoying the novel sensation of
his body against hers and the sight of his handsome
face so close to her own in the gentle morning light.

The advice provided by her sisters had proved to be
accurate—not least the part where they had tried to tell
her how delightful it all was. That part, in fact, they
had significantly understated.

How many times they had made love in the night, she
could not be sure, for her head was delightfully sleep-
lacking, and her mind was wonderfully foggy. Her body
knew what it wanted, though, so she stretched a little

as she lay beside him. He groaned, moving a little, then opened his eyes.

'Good morning, my love.'

'Good morning, Will.'

His eyes softened. 'Our first morning waking up together. I still can hardly believe it.'

'It does seem improbable that anyone should feel so happy.'

'True.' He kissed the tip of her nose. 'When I recall all those balls and soirées during the season, when you acted like you did not know me… How far we have journeyed, from that to this.'

'And now we are here, safe and married.'

'And in a bed. And naked.'

She moved against him. 'Why, so we are!'

He rolled on top of her. 'Kiss me then, my lady!'

Gladly, she obliged.

* * * * *

MILLS & BOON®

Coming next month

ONLY AN HEIRESS WILL DO
Virginia Heath

Book 1 of **A Season to Wed**
The brand-new regency series from
Virginia Heath, Sarah Rodi, Ella Matthews and
Lucy Morris

Gwen laid down her quill and steepled her fingers. 'This is a surprise, Major Mayhew—although I must say, a timely one. I've been thinking about earlier and—'

'So have I. Incessantly. But I'm in. Obviously I am in.' He suddenly smiled and that did worrying things to her insides. However, if his smile made all her nerve endings fizz, what he did next made them melt. 'I would have been here sooner but I had to collect this.' He rummaged in his waistcoat pocket—this one a vivid turquoise peacock embroidered affair that shouldn't have suited anyone but did him—and pulled out a ring. 'This was my mother's. I hope it meets with your satisfaction.'

She stared at it dumbstruck. Shocked that he had thought of it and yet unbelievably touched that he had. 'You brought me a ring...' She had assumed, when her engagement was announced, she would have to buy her own and that it would be a meaningless trinket—not an heirloom. Not something that meant something to someone. Something pretty and elegant, a simply cut oval ruby the size of her little fingernail surrounded by diamonds, that she probably would have chosen for herself before she talked herself out of it for being too bold.

He shrugged awkwardly. 'It seemed the very least I could do after you proposed.' Then to her utter astonishment he reached across the table, grabbed her hand and slipped it on her finger. 'It fits perfectly. Perhaps that's an omen?' He held her hand while he stared at it, twisting it slightly so that the lamplight caught the stones and made them sparkle. Gwen barely noticed the gem, however, as his touch was playing havoc with her senses.

He let go of her finger and, for a fleeting moment, common sense returned, warning her to yank the thing off and hand it back to him. Except...

It felt right on her finger and she couldn't formulate the correct words to tell him that she had changed her mind. That he wasn't at all what she was looking for, but she hoped he found another, more suitable heiress, to marry as soon as possible. Instead, there was another voice in her head overruling that of common sense. One that was rooting for Major Mayhew, no matter how wrong she already knew him to be.

Continue reading

ONLY AN HEIRESS WILL DO
Virginia Heath

Available next month
millsandboon.co.uk

COMING SOON!

We really hope you enjoyed reading this book.
If you're looking for more romance
be sure to head to the shops when
new books are available on

Thursday 27th February

To see which titles are coming soon, please visit
millsandboon.co.uk/nextmonth

MILLS & BOON

LET'S TALK

Romance

For exclusive extracts, competitions and special offers, find us online:

- **f** MillsandBoon
- **X** @MillsandBoon
- **◉** @MillsandBoonUK
- **♪** @MillsandBoonUK

Get in touch on 01413 063 232

MILLS & BOON
A ROMANCE FOR EVERY READER

- **FREE** delivery direct to your door
- **EXCLUSIVE** offers every month
- **SAVE** up to 30% on pre-paid subscriptions

SUBSCRIBE AND SAVE

millsandboon.co.uk/Subscribe